The Six

and the

Gardeners of Ialana

Katlynn Brooke

Book Two of the Ialana Series

For my mother, who always wanted me to write.

Contents

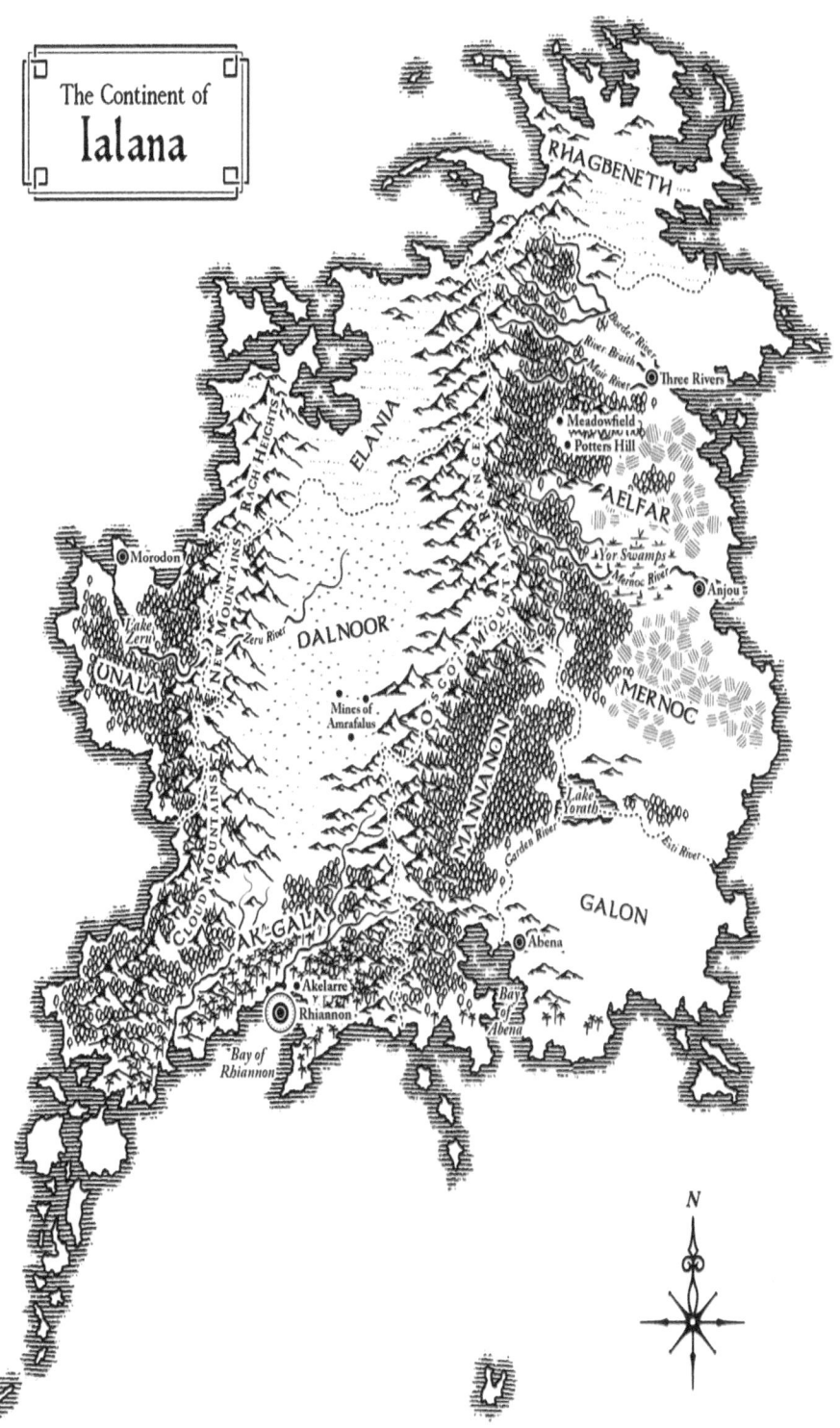

The Continent of
Ialana

RHAGBENETH

Border River
River Braith
Muir River
Three Rivers

Meadowfield
Potters Hill

ELANIA

AELFAR

Morodon

Yor Swamps
Mernoc River

Anjou

Lake
Zeru

Zeru River

DALNOOR

UNALA

Mines of
Amrafalus

MERNOC

Lake
Yorath

Esti River

Garden River

GALON

Abena

AK-GALAL

Akelarre

Rhiannon

Bay
of
Abena

Bay of
Rhiannon

N

1.

To Galon

I t took several hours for the dust cloud over Rhiannon to disappear. It hung like a dark mushroom in the sky, just over the horizon, as the fishing boat headed east through the Sea of Alania. The Six, along with Irusan, Yared, Askia, Shogna, Holgar, and Adne, sat silent in the boat, awed by the remarkable power that had unleashed itself from what used to be the Citadel of Amrafalus. Finally, the cloud disappeared from their sight, sinking behind the trees and hills of the southern shoreline.

For a while, they were each lost in thought. Death had come too close in the tunnel that Irusan, with his rock-melting crystal, had carved out for them under the bay and into the Citadel where they'd been imprisoned. They had time now to reflect, recalling with shudders how the tunnel had collapsed behind them just before they had emerged from it onto the shore, and how they'd made it out only just in time. The generator crystals that Amrafalus, the Reptilian ruler, and Blaidd had forced them to awaken under the Citadel had released their pent-up energy with a ferocity that had brought the Citadel down. They assumed it must have crushed not only Amrafalus, but everyone still in it.

As soon as he thought they were a safe distance from shore, Irusan shape-shifted back from his natural cat-man form into one of an albatross. With a farewell squawk, he launched himself up into the air, glided effortlessly in circles around the boat a few times, and then disappeared into the distance. The Six were always sorry to take leave of the cat-man. They wished that he would stay with them forever, but they knew he found it difficult to stay in their reality for long. He'd once told them that the longer he stayed, the more difficult it became for him to return to his natural state. He would visit them whenever the situation warranted it, but not until then.

Jarah sighed. He was now, once again, the leader of the group. He rested his chin on his hands, his elbows on the side of the boat, as he stared out over the water towards the setting sun. He didn't want the others to know how he really felt. He had never wanted to be a leader, but Irusan had stressed before flying away that this was his role, and that he was perfectly capable. Jarah had sent his thoughts to Irusan soon after the boat had left the shore.

Tristan should lead, since as a soldier, he's done it before and he is, after all, the eldest in our group. If it were not for Tristan, he'd added, they would never have made it over the Osgoi Mountains. Tristan had helped them escape their capture by King Brenin's army recruiters. It had been no small feat. If it were not for Kex, he'd said, none of them would be alive now. If it were not for Djana, they would not have found their way through the mountain tunnels, and, of course, if it were not for Tegan, he added, they would never have found Irusan. What had he done, he asked Irusan, to ensure their safety and well-being? He'd simply located the Healing Crystal, and he felt that even that had been an accident.

Irusan had looked at him strangely with his large, cat-blue eyes, and thought back to him. *Do you feel your role was merely accidental, and you have not contributed? A foolish thought, Jarah, and not one worthy of a leader. Think before you speak. You and Tegan are the only ones in your group who know how to use telepathy. Without your skills, I would not have been able to communicate with you and your companions as well as we do.*

This so-called humility does not serve you well. If you can't appreciate yourself and your own contributions, how are you going to value that of others? You will always be second-guessing your guidance, and it will become a self-fulfilling prophecy. You will become the ineffective leader you fear.

Jarah had turned red, but not out of anger. He'd been embarrassed. Irusan's words were true. He'd never valued himself, and he could hear his parents' voices—mostly his mother's—echoing in his head.

"Jarah, you are bone-lazy! Jarah, you lack responsibility!" and the worst, *"You will never amount to anything if you don't stop your incessant day-dreaming!"*

He looked at Tegan, standing at the prow of the boat, hair flowing like silk in the breeze. What did she see in him? A nineteen-year-old who blushed easily, and whose red hair never lay flat no matter what he did. On the other hand, did she see the man he only wished he were, the man he could still be? He decided that whatever it was she saw in him, he was lucky. Their connection was strong. She turned and gave him a comforting smile. She knew what he was thinking, and she answered with the thought, *"I love you too! Irusan was right. You are our leader, and we're all happy with that."*

"I consider you all leaders, Tegan," he returned. *"I am merely the one who holds the Crystal, and that is not false humility!"*

"Yes, we all have an equal say, Jarah, but we also chose you to lead us because of your healing skills and knowledge of crystals. We decided all this before we set out on our original mission five hundred years ago. As far as we're concerned, you are still El-Azar, and that has not changed."

He looked at Djana, who sat with her parents Holgar and Adne. Yared, the Trueni, and his wife Shogna, sat with them as they fussed over Shogna and Yared's baby girl. They all seemed happy to leave Rhiannon, but he sensed a sadness there too. Rhiannon and Akelarre had been their home for so long, and they didn't know if they'd ever see it again. Askia, at the helm, did not look too sad to be leaving. He was now the proud owner of a beautiful fishing boat, thanks to Blaidd who had used it to find Mu'A.

Jarah and the Six now knew how Amrafalus had used his destructive memory crystal on Blaidd so that he would remember his lifetime in Mu'A. It was how Blaidd had eventually located the island and the Six. It was how Blaidd had lured them back to Rhiannon with false promises and lies. But Blaidd had not known that they, along with Irusan, had seen through his deception, and arranged the destruction of the Citadel, and how they'd kept the Healing Crystal safe from him and Amrafalus.

"What do you think happened to Blaidd?" asked Kex, as if she too had read his thoughts. He straightened up, and turned around. They stood just behind him, Adain's arm draped protectively over Kex's shoulder. There was no doubt how they felt about each other, thought Jarah, and he felt pleased but not surprised. Kex had been smitten with Adain right from the beginning.

"I have no idea. I hope he made it out. I wonder more about Amrafalus. Is he still alive? I wish we knew."

Tristan joined them at the stern. "I think they're all dead. No one inside that Citadel could have escaped."

"I suppose we'll never know," said Adain. "We probably won't be back in Rhiannon ever again."

"Don't tell that to Djana," said Jarah. "It will break her heart."

"Askia says Irusan told him to head for Galon—the port of Abena," said Tristan.

"We no been there," said Yared. He put his hand on Shogna's shoulder. "We both like go there, maybe make fresh start for child."

Well, at least some were happy to be leaving, thought Jarah. Maybe they could all make a fresh start in Galon. As long as they weren't being hunted, it might be a good place to settle. He did wish that he could go back to Aelfar, but only for a visit. He knew Adain and Tegan wanted to return as well. They all needed to make sure their parents were safe; although Tegan seemed sure that hers were dead. The last she'd seen of her village, she'd witnessed soldiers on a killing spree. Captain Eglog, King Brenin's army recruiter they had escaped from, had tracked the five runaways to Tegan's village, Potter's Hill, where her father Rhaol had sold them new boots. When the villagers were unable to tell him where the runaways were, he'd torched the village.

Jarah and Adain thought their own parents were still safe in Meadowfield, but they had to be sure.

Kex had no desire to return to her clan in Rhagbeneth. She made that clear when they discussed it on the island. "My clan will kill me," she said. "I am now dead to them." They knew the story behind her own escape from an arranged marriage. She decided she'd settle wherever Adain wanted to be, and he wanted to be with her and the Six.

Tristan said he didn't care where their healing mission took them. He might return to his family in Mernoc one day, but he was in no hurry. Soldiering had once been his life, he'd added, but he now considered the Six his family.

Djana had said that she wanted to see her parents settled in a safe location before going anywhere, and Tristan and the Six agreed about that. They also wanted to be certain of the safety of Yared and his family, and Askia. Galon seemed as good a place as any other place.

No one had even suggested they return to Mu'A, the island where they'd been so happy and carefree, and where they'd continued their education in the old skills: the Basajaun command of crystal technology. They had all felt, after their escape, that their mission must continue. Their mission, five hundred years ago in different bodies and presently, was to heal those with distorted templates—the Trueni slaves—using the Crystal. They could not do this from the safety of Mu'A.

Jarah noticed now just how much Askia, the Trueni fisherman at the helm, had healed. Although he still had a slightly piggish look around the face, he had lost most of his speech defects. He now spoke with a more sophisticated speech pattern, like that of a human. He looked over at Yared and Shogna. They had not yet had the opportunity to partake of the crystal's healing, but, he hoped, they would soon be able to once they reached Galon.

Jarah was left to his own thoughts again as the sun slowly sank over the western horizon. Shogna and Yared were preparing their evening meal with the help of Holgar and Adne. Shogna had fed the baby, and she was now sleeping peacefully in a little hammock between two crates. Tegan, Djana, and Kex softly sang a Bhajan, or song, that Irusan had taught them. He felt more at peace now than he had in a while. The sea, like the sky, turned a brilliant orange, and purple, fair-weather clouds overhead promised them smooth sailing.

He wished he could bottle this moment and keep it forever, to take out and breathe it in whenever needed. He knew the time would come when he would long for these peaceful moments in the future. He felt the certainty in the pit of his stomach that their return home would not be as uneventful as they hoped.

He wondered again about Blaidd. As much as he still disliked Blaidd, he now felt that he should have done more for him. He should have seen the direction Blaidd was headed. He could have pulled him aside and tried to gain his confidence. He felt badly for his former friend, with his lazy and drunken father, and no mother. He could have shown him more compassion.

It was too late now, he thought. Blaidd was probably dead.

2.

Blaidd

Blaidd was not dead. Far from it. His legs shook, his head was wet with blood from being hit with falling debris, and he looked like a grey, stone statue from all the dust, but he was still very much alive. He had barely escaped a falling tower—one that almost crushed him like a mosquito. Riderless horses hurtled past him, their panicked hooves dangerously close to his head. Soldiers dashed past on foot, making for the gate in the wall where there was already a crush of horses and men all attempting to go through at the same time. He knew people must have been screaming because their mouths were wide open, but he couldn't hear them. The popping noises in his ears muffled all sound. Some, like him, simply stood rooted in shock as they gazed with empty, uncomprehending eyes at the devastation around them. He still held the Crystal in his hand. He staggered and almost fell, but felt a firm grip under his arm. Startled, he turned.

A woman stood behind him. A woman he'd never seen before. A woman with glossy, raven black hair that framed a porcelain, oval face. As he looked at her, he felt as though his breath left his body. A wave of dizziness hit him, and his vision dimmed. The last thing he remembered was being lifted up, and then there was blackness.

He sat up. The dark, silent room was not familiar; he had no idea where he was. He looked around and blinked. His eyes felt fuzzy. For a moment, he couldn't remember what had happened, but then it all came back to him in a rush. The five crystals under the Citadel ... not working ... the overload of energy and running ... running up stairs as the Citadel collapsed around him. Oh yes, and the Healing Crystal! He felt a surge of panic as his hands went to his neck. It was still there in its pouch! He breathed a sigh of relief and smiled as he remembered how he'd taken it from Jarah.

Did Amrafalus make it out? He had no idea. Amrafalus had been at the other end of the cavern. He hadn't looked back as he ran, but he'd heard pounding footsteps behind him. He'd just barely made it out himself, and he didn't know how anyone else behind him could have escaped. Thanks to the gods of his ancestors, he'd always been a fast runner. He wondered what had happened to the Six. They'd mysteriously disappeared from the cavern below. His instincts told him that Irusan must have had something to do with that—

His head jerked as a sound came from the door. It swung open, and a woman walked in— the same woman who had appeared behind him at the Citadel, and who'd held him up before he lost consciousness. She must have been the one who brought him here. The glow from the lantern she carried accentuated her beauty. Her dark sapphire eyes radiated love and concern. They also seemed to bore into his soul. He didn't know what to say as his mouth opened and closed, carp like, and he knew he must be staring at her like a fool. She merely smiled and set the light down next to his bed.

"So you're awake, Blaidd. How do you feel?" Her voice was as gentle as her demeanor, and all he could do was gape. "You are probably wondering who I am. My name is Branwyn."

"H-how do you know my name?"

"I know a lot of things about you, Blaidd. Or should I call you Seryn?"

Blaidd felt his heart racing, but whether from fear or excitement, he couldn't tell. Maybe she wasn't as benign as she looked. She knew too much about him already.

As if she read his mind, she responded. "Yes, I do know all about you. I've probed your mind, and there is nothing I don't know about you, Seryn. But don't worry. I'm not here to harm you. I know what you want, and I think I can help you."

"Call me Blaidd," he said. He was feeling more confident now. In spite of Amrafalus having previously called him Seryn, he felt he should return to being just Blaidd. The name 'Seryn' had not brought him much luck. Seryn was the man he had once been five hundred years ago, the man who had betrayed the Six, and lost his own life in the process. He would not make the same mistakes again.

A part of his memory was returning ... Or had *she* had placed it there? He wasn't sure. She reminded him so much of Irusan by the way she spoke and the way she read his mind. *Was she*—?

"You're right, Blaidd," she said. "I am one of them, or at least I *was*, until they threw me out. You probably remember the old stories about us from Mu'A. The Guardians, and how they promised to help the Basajaun and the Mu'A—how *dare* they judge *me*!"

Her voice changed. It was no longer soft and loving. A harsher tone had crept in, and he drew the covers up to his chin as if he could hide from her. Her sensuous mouth pouted.

"I did not want to get involved with idiots who could not protect themselves from invasion—who'd caused it to happen in the first place. I expressed myself strongly, and many agreed with me. I said our crystal experts should train the Basajaun in the weaponization of crystals, but the Council of Twenty-Four decided otherwise." She paused as her mouth turned down again. *"We will never turn crystals into weapons,"* she mimicked, in the voice of a council member. Her voice returned to its normal pitch and she continued. "But I went ahead with the project without their permission, or their help, and created a crystal, a weapon, that would kill."

Her mouth twitched, lifting in a brief smile.

"But just as I was going to hand it over to the Basajaun, the Guardians intercepted me, and the crystal was destroyed. Months of work, *just destroyed*! They exiled me from Agra'Tan. And guess who escorted me out personally? Your friend, Irusan."

"He isn't my friend," said Blaidd. "He helped the Healers escape, and he doesn't like me anyway."

Branwyn's hand rose and she stroked Blaidd's cheek lovingly. "Yes, I know, dear. I meant that sarcastically. That is why I know you will help me, and I will help you. Together, we can make Rhiannon great again, and not only Rhiannon. We'll rule the whole *continent*, you and I. Now, let me take a closer look of that crystal of yours. I didn't have time to examine it before."

Her eyes went to the pouch around Blaidd's neck, and his hand moved towards it protectively.

"No, don't worry; I am not going to take it away from you. It's yours. I took it out of your hand and put it back in your pouch. I just want to see it."

Slowly, he lifted the pouch from around his neck and shook the crystal out into the palm of her hand. Branwyn looked at it for a moment and closed her eyes. He sensed a probing energy directed towards the crystal. She smiled. It was not a pleasant smile, he thought. It was tight-lipped and angry.

"Oh Blaidd, dear, I am so sorry. They have fooled you once again."

His heart stopped. *What?*

"What do you mean '*they fooled me*'? This *is* the Crystal—I saw it—Jarah always wore it around his neck!"

"It's a rock-crystal, honeybunch. Useless, I'm afraid. They must have done a sleight-of-hand. I believe they're rather good at that considering they fooled you and Amrafalus to bring the Citadel down."

Blaidd thought he would cry and he put his head in his hands. In spite of the dreadful day, he'd still felt as if he had so much to live for now that he possessed the Crystal—or thought he did.

"Oh, don't cry, sweetie!" Branwyn enveloped him in her shapely arms and he could smell her scent—roses—as he rested his head on her breast. "We'll get it back for you, I promise! I have plans, and I need your help."

He raised his head and gazed into her eyes. They were deeply blue, so dark they almost appeared black. He could lose himself in them forever. *Yes, they would get it back!* He would do anything to help her. *Anything!*

Trapped

His slit eyes opened, and he blinked furiously, trying to clear the fuzziness from his vision. Wherever he was, it was dark, but that did not matter. His pupils were capable of perceiving in the ultra-violet range, and he could see just as well in the dark as he could in daylight.

Pain.

It was like being caught in a vice. His head pounded in rhythm to the beat of his heart, and there was something heavy pressing on top of one of his legs. A cruel, wet cold enveloped his body. Under him the water was rising, and nearby, he could hear the trickle of running water.

Finally, his vision cleared, and he scanned his surroundings. He was in an underground cavern of some sort. What had happened? He couldn't remember anything. Who was he? He had no idea. All he knew was that he should get out of this place before his blood became too sluggish. He needed heat. He longed for the sun.

He tried to move, but whatever was on top of his leg—it looked like a large rock—had pinned him to the floor of the cavern. He groaned. The water continued to rise, and if he knew that if he didn't get out of here soon he would drown. He strained again, and again, until he felt the huge rock shift. Summoning all the power he could muster, he heaved one more time and pushed at the rock with his gigantic hands. It shifted a bit more, and he screamed in agony. Encouraged, he pushed and pulled, and at last, with a final heave, the rock rolled off him, with a heavy splash, to one side. He massaged his leg, trying to bring the life back into it. It hurt so badly, but he couldn't afford to rest. He must keep moving. Shakily, he stood up and looked around. Not too far away, he saw something—what was it? It looked like ... a crystal? Whatever it was, it was immense. It towered over him.

Except for the sound of water, the cavern was silent. He wondered how long he'd been down here. He began to move and his foot hit something, something soft. He bent down to look, eyes locking on a blank, fish-eyed stare of a soldier. The soldier was half-submerged, trapped under a rock. There were more bodies. He didn't recognize any of them. He could see rocks and rubble everywhere. He must find an exit.

With his good leg, he kicked the bodies out of his way, and stumbled through the water. Bellowing with each painful step, he followed the wall of the cavern as far as he could go, but there was no exit. It looked like there had been a cave-in, and that he was trapped on the other side of it. He continued to follow the wall until he came to the source of the trickling water. He could see a small hole in the rocky wall of the cavern, and he noticed that it was getting larger. The trickle was gradually widening, and soon it would become a torrent. But that was good, he thought. If he could find the underground river or source, perhaps he could get out that way. He scratched, dug some more, and pulled at the sides of the hole until the small torrent became a gushing cataract. With much difficulty, he kept his footing and continued to dig until the forceful rush of water nearly knocked him over, but he knew he must make the effort to get his bulky body through.

Desperately, he pulled at the last rock and felt it move. With a roar, it gave way to the pressure of the water behind it. The deluge coming through the hole now was too strong to allow him to stand upright, and the cavern was filling up fast. Taking a last, deep breath, he plunged into the water and fought for his life against the current. He felt it push him out of the hole again, and using every bit of strength he still had left, he forced his body through the opening, but to no avail. The current was too strong. He fell back exhausted, into the cave. The pain was now continuous, but he knew he had to work through it. He could feel the cold overtaking him, making him sleepy and even more sluggish.

As the water slowly rose, he rose with it, until it reached the roof of the cavern, and then he took the deepest breath he was capable of, and dove back down, back into the hole. His instinct to wait had been correct. The current was no longer too strong for him. He swam through the hole that became a water-filled tunnel, but he kept on swimming. He knew, although he didn't remember how, that he had the ability to stay underwater much longer than humans. He remembered humans now, and he remembered a city, but everything else was lost in a dark fog.

The tunnel stopped abruptly. In front of him, a pile of rocks and sand completely blocked his passage. There had been a cave-in here too, he thought. Scrabbling quickly with both his hands, he moved as much of the rubble out of the way as he could, and at last a hole appeared in the roof of the tunnel. As it grew bigger, he forced his way out, pushing away the debris that surrounded it, feeling his body rise through the hole as he cleared the last of the rubble. Far above him a light danced tantalizingly, and as he drifted upwards the darkness began to dissipate. He was at the bottom of a shallow seabed.

There were spots in front of his eyes, and even his strong lungs could not keep him underwater much longer. With a final firm kick, using his good leg, he rocketed upwards, faster now, towards the light above as air bubbles jetted out of his mouth. It seemed to take forever, and he hoped he would not lose consciousness, but at last, his head broke through the surface. He coughed, choking, water spewing from his nostrils. His lungs expanded once again with welcome air.

He was in a bay. Behind him, a city loomed through a dark cloud of swirling grey dust, but he didn't want to go that way. Something terrible had happened there. *Something* ... He couldn't remember what it was though. He looked in the other direction and saw a distant shoreline rimmed with trees. He would go that way.

He swam slowly, his snout just barely breaking the swells. It took a while, since his leg hurt so much, but his strong arms and other leg did not let him down. Finally, he felt firmness under his feet, and, exhausted, he dragged himself up onto the shore. There was no one else around.

He rested for a while, warming his unresponsive body in the heat of the sun. By the position of the sun in the sky, he thought it was morning. He wondered again how long he had been in that cavern. He looked around. He could see other footprints here in the wet and muddy ground; human ones, and that of something other than human. Someone else must have used the tunnel before the cave-in. Its exit had to be close by, but he was famished, weak with hunger. He needed to find food and then he would have to decide what to do next. He wished he could remember who he was.

Admiral Udfa

Admiral Udfa ran his fingers lightly down the edge of his knife blade. *Not sharp enough.* He held the beveled edge to the flat, granite stone again, scraping it slowly back and forth. His thoughts were bitter, and they were not about the knife. He'd found it difficult to focus on daily activities since the death of Amrafalus, and his own narrow escape from the Citadel. There was still much for him to do, and the only question in his mind was "how?" He remembered that his overriding goal had been to kill Amrafalus' monkey, Blaidd, but the Raven had cheated him out of that. Just as he'd caught up with him outside the falling Citadel, a bird had flown down, and in a flash it had turned into a woman. That had been the last thing he remembered. He had only regained consciousness when a soldier had mistaken him for a dead body and tried to load him into a cart.

She must have put a sleeping spell on me, he thought.

He knew of the Raven. Amrafalus had warned him about her many times, but he'd thought she was merely a legend—a superstition of the masses that Amrafalus had bought into. He'd realized, when he'd seen the woman materialize—shape-shift—from bird to a woman, that she was no myth. He understood now that she was a powerful enchanter and that he must proceed carefully.

He tested the knife blade again. A small drop of blood welled up on his palm, and he smiled, but his eyes were cold. He picked up his sword. He needed to be ready. He was one of the "old guard" and the new rulers of Rhiannon may not trust him. They were right not to, he conceded. He placed the beveled edge of the sword onto the stone, and rhymically moved it up and down. He found weapon sharpening a comforting task; one that allowed him to think of more important things.

He wondered what the Raven wanted with Blaidd. If the sorcerer wanted Blaidd then there must be a reason. He knew too that Amrafalus had kept Blaidd on as his useful idiot so that he could assist him in finding the Six and luring them back to the Citadel. It had worked. Udfa decided now that, instead of killing

Blaidd, he needed to find him too. He would capture the Six as well, before anyone else could beat him to it. It still rankled him that they'd escaped his net so many times in the past. It left him looking foolish, and he couldn't have that.

He grimaced as he thought of Madfall, the leader of the Council of Ten. Madfall had taken over the leadership of the land right after the Citadel fell. But Udfa felt it was his own destiny to be the Great Leader of Rhiannon and Ak-Gala, and maybe all of Ialana too. If the Six could help him accomplish that, so much the better. He'd never paid much attention to why Amrafalus wanted them so badly. He'd simply obeyed orders. Now though, it seemed that his future rested on finding them, and he would soon remove from them all their knowledge and put it to use.

He put the sword down. Reflecting, he fingered the pouch that he kept at his waist. Inside the pouch was a small, lead-lined box. Inside the box were two small crystals. He knew something about Amrafalus' crystals. He'd not only stolen some of them for himself— Amrafalus had so many and he was careless with them—but he'd also watched him many times, observing how he turned men into *things*, and how to extract thoughts from spies. Amrafalus had done it to Blaidd, and Udfa knew Blaidd would be forever changed by this process. He may not even look the same, but he'd find him, and then he'd kill him after he'd first extracted his knowledge of crystals, and the Six, of course. He was not sure of the exact function of these two crystals, but he remembered Amrafalus saying that they shouldn't be taken out of the box, that they were dangerous.

He knew, without any doubt in his mind, that one day he would find a use for them.

3.

Ibai, Galon

It was on the morning of their fourth day at sea when they reached the coastline of Mannanon. Askia told them that Galon was still over the horizon to their east. He possessed an uncanny instinct about what was under or ahead of the boat and skillfully avoided shoals, reefs, and rocks as he navigated around an island chain south of the mainland. The next day they turned north, and a few hours later sailed into a large bay. They did not know exactly where Abena was, but Yared said he thought it was located at the northern end of the bay.

They were feeling nervous now. They had no idea what awaited them at landfall, whether it would be friend or foe. Yared had heard many stories about Abena from his fellow-Trueni. They knew that there was a Trueni community, just like Akelarre, near Abena. They decided to hug the western coastline of the bay and keep a close watch for other fishermen.

It was on the second day of their journey into the bay when they sighted the fishing boats. As they drew nearer, they found themselves the objects of curiosity. Their boat was different to the fishing boats of Galon. Their own sails were light colored and square, while the Galonese sails were colorful triangles. Carved prows curved gracefully to the sky, and mermaids, painted eyes, and sea monsters adorned the boat's hulls. As they approached the vessels, Tristan kept his hand on his knife. A large fishing boat came towards them, as close as it dared in the swells. They could see now that there were Trueni on board, and Askia hailed them.

"We come in peace, brothers!"

The Trueni captain looked at Yared and Shogna carefully, then raised a large hairy hand and said, "We greet in peace too, brother!" They all raised hands to show they were unarmed, and Tristan took his hand away from his knife. The Trueni captain signaled that they should follow him, turning his boat and sailing north. The other fishing boats continued with business as usual and did not follow the larger boat. After a few hours, they arrived at the northern end of the bay and began to head east. The Trueni captain continued with his fishing on the way, throwing out nets and hauling them back. Apparently, he wasn't going to waste time.

At last, they saw where they were headed—a fishing village on the eastern banks of a large river mouth that emptied into the bay. Avoiding the shoals and tides at the mouth of the river, they navigated around the muddy waters into a cove. It looked much like Akelarre, only smaller. The captain indicated they should pull up at a dock alongside his boat, and they threw out a rope to a Trueni fisherman who made the boat fast to the dock.

"Wait here," said Askia as he jumped onto the dock, then walked over to the Trueni captain who was now on the dock. They saw him speak briefly to him, and then he waved to them to come over. "This is Bakar. We are in the village of Ibai, in Galon. Mannanon is over the Garden River." He pointed to a wide, brown river mouth. "It a wild place and Bakar say we should not go there."

They all introduced themselves, and the Trueni boat captain invited them into his small and humble home nearby. His wife, Erlea, greeted them all in a friendly way and immediately offered them food. The Trueni here looked the same as those in Akelarre: all with various animal snouts, ears, tails, or horns. Some were completely covered in fur, while others had more human skin showing. Their speech was the same—broken, but understandable. Bakar told them that many of them were escapees and refugees from the mines in Dalnoor. Some were recent arrivals, but most of them had been here for generations. He said that they were better treated here than their counterparts over the mountains, but they were still not acceptable to humans, and were used mainly as servants or fishermen. They weren't allowed to live in Abena unless they had jobs there, and were confined to Ibai, shanty-towns on the outskirts of the city and the banks of the Garden River. They were peaceful, and did not offer resistance to their lower status since they felt they were here by sufferance of the Galonese and did not wish to anger them. They felt it was better to be of lower status here than in Dalnoor and Ak-Gala. At least there was no overt cruelty here towards them, such as killings, whippings, and slavery, as there still was in the land of Amrafalus.

"Galon people not bad," said Bakar. "We work hard—they not send us back." Bakar explained, in his broken way, that a man called Ortzi was the Lord of Galon. He was a respected leader. He left the Trueni alone, and was more preoccupied with the defense of the province from the northern aggressors, or an invasion from across the mountains and sea. His army and navy were formidable forces, and that is why their neighbors had not invaded them—yet. They defended their territory fiercely. Bakar said he knew Trueni who gathered bat guano from caves for Ortzi. They believed he used it to make a weapon that made fire and a loud noise. Stone

castles that overlooked the bay housed these weapons. The Galonese were also skilled builders. It was the opinion of Bakar that
it would take a large fleet and army to invade their sheltered city.

As much as he wanted to see the city of Abena, Jarah felt that
they should stay here for a while and help these people, so after
they'd eaten he indicated that the Six should return to the boat
for a private discussion. They all agreed that this would be a good
place to begin the healing process for the Trueni. They could live
on the boat and not be a burden to Bakar, or the people of Ibai,
and it would give them privacy during the healing sessions. They
returned to the shack.

"Bakar," said Jarah, "We would like to help you and the Trueni
of Ibai. We have the ability to heal and return you to your human
form, like us, or the people of Galon." Bakar and Erlea looked at
them, astounded. "Askia was one of you, and in a way, he still is,
but you may have noticed he is more human and speaks more like
one of us. We are still in the process of healing him. Yared and
Shogna too, but it takes a little time. We can start this healing for
you, and any Trueni, who wish it. We will not force it on anyone,
and you may decide if this is what you would wish for, or not."

"Yes, I see Askia like us, but also not like us. He speak different
too. We would like much to be healed!"

So, with the decision sealed, Holgar and Adne agreed with the
Six that it was a good plan.

"We will help where we can," said Adne. "I can help with the
language. Teach them how to pronounce words correctly and put
together sentences that are more understandable."

"And I can teach them other things, such as business and
building skills, and then they won't be so different from humans,"
Holgar added.

They constructed two shelters on deck, one where they could
live and eat, and another just for healing. Word spread in Ibai, up
and down the Garden River, and soon they were swamped with

Trueni who lined up on the pier for healing. Yared and Shogna helped them organize the sessions, turning some away for the next day, and handling those who were growing impatient with the wait. Shogna handed out water all day long, and Erlea fed those who had waited all day. The Six were fast becoming exhausted, but they did not flag in their marathon sessions. They retired early to bed and were up with the sun the next day.

They could see that Yared and Shogna were losing their animal-like appendages, and their speech, thanks to Adne, was now becoming more sophisticated.

"I could not do this with them before the healing," she explained. "Their mouths were not suitable for human speech as ours is, and it would have been cruel to try. Now it is different. They can articulate as well as I can!"

Even the Six were amazed at the speed of the Healing Crystal. It took two or three sessions per person for noticeable and dramatic results. Horns simply disappeared overnight. Tails fell off painlessly and did not regrow. Mouths, noses, and ears reformed and new, human hair grew in places where it should. Babies seemed to heal faster, and Yared's daughter was now fully human. Yared and Shogna named her Zuri, which meant "happiness."

Not all Trueni desired healing though. One in particular, a fisherman named Mikel, was vocal in his opposition.

"Healer's witches and wizards. I no go near. I happy with face and horn." He would not allow his wife and children near them either, and glared at them as he sailed by on his rainbow-colored boat. There were a few more who felt the same way Mikel did, and they resented the newly-healed, calling them traitors to the Trueni and mocking them for their desire to be human. Some of them threw rocks or sticks at the boat as they passed, but they were quickly chased off by the Trueni lined up for healing.

Gradually, the lines became shorter, their days now punctuated with more free time as the Trueni healed. Many of their lean-tos' and shacks were reconstructed with the help of Yared and Holgar. Shops were set up with new businesses, and Ibai transformed dramatically into a clean and well-planned village. Holgar encouraged many to build on land rather than the rickety piers. They spent months in Ibai, and even though they'd never worked so hard in their lives, the Six felt they'd never been happier.

It couldn't last, thought Jarah.

Thane Awstin and King Brenin, Three Rivers

There had been another beheading today. King Brenin was pleased. His eyes swept around his chambers, raking over each member of the Witan—his council—who had gathered there. He noted the raw fear in their eyes, and he felt a sense of achievement. It had been an adequate demonstration to his subjects of his resolve and strength. He would not tolerate any further resistance to his government, or his decrees.

"If I have to raise taxes, I will raise them," he looked pointedly at Thane Awstin, head of his Witan. "The people must know that it's for their own good. Enemies, those who would invade our borders and overrun our land, surround us. I've only raised the rates by one ma'ah for most households—"

"Yes, Your Majesty, I do understand," Thane Awstin the Forkbeard was the only one of the Witan who dared to interrupt the king. As his closest friend and advisor, he often tried to express his opinions in the most diplomatic way possible. "And that is well within your rights to do so. However, most households in Aelfar and Mernoc are simple farmers. A silver ma'ah represents many months of hard labor—"

"Don't interrupt me again, Awstin." Awstin turned pale. Why had he opened his mouth? He knew the King hated disagreement.

"Maybe you'd like to join our headless objector out there." Brenin nodded towards the courtyard outside. "My army needs to pay our soldiers. I'm building up our army, and our navy is still sadly lacking. Where do you think the money is going to come from?" No one responded, their faces still ashen.

Awstin privately decided that he'd like to keep his forked beard intact. He took pride in it, and he spent hours having it trimmed to his satisfaction. He too had threatened many barbers with a beheading if they didn't get it just right, so why should he worry about a few malcontents who objected to being taxed?

The King was right, though, thought the Thane. They needed more money, more soldiers, and a fully equipped fleet if they were going to defend themselves from the Rhagbeneth and the Galonese. Word was that Ortzi, the Warlord of Galon, was building up his own army and navy, and who knew what was going on over the mountains? Amrafalus was the main threat, but no one knew exactly what he was up to. Crossing those mountains was a death sentence, and sending spies by sea was risky. Few of them ever returned, and those that did return remained changed. A quick death was better than what Amrafalus did with them.

"You, the Witan," said Brenin, "will determine exactly how much more in taxes our citizens will pay. Every citizen, starting today and regardless of their income, will pay more, even if it's a copper issar."

"Your Majesty, does this include our peerage and noble classes?" A Witan member asked, timidly.

"Of course not, you fool. Taxing ourselves is ridiculous. Now get out of here. Send our collectors out into the city and farmlands immediately. If they don't have the money, take their livestock. Take whatever they might have of value."

The Witan scurried out, and the King sat and thought for a while before calling for Sweyn, Earl of Aeynsham and Keeper of the Privy Purse. Sweyn appeared magically, as if he'd been waiting just outside the door. Brenin knew that eavesdropping was a typical palace pursuit. The only place he felt safe from listening ears was in his private chambers, where the door was too thick for even Sweyn's ears.

"Sweyn, send someone to get that bracelet I saw in the jeweler's shop yesterday. I have a lady who will appreciate it."

Sweyn bowed and left. He'd told the king yesterday that unless taxes were raised, he, as Keeper of the Privy Purse, could not justify its purchase. Therefore, he was not surprised to hear at the door what the King had done.

Yesterday, one of the Witan had protested, and now his head decorated a stake in the courtyard. The king would be looking for a replacement. He knew that his own position in the royal household was precarious, and he'd not slept well last night, worrying about how his refusal yesterday to buy the bracelet had angered the king. He knew whom the bracelet was for. Not Queen Catrin, but a lady-in-waiting. A lovely young thing, for sure, but not the queen.

4.

The Keep

Early one morning, towards the end of the dry season, the sound of loud voices and shouts on the pier awakened the Six. Curious, but still sleepy, they emerged from their shelter and onto the open boat deck to see what the commotion was about. The dock swayed perilously as a troop of a dozen soldiers, armed with swords, spears, and knives strode purposefully towards them. They were a fierce lot: unshaven and dirty with wild, coarse hair bristling out from under their horned helmets.

Djana noticed her parents as they tried to push their way forward in the crowd, with Yared and Askia right next to them, but she gave them a warning look and shook her head. To her relief, they stopped where they were. Dark eyes flashed as the soldiers spied the Six on the boat deck. A soldier, who seemed to be their commanding officer, stepped forward.

"Come with us. Ortzi wants to see you." The Six agreed amongst themselves that resistance would serve no useful purpose, so they quietly pulled their boots on and accompanied the troop off the pier.

They made their way through the village and headed towards the road to Abena. Djana thought there was a small chance that Ortzi and the soldiers did not know of the existence of her parents, Askia, or Yared and his family. As they led the Six away, Holgar and Adne had looked on helpless and stricken.

Djana wished she could have comforted them before they were taken, but they'd had no warning, and she did not want to draw attention to the rest of their party. Her parents did not stand out from the crowd now that so many of the Trueni in Ibai looked fully human. She believed that Ortzi did not want to harm them, and that they'd soon be back in Ibai.

The soldiers refused to answer their questions, no matter how many times they asked. They continued to march them down the road, occasionally prodding them with their spears if they moved too slowly. Jarah did not sense a lot of hostility from them, only a desire to obey orders. Tegan agreed as she picked up his unspoken thoughts. *"Perhaps we'll be back by the end of the day, and at least we'll get to see the city."*

After about an hour of marching with the sparkling bay on their right, the city appeared in front of them. Abena sprawled across the half-moon curve of a smaller bay. It rose steeply up the surrounding hills from stone piers where large warships flying a yellow sun crest were moored. It was an attractive city sporting ochre stonework, red tiled roofs, bustling market places, and cobbled streets. Rocky hillsides and sheer cliffs tumbled to the edges of the bay. They could see that that the bay was fortified with castles that clung dizzily to the cliff's edge. They did not enter the city, but circumvented it, ascending narrow steps that zigzagged up towards one of the stone fortifications. They wondered what their fate was to be, and what Ortzi wanted with them.

Jarah had an unsettled feeling in the pit of his stomach. Whatever it was, it couldn't be good news for them.

Blaidd has Doubts

Blaidd, now fully recovered from his trauma, sat basking in the sun on the open-air terrace that overlooked the Bay of Rhiannon. Several months of sitting in the sun, breathing in the fresh sea air and enjoying the flowers and aromatic shrubs that proliferated on the terrace had passed him by as he slowly recovered from his ordeal. Today, as usual, his thoughts lingered on Branwyn. He wondered why he still did not trust her. She was the most fascinating woman he'd ever seen, and his feelings veered from absolute adoration to distrust and fear in the space of moments.

When he awoke in her home in Rhiannon, he knew all his dreams were now a reality. Branwyn lived luxuriously. She owned slaves—Trueni—who did her bidding with a snap of her fingers. Silently, they brought food and drink, tending to his every need and then melting unobtrusively away when they were through. He was of the mind that he could live like this forever. Amrafalus had treated him well too, but the Citadel had felt to him more like a military barracks than a home.

Nearly every day, he noticed a raven that sat on the terrace with him. It seemed as if the raven was curious, and he often spoke aloud to the bird. The raven hopped nearer each time until it came to rest on the back of his chair. As he gained the raven's trust, it sat in front of him as he talked, and it wasn't long before he bared his soul to the bird. He told it his life story, his past as Seryn, his wishes—to marry Branwyn—and his ambitions to rule Rhiannon. As he spoke, he ran his hand unconsciously over the bumps on his head.

There were two of them—hard, bony protrusions. His hair was falling out, and he hardly recognized himself now when he looked in the mirror. Even his ears seemed longer and hairier than normal. His thoughts were slow, and it took him forever to plan his day. He had been aware of the changes in his thoughts and body soon after Amrafalus had used his memory crystals on him, before the fall of the Citadel. What else had Amrafalus done to him in those sessions under the Citadel? He'd been unconscious most of the time, as if he'd been drugged.

A spasm of fear skittered through his mind, and he pushed it down, as he'd done so many times before. Perhaps it was nothing—he'd bumped his head without realizing it, and everyone felt a little hairier than normal at times.

His thoughts went back to the raven. He felt the raven was a friend, and the only thing in the whole world he could really trust. Day after day, he talked to it. He told the raven about the changes of his body and his thoughts on them. A bird would not judge him, and it would be their secret. He didn't tell Branwyn about his conversations, and she never asked. It was something that he felt embarrassed about, and he was glad no one could see him talking to the bird.

It was now several days since he'd last seen the raven. Branwyn had also mysteriously disappeared, leaving a message with a slave that she'd be back soon and that he was to remain in the house. He felt lonely and abandoned. There was nothing to do and he was bored. He wondered if the raven was all right and hoped it would return. Then, to his delight, it did. He was sitting out on the terrace, as was his custom, when the raven appeared on the low wall in front of him.

"Hello, old friend," he said. "Good to see you again!" The raven cocked its head and observed him with a bright eye. "I missed you. Where did you go?" He turned his head to look out over the bay, not expecting an answer of course, but to his amazement, a voice spoke back to him.

"I will always come back to you, my love!"

He jerked his head back around, and there in front of him, sitting on the wall, was Branwyn.

"W-Where did you come from? What happened to the raven?" He blinked, and the raven appeared again on the wall. Branwyn was gone. Like a slap to the face, he realized what she ... what the raven, was. He felt the rage bubble up, rising from deep within him. His arm snaked towards a loose rock on the wall, and picking it up he hurled it towards the raven. It vanished again, and now Branwyn stood behind him. "You're a loathsome shape-shifter—a sorcerer—just like Irusan!"

"*Tut, tut!* You really need to work on that temper, Blaidd!" He whirled around again, flying at Branwyn with fists pumping and arms wind milling, but he met again an empty space. Branwyn stood behind him. She shrugged, an amused smirk on her lips, as if he were a toddler having a tantrum. "We can do this all day, it's up to you."

"Why didn't you tell me?"

"Well, if I had, then I wouldn't have gained your trust so quickly, would I? You've told me a lot, much more than if I'd simply asked you to be honest with me. Deception is my game, Blaidd. I can learn a lot more, much faster. We don't have a lot of time, and I didn't want to have to extract it from you through mind probes since you're already in an unbalanced state, thanks to your sessions with Amrafalus' unreliable memory crystals. I knew you'd enjoy my company more as a raven, so that is why I decided upon that strategy. One day, it will make sense to you."

Blaidd sat down again, his anger quickly dissipating. He couldn't stay angry with Branwyn for long. "It already does, Branwyn. Yes, I *am* furious—and humiliated. I told you some things I've never told anybody, but you're right—you have it all now." He thought a bit more, and then asked, "What is it we don't have a lot of time for?"

"I told you. I have plans. I've been in Rhiannon a long time, Blaidd, just waiting for my chance, and finally it has arrived. Amrafalus' body has not been recovered, and he would have surfaced by now had he survived the collapse of the Citadel. We can only assume he's buried below the Citadel. Madfall, the only council member to escape the collapsing Citadel, is running things. Udfa is still in charge of the Navy. I am now a member of the new Council of Ten, and everything is going my way. I haven't been idle. I've also cultivated a friendship with Anfawl—you'll remember him as the Captain of the Guard, who, fortunately, was not in the Citadel when it collapsed. He's not happy about Madfall's takeover of the leadership reins, and he has an ongoing feud with Udfa—"

"How did Udfa make it out of the Citadel? I thought he was dead, too."

"Udfa doesn't die easily. He, along with Madfall, were right behind you." Blaidd remembered the pounding footsteps he'd heard just behind him. "The falling door nearly crushed them both but, like you, they managed to get under it just in time. Madfall collapsed in the courtyard, but Udfa headed towards you with sword drawn when I put a sleeping spell on him and he fell unconscious. So, you see Blaidd, I really saved your life." Branwyn stroked his cheek with a soft hand, a gentle touch that made him want to cry, to sob out loud for the mother he'd never had. But then her voice changed: a metallic rasp, and every hair on the back of his neck stood up. "I don't expect gratitude, but I do expect your help. You are the only person on Ialana, other than the Six, who understand the big generator crystals. Amrafalus tried to make use of you in this respect in both your lifetimes, but Amrafalus was a fool. He was distorted in his thinking and nuances escaped him. He was incapable of really understanding the situation and thinking it through. Instead, he wanted to get his way by brute force, hasty action, and fear." She snorted, her gaze focused now in the direction of where the Citadel used to stand. "I knew that it would eventually guarantee his downfall, and it took a long time, but it finally did. It was easy enough for six youngsters to outsmart him, but it's not so simple to outsmart *me*, Blaidd." Her blue-black eyes whipped back to him. "The Six, when we locate them and bring them back, will not find me a pushover."

Blaidd tried to look away, but no matter how hard he tried, he could not pull his gaze away. He could not even move his head. She terrified him, his knees knocked together, but how could he hate her? She was so beautiful, and she *loved* him. No-one, not even his father, had loved him before. He'd worked with Amrafalus to get the Crystal, but he'd never felt any loyalty towards him. He was glad he was dead. Branwyn, on the other hand ... he knew he would do anything for her. He did not wish to displease her, ever.

"Madfall is almost as stupid as Amrafalus was." At last, Branwyn's eyes released him, and her voice took on a conversational tone, as if she were discussing what they were going to eat for lunch. "He's not a threat to me, but I do have plans to remove him, as well." She snickered, hand in front of her mouth, like a schoolgirl planning a joke. "This is where Anfawl comes in. He's to lead a coup against Madfall with the Army. The Navy is not equipped to deal with this, and Anfawl will be placed on the throne of Rhiannon, with me as his queen and bride."

Blaidd felt the shock of her words. They pierced through his heart like an arrow, and he went pale. Branwyn marry *Anfawl*? What about him ... didn't they ... didn't she ... ?"

"Oh, don't be so sentimental, you ass. Yes, of course, I love you. How long do you think Anfawl is going to live, married to me? Accidents do happen." She laughed and Blaidd sighed a long sigh of relief. "Together we'll rule, my love, just as I promised. Now that I know what your heart truly desires and what to expect from you, we can work together to make this possible. I went on a long journey that took me far away—which is why you did not see me in my raven or physical form—so sit down and I'll tell you all about it."

They sat together, companionably, on the wall and Branwyn told him exactly what she'd been doing for those several weeks that he had been recuperating in the sun on her terrace.

5.

Three Rivers, Aelfar, Queen Catrin

An icy wind howled down from the tundra of Rhagbeneth towards Three Rivers, with the Border River, the River Mair, and the River Braith, solidly iced over in the severest winter in living memory. Catrin peered intently at her image in the burnished shield that was her mirror as Corrick, her lady-in-waiting, brushed her hair. She wasn't getting any younger, and she was sure she saw some more grey in the brown, and wasn't that another wrinkle? How, she asked herself, could she compete with the beautiful ladies of her court if she kept appearing older?

She'd caught Brenin looking at Corrick, just recently, in a way that she hoped he would one day look at her again. But, she thought, a long time had passed since he'd looked at her like that. How could she produce another heir if he refused to come to her chamber at night? Deryn was the successor to the throne, of course, but he—she stifled a sob. She didn't want Corrick to see how anxious she was.

"All done, milady. Is there anything else you wish me to do for you tonight?"

"No, Corrick, you've been a gem, as usual. Go get some sleep yourself and I'll see you in the morning." Corrick curtsied before she left the Queen's Chamber, and Catrin continued to sit and stare, gazing into the mirror. She didn't really see herself there, anymore. The spirited Catrin, who had arrived at the palace from sunny Mernoc so long ago, was gone, replaced by this empty shell of a woman. It was this woman who looked back at her with blank eyes; eyes without hope.

She'd not always felt this way. She remembered the birth of Deryn, a joyful event, one celebrated with feasts and laughter. Her husband was playful and loving with her. Nothing was amiss with their marriage, until it was noticed that Deryn did not walk when he was supposed to walk, and did not speak until he was almost three years old. His leg muscles seemed withered, and she spent her days and nights teaching him how to use them, calling in healers—who were mostly charlatans—but nothing seemed to help her son. He was now ten summers, and although he walked, it was with great difficulty, as his withered legs could not easily hold up his little body. He used a cane to stay upright, and he walked in a limping fashion if he walked at all.

Brenin did not disguise his disgust with her. She felt that he thought it was her fault their son was not fit to be a king, and he ignored both her and Deryn, as if they somehow caused him shame. She knew that he consorted with other women, and he openly talked of finding another queen consort who would produce a healthy son as his heir. Up until now he'd not found a suitable replacement. She knew that, because she too had a secret.

Some years ago, with the help of Corrick, she'd tried to move a large armoire in her bedchamber. After they pulled it away, Corrick noticed that it covered a panel of wood that seemed different to the others surrounding it.

"What do you think it means, Corrick?" she asked, running her fingers over the smooth wood.

"Why, I am sure I have no idea, milady. Maybe they ran out of the other kind of wood and put this one in thinking no one would notice, especially with the armoire in front."

Catrin was just about to walk away when Corrick's hand reached up to wipe at a dark stain on one side of the board. That was when they heard a *click,* and the panel swung smoothly away from the wall. An opening, just large enough for a person to go through, appeared.

Corrick protested as Catrin squeezed through the narrow doorway. "No, milady! Don't go in there! You don't know what's in there or where it leads to!"

"Oh, come on, Corrick. Get a candle, let's go together!" They moved silently down a small and dark corridor that twisted between the palace walls. The candle guttered and cast grotesque shadows in front of them as they descended a narrow flight of stone stairs. Spider webs brushed their faces and Catrin wanted to sneeze. There was a lot of dust in a passage that had lain undisturbed for countless summers.

They walked some more, went down another flight, and after more twists and turns came to a wooden door bound with iron set in a stone wall. Catrin pulled at the ancient, rusted padlock. It fell apart in her hands. She and Corrick pushed and pulled on the door until finally it creaked open. Rust and must fell away like dark snowflakes. The warm sun touched their faces as they cautiously peaked out.

"We're outside the palace walls!" The door was set into the wall that surrounded the palace, and below them, the green banks fell away to the silvery waters of the gently flowing River Mair. "Well, at least we know where this comes out. Tell no one what we've discovered, Corrick. It may be to our advantage one day to know of this."

Corrick nodded, and they made their way back after closing and latching the door behind them.

THE SIX AND THE GARDENERS OF IALANA

As they walked back along the way they came, the candlelight glinted on something Catrin had not seen before: a small metal grate in the wall. Catrin stopped, and, standing on tiptoe, looked through the lattice. She gasped. She could see right into her husband's private bedchamber. It was the place he went to when she wearied him with her company, or when he needed to speak privately with his advisors. But tonight he was not in his chambers. She could see one of his manservants cleaning the room, and she quickly withdrew. She did not tell Corrick what she had seen, and when Corrick asked where the grate came out, she said, "Oh, it's only a ventilation duct to another room. Nothing important."

They pushed the armoire back and Catrin did not speak of their adventure again, but she had not forgotten. Many nights, when sleep was slow in coming to her, she laboriously pushed the armoire back just enough so she could squeeze into the corridor and feel her way, without a candle, to the metal grate in the wall. She knew exactly where it was, and she stood quietly listening to the voices on the other side. She could see the room clearly, and she was careful that no one glancing at the grate from the other side would see her. Most of the time, the conversations she overheard were mundane, simply her husband speaking with servants. Nevertheless, there were times when he conversed with his State Advisors and confidantes.

She'd heard all the plans he refused to tell her about—affairs of State, the wars continually being fought on their borders, and other things that she'd not been aware of. She often found him entertaining women of dubious character, some of whom she never thought were untrustworthy, and most of those who claimed to be her friend. She always withdrew when this happened. She did not wish to torture herself with a sight she could never take back, but now she fully understood whom her friends really were. That is why she trusted Corrick, and Corrick only. She'd never come across her lady-in-waiting entertaining her husband.

For years, she kept her secret, and she did not confide in any-one, not even Corrick. She did not know if the King might se-duce Corrick in the future, since he could be very charming to the unwary, and she did not want to give away the one advantage she held by being too trusting. Although Corrick knew about the secret passage, they'd not discussed it again and she hoped that Corrick had forgotten about it.

A few nights ago, she'd again made her way back to the grate. She didn't think she'd hear anything new. Lately there had been little happening, and her husband had not entertained any women in his private chambers for a long time. She wondered if he was losing his virility.

The room was dark and she heard her husband snoring in his bed. She was just about to turn around and return to her room when a knock came from his chamber door. The snores stopped. Brenin muttered something, and the knocking came again.

"*Yes, come!*" Brenin lit a candle on his bedside stand and got out of bed. The door opened. The Captain of his personal guard stood there.

"Your Majesty, I beg your pardon for the disturbance, but there's someone in the courtyard who demands to see you!"

"Who would ask to see me this time of night?"

"She says she comes from Dalnoor, Your Majesty, and she has news of Amrafalus!"

"What? All right—bring her here."

To everyone's surprise, including Catrin's, a figure stepped out from behind the guard and walked into the room.

"Uh, begging your pardon Your Majesty—I didn't know she was right here!" said the flustered guard. "I told her to wait in the courtyard."

"I wait for no-one," said the figure as she stepped into the light. Catrin heard Brenin's sharp intake of breath, and it was all she could do not to gasp aloud herself. She quickly put her hand over her mouth. She had never seen such a beautiful woman.

Brenin stood slack-jawed, and he didn't seem to know what to say. He waved for the guard to leave, and the startled guard left, closing the door behind him. "I am Branwyn," said the woman, "soon to be Queen of Rhiannon."

Finally, Brenin found his tongue. "What do you mean, 'soon to be'?"

"There is soon to be a military coup in Rhiannon. My future husband will be King, but, unfortunately, he will not live long."

"Well—I'm not sure if you are an insane woman or a witch who knows the future," said Brenin. "Tell me, what about Amrafalus? You said you had news—"

"Yes. Amrafalus died about a month ago. His Citadel collapsed upon him, poor man, if one can call him a man. He was just as the rumors said—a reptile. His right-hand man, Madfall, head of the Council of Ten, now rules. However, rest assured it would not be for long. My future husband has the army on his side, and there will be a coup."

"So what do you want from me?"

Branwyn walked over to the King and placed her hand on his cheek. Catrin was stunned. He had beheaded people for less—did this woman have no sense? Nevertheless, all Brenin did was stand there as if hypnotized. "I want your army and your navy. I want the Six, and I also want you."

She leaned over and kissed Brenin full on the mouth. Catrin put her hand out to stop herself from falling. Her knees felt weak with shock. She could not believe the temerity of this woman! Who did she think she was? She must be crazy.

But Brenin still did not move, and finally, his arms came up, pulling the woman roughly towards him. Catrin decided that she would not remain for this, and, trembling with fear, she walked back to her room. Her last thought before falling asleep as the sun came up was, *who, or what, were the Six?*

She went back to the grate every night, and every night she saw Branwyn in her husband's chambers. She felt a compulsion now to return, to find out all she could about this Branwyn. It was obvious to Catrin that Brenin and Branwyn now shared a bed. In addition, much discussion that went on between the sheets, and between other activities. Catrin now felt immune to these spectacles, and her mind was razor-sharp as she focused on what had been said. It had only been four nights ago that her world came crashing down, but hope too was offered, and it was hope for her and Deryn that kept her going back to the grate. She recalled the conversation exactly as it happened. She replayed it in her mind repeatedly.

"So what about your queen, dear one?" Branwyn had asked as she seductively caressed the king's face.

"What about her? She's of no consequence."

"Well, she will be if I am to be the Widow-Queen of Dalnoor and Ak-Gala. How will we combine the lands we rule over if we do not marry?"

The king thought for a while, and then said, "I'll cross that one when I get to it. Catrin is weak of mind and spirit. No one will be surprised if she throws herself into the river and takes her lame son with her."

"My love, I'll give you a strong and healthy son, and he will be everything you ever wished for. But first, we must find the Six."

"What is this Six you keep on about?" asked Brenin, smiling.

"Not 'what', but 'who.' The Six are powerful healers who know how to manipulate crystals. They also know how to find a passage and activate the key that opens these passageways through the Osgoi Mountains—a passage that will enable our armies to pass through with the greatest of ease. We'll conquer Rhagbeneth and Mannanon from the west while we pincer them in from the south and east with our combined fleet. They'll be surrounded on all sides, and the Continent of Ialana will be ours!"

"So where do we find these healers?"

"I believe they'll make their way back to their homes in Aelfar. I know some of them originally came from the villages of Meadowfield and Potter's Hill. It would be surprising if they did not return there after their escape from Amrafalus. They still have families there, and it is likely they'll want to see them. If you send a detachment to stake out these villages, you might get lucky and catch them."

"I like it," said Brenin, kissing Branwyn's glossy hair as Catrin shakily withdrew.

Amrafalus

He sniffed the air, his monstrous body crouching low on the ground as he stalked his prey, a sleeping wild pig that had made its bed in the forest undergrowth. The rock had badly mangled his leg, but now it was healing and he was able to hunt for food. The sensors in his gaping jaws told him when he was close enough. He could feel the body heat of the pig, and he could see its outline in the dark with his night-vision. Like an arrow from a bow, he launched himself at the pig. It never knew what hit it as the enormous jaws closed around it, swallowing it whole.

He spent the rest of the night up a tree where he was safe from other predators, giving his meal a chance to digest. He would continue his journey in the morning.

After his escape from the cavern and tunnel, he felt the urge to keep moving. He had looked back again across the Bay as he moved further into the forest and seen the city in the middle of the bay, the dust still rising from a pile of rubble at its center. Whatever happened to him back in the city must have been personal, but his memory was still spotty. He remembered that there was an escape, and that he, at any cost, must find the escapees. It was important.

A number—six—kept flashing in his mind. He didn't know what it meant, but he had to find out. His survival depended upon it.

He felt rage boiling up in him, and he nearly vomited up the pig. Instinctively, he felt that whoever it was he needed to find had gone east over the mountains. He too would go east. His memory would return.

6.

Ortzi

The Six reached the top of the cliff via a rocky path that twisted between boulders, shrubs, stunted pines, and cypress trees, all the way to the top where a stone staircase wound between crenellated walls to the Keep. The Keep was a single tower, surrounded on three sides by a courtyard. Buildings with red tiled roofs enclosed the courtyard. Guards were posted at the entrance gates of the tower that overlooked the bay and the city. They noticed heavy metal objects positioned atop the walls, but they didn't know what they were. They looked tubular, and the tubes were cradled on metal stands, metal balls piled next to them.

The Captain led them into the courtyard, then ushered them into the hall of the largest building. A central table ran nearly the full length of the long room where men, clad in fine silks, sat. An imposing man, even when sitting, stood up as they entered and lifted his hand—palm forward—in greeting.

THE SIX AND THE GARDENERS OF IALANA

"Blessed day to you! I apologize for having to disturb you in this fashion, and I hope you forgive me, but I had to see you. I am Ortzi, and I lead this nation of Galon. This is my Cabinet." With a sweep of his hand, he indicated the men at the table. "We are all curious to see the healers we have heard so much about!"

"I am Jarah, and these are my friends and fellow-healers—Tristan, Adain, Tegan, Kex, and Djana. May you inform us how long we are to remain here, or are we free to return to Ibai?"

"You are free, but first I must ask you what your purpose is. Where are you from, who are you healing, how, and why?" Ortzi waved his hand again towards several seats on one side that were empty. "Please, sit!"

Jarah hardly knew where to begin. How much should he tell this Ortzi, and should he be trusted at all? He felt inadequate as the group's spokesperson, but as he looked at his companions they all looked back at him, and he could clearly see they were waiting for him to speak. He had no choice. He would have to decide.

"We are healers who use a crystal to heal. We were trained in the use of crystals by the descendants of the Basajaun."

Ortzi looked startled, as did the Cabinet members. "Basajaun? We've not heard of any Basajaun in Ialana for thousands of years. Our records clearly show they disappeared a long time ago. No-one even knows what happened to them."

"Well, there are many descendants of the Basajaun still on Ialana. You need look no further than yourselves. Ialana was overrun fifteen hundred years ago in the area of Rhiannon and Dalnoor by the Dherog—the Reptilian race that Amrafalus came from. As a result, the Basajaun were scattered over the continent and settled in areas such as this and other places. Most forgot their knowledge and reverted back to savagery and ignorance—"

Ortzi's eyes flashed. "Are you calling us ignorant?"

"No, sir, but you have forgotten your own history and origins, as did my people in Aelfar."

"You are from Aelfar?" Ortzi leapt up, his chair crashing nois-ily behind him. They jumped as he yelled, "I will have you put in chains! You are spies for Brenin!"

"*No*, we are *not* spies! We did not come here to spy. We have no alliance with Brenin, or anyone else!" Jarah drew a deep breath. Things weren't going well for them, and he was botching it up bad-ly. He wished Irusan were here so he could consult him on what to say. Why weren't the others helping him? He noticed then that Tegan was opening her mouth to say something.

"My friend is right, we are not spies—"

"Curb your female!" yelled Ortzi, his face turning purple. "We do not allow women to speak in our Hall of Justice!"

Jarah now felt his own anger, and he too stood up, pushing his chair over the tiled floor with a screech as it moved back.

"Our women speak whenever they want to," he said. "They do not wait for our permission." Ortzi opened his mouth to say something, but Jarah held up his hand. "Let me finish. I say again, we are *not* spies. If we were, we would have come straight into Abena instead of Ibai. What is there to spy on in Ibai? How many fish they catch? We are not war-makers, but healers. Our purpose here is to heal the Tru-eni and others like them whom by foul means have been altered. I do not understand why anyone would object to this. Let us sit down like men and talk calmly, and everything you desire to know about who we are, and our purpose here, will be made clear to you."

Ortzi picked his chair up and sat down. He looked long and hard at Jarah and the others. Then he laughed.

A deep, belly laugh went on and on, and soon all the Cabinet were chuckling too, except their chuckles sounded forced and did not match their eyes. Jarah did not know if he should laugh as well, and his companions looked as puzzled as he did. This Ortzi was a difficult man to understand. Mercurial, perhaps, but not an evil man. It was even possible, he thought, that Ortzi could be reasoned with.

Finally, the laughter stopped and Ortzi wiped his eyes with a cloth. "You are lucky I did not put you all in chains and throw you over the cliff, but yes, we shall talk. It's possible you are not spies. If you are, I will find out, and it won't go well for you. Tell me more about this *healing* and what you are doing in Ibai."

Jarah told him about their escape from Amrafalus, and how they thought Amrafalus was dead. Ortzi's eyes lit up at this news. "But we don't know if Amrafalus is *truly* dead, and we won't go back until we know for sure. It's too dangerous for us. He will use us to make weapons out of crystals."

"Weapons from crystals? *Hmmm* ..." Ortzi stopped and thought a bit, then continued. "But if he *is* dead, that is good news indeed! I still don't trust those people across the mountains. We won't let our guard down." The Cabinet nodded in unison. "Go on."

Jarah continued. "We came to Galon several months ago. It's one of the few places we thought was safe for the Trueni and us. We have a crystal that is able to change back the pattern of the Trueni to that of a human one. It is our mission to heal as many as we can before we go back to Akelarre."

"Yes, I've heard from others that the Trueni are becoming human. I have seen this with my own eyes. Some of our servants are Trueni, and the change has been noticeable. Everyone is talking about it."

Jarah relaxed a bit. Things were going better. Then the hammer blow struck. "But I can't allow it." The Six looked at Ortzi, stunned, then at each other.

"What do you mean—you can't allow it?"

"Just what I said. Are you deaf? I can't allow it." Ortzi shifted in his chair. "Look, these people are allowed to remain here by my sufferance, regardless of what my predecessors decided about them. They have places to live and jobs to keep them busy. They're perfect in these roles, and we've had no trouble from them since they first came here several hundred years ago. They know their place and they stay there. We have cheap labor and everyone is happy. Why upset the balance?"

"Who says the balance will be upset? They are the same people, they just look different."

"And behave differently too. My subjects have reported that some of their servants are demanding to be educated. Imagine that! An animal that speaks wants to be a scholar! Next thing, they'll be demanding equal status, higher wages, and that will lead to unrest, and before we know it, they'll be arming themselves against me. I can't allow it. This must stop today."

There was silence for a while, the cabinet members nodding sagely. The Six had not seen this coming and they were shocked. Who would have thought anyone would object to their citizens being healed? They looked at each other, at a loss for words.

"You can continue to heal if that is what makes you happy, but not the Trueni. My people have various health problems our own healers have not been able to help with. You can heal the sick, the lame, and the blind. We'll bring them to you. But no Trueni."

"You misunderstand the ability of our Healing Crystal, sir. The reason for its creation is to change the distortions to the natural pattern, and that that caused by other crystal misapplications, such as that of the Trueni. It was not programmed for healing those with ordinary ailments—"

"I do not know this *program* stuff. You will heal our people or I will put you in my dungeon and leave you there. I understand you have others with you—other Trueni. I will round them up too and—"

"*All right.* We'll do what you ask. Nevertheless, don't be surprised if it doesn't work too well. We can't guarantee the outcome."

"Another thing; if you need more crystals, I have plenty." Ortzi sniffed as he saw the surprised looks on their faces. "You didn't know, did you? Why do you think Amrafalus wanted to conquer Galon so badly? Not for our fish, as you so aptly said earlier. He knows—knew—that we have crystals. Yes, the Basajaun obtained all their crystals from Galon. No one wants them now, except Amrafalus. Or he once did. I still can't believe he's dead. So, we will take you to our crystals, and you will find crystals that will heal our people and protect my country. Now, my Captain of the Guard will take you to your quarters."

With that, Ortzi rose and strode out of the Hall of Justice, and then the cabinet disbanded and left, leaving the Six to go with the Captain.

Admiral Udfa

Udfa felt little gratitude that he was still Admiral of the Fleet, and that no one had ended his life—yet. He had hoped, though ... He turned to face the Council of Ten. Anfawl was now a member of the committee and a senior officer. Madfall, the only member of Amrafalus' original Council of Ten to make it out of the collapsing Citadel, sat at the head of the table with Anfawl at his right hand. They had not made a seat at the table for him. Instead, they had summoned him as if he was a low-ranking junior officer. He wondered if he could still be nominated as a member of the new council.

There were now nine members, not counting Madfall, and they would need another one. Udfa realized now he had not moved fast enough to seize power after the collapse of the Citadel. He should have killed both Madfall and Anfawl instead of chasing after Blaidd, but hindsight was always better, Udfa thought, bitterly.

He had swallowed his pride though, and did his best to ingratiate himself with the new council members. It would not be wise for him to oppose the new government directly, at this time, he thought. He had more power as an admiral than as a hunted fugitive, and becoming a council member would place him on a level equal to Anfawl.

"Yes, my lords," he responded to their question. "It is always my goal to increase the weaponry of our navy. Now, we have little in firepower. I would suggest we concentrate our funds on improving this situation instead of focusing only on the army." He glanced sideways at Anfawl, whose face resembled that of a dark thundercloud. "I mean no disrespect to the army," he added hastily. "But with the navy at such a disadvantage, we would be pressed to win a battle against Trueni fishermen, never mind a well-armed foe."

"What do you suggest?" asked Madfall, who was well aware of the rivalry between the two men.

"I hear the Galonese possess a weapon that is able to catapult fiery balls from a distance, my lord. My spies have observed this during their training exercises in Abena. We do not have that capability, but we could construct something similar on the decks of our ships using flammable missiles that we can propel onto other ships—"

"And thereby burn our ships down as well?" asked Anfawl with a smirk on his face. "No! I say we use the fleet for carrying my troops so that they can attack from the sea. We can board their ships and fight to the death like men. We give our men better weapons, train them in ship-boarding and how to keep the enemy distracted while our ground troops move in."

The council members nodded as he spoke. Udfa realized that things were not going his way. The fool outranked him now, and he *almost* wished Amrafalus were back. At least he would have seen the sense in his suggestions.

At that moment, the sorcerer walked into the council session. Udfa gasped. Who did she think she was? He looked at the members in astonishment, but they merely smiled and showed her to a seat next to Anfawl.

"Meet our new member," said Madfall. "Since I became our land's leader, I felt we needed another member to replace me, and Branwyn has convinced me that she is the right choice."

It felt as if the floor swayed beneath Udfa's feet. He clenched his fists, but kept his expression calm. This was Anfawl's doing, he was sure of that. Anfawl was besotted with her. He would find out what she'd done with Blaidd. He knew she had him, and that she was planning to use him to find the Six. He would keep a close eye on her.

He'd tried many times to follow her, but each time she simply disappeared or turned into her raven form. There was no doubt in his mind that she was a sorcerer, and he must be careful. There was no telling just what exactly she was capable of doing.

"Excuse my lateness to this meeting," Branwyn said, her face slightly flushed from the triumph she felt at her appointment. "I will dedicate my life to serving this land and its people."

She went on for a while, about her commitment and love for humanity, but Udfa wasn't listening. His thoughts were dark. It took all his strength and self-control not to pull out his sword and run it through her while she sat there in the midst of her web of lies. She was within his reach. Nevertheless, he must not ... he swallowed. He must be patient. One day, he would have his opportunity. One day.

7.

Three Rivers, Lady Corrick

Catrin had many sleepless nights after learning of her husband's plans for her and their son. What was she to do? Brenin was the most powerful man in the kingdom, and his army was unquestionably loyal. She carried no weight at all with the army or court, as Brenin well knew. She was "*of no consequence*." She didn't even know who she could confide in. She had no one. She was no longer included in the meetings of the Witan, and she never trusted any member of the Witan. The last Witan member who defied her husband lost his head.

She spent more time with Deryn and hardly let him out of her sight for a minute. She knew he felt that his mother was stifling him, but she didn't dare let down her guard. Could she tell him? He was too young. She didn't want to shatter his world. He already knew, or instinctively felt, that his father was not eager to spend time with him, or in teaching him how to be king one day. She had no answers for him other than hollow-sounding platitudes.

THE SIX AND THE GARDENERS OF IALANA

Today they were sitting in the terrace room that overlooked the city of Three Rivers. They could see two rivers, the Border River and the River Mair, glinting in the pale winter sun. There was snow on the ground and winter trees silhouetted starkly against a grey sky. Corrick stoked the fire in the large hearth, and Catrin felt that if she'd never found the secret passage she would be enjoying the warmth and coziness of the fire in the company of her son. Then, she would be in a fool's paradise, never knowing what her fate would be. She felt she would rather know than not.

She'd kept an eye out for the woman, Branwyn, but she was nowhere to be found. After the first few nights with Brenin she'd simply disappeared. Brenin stalked around the palace grounds silently with a sour look on his face. He snapped at anyone who spoke to him, and Catrin was probably the only person who knew why. Branwyn had left as quickly as she'd arrived, and her husband was not one to play around with. She stayed out of his way and felt the less she spoke to him the better it would be for her and her son.

"Mama, I want to go out riding today after lessons."

She looked at Deryn. He was bored. She often went out riding with him, and she felt it helped to strengthen his leg muscles as they walked or trotted through the woods on the banks of the river. Today though, she did not want him to go out. There was ice on the ground, and if the horse slipped, her son did not have the strength to stay on. The "accident" her husband would hope for ... maybe he would even arrange something on a day like this. Who would know? "No Deryn, it's too cold. Let's wait for spring. Then we can go outside."

Corrick looked over at her curiously. "Milady, I can ask the Captain of the Guard—"

"*No!* Corrick, do not undermine me. We are *not* going out today."

"Yes, ma'am." Corrick gave her another strange look. Her mistress had not been herself these past few days. Something seemed to be troubling her, and she wished she could help. She was fond of the queen and Deryn. She felt sad for Deryn, as he did not live a normal life, even for a prince. She could see he was bored and restless, and his inability to walk properly weighed heavily on him. He had few playmates—he was limited to the sons and daughters of courtiers and the Witan, and she knew they made fun of him behind his back. She would chastise them when she caught them at it, but as soon as her own back was turned, they would continue.

She waited until Deryn's tutor arrived and they had moved to another part of the terrace room, where Corrick knew they would be out of earshot, before confronting the queen.

"Milady." She curtsied. "May I speak?" Catrin nodded, still distracted as she watched her son with the tutor on the other side of the room. Could she trust the tutor to be alone with her son? "I have noticed that you do not seem happy. Is there something I can help you with?"

Catrin tore her gaze away from Deryn. "What? What is it, Corrick? What have you noticed?"

"It seems that you are more distracted, and there is a sad and frightened look on your face, especially when you look at Deryn. Is there something I can help you with? I am here to do just that as your lady-in-waiting. Did the Royal Healer have bad news about Deryn?"

"Oh, no—he did not. Deryn's health is stable at this time, thank the gods, but you are right. I need to talk about this, Corrick, although maybe you'll wish I hadn't," Catrin sighed. The burden of her secret was too heavy for her to bear alone. Perhaps she could get some advice from her friend.

"If I asked, then I have already committed myself to what it is that saddens you so. Your problems are my problems, milady."

Catrin began to talk, softly and with frequent glances towards her son and his tutor. She told Corrick everything, how she used the secret passage to learn of her husband's secrets, and of the woman who mysteriously appeared and disappeared, along with the substance of their conversation. When she was finished, Corrick looked at her with compassion in her eyes.

"This is far worse than I thought, milady. Your life, and that of your son, is uncertain. We must take steps to ensure safety for you both. Tell me more about the six healers that they spoke about."

"There is really nothing more to tell. They are from small villages in Aelfar—Meadowfield and Potter's Hill. I had not heard of them before, but now, they are branded forever in my memory. If these healers can help me, perhaps ... but how will I find them?"

"It seems that this Branwyn fears these healers, for some reason," Corrick commented. "She wants them too, but not to heal. To do something ... some devilry, with their skills. If they can heal, perhaps they can help Deryn?"

"You've read my mind. We must find them, Corrick. We must also protect them since the king and Branwyn have plans to further their own ambitions using these healers. We cannot allow my husband, or her, to find them. Who in this court do you trust the most?"

"Do you know a member of the Witan named Callum, milady?" The queen shook her head, frowning. "Callum's father was a Councilor—a Witan member—for many years. He was the Earl of Mercia."

"Oh, of course—I knew him. He was the Master of the Horse. He died just last year, did he not?"

"Yes, milady. After his death, Callum was appointed to be Master of the Horse, but since the beheading, he has replaced the unfortunate member of the Witan. I've formed a friendship with him," Corrick said as she blushed, and the queen smiled. "I know him well. In fact, we plan to marry soon!"

"My congratulations, Corrick! I am pleased for you. Tell me more about him."

"He told me his father revealed many of the king's secrets on his deathbed. He was delirious and spoke of things that shocked him to hear. He never knew that our king was capable of these deeds, and that they had obviously bothered his father, who never spoke of them. That is why I wasn't surprised when you told me what you heard from behind that grate. You and Deryn are in danger, milady, and I will do my best to help. I'll talk to Callum, and between us, we'll find a way."

Catrin breathed freely. She was right to trust her favorite lady-in-waiting. Now it was just a matter of biding her time. She did not think that her husband would make a move towards her if she kept herself surrounded by people. She felt that his deeds were done in shadows, and he only showed his real face to those who were like him. From what she could tell by their public appearances in the kingdom, his subjects worshipped him and thought he could do no wrong. Surely, they would not go to war and sacrifice their sons for an evil king, and he well knew that.

In her opinion, he kept his public face shiny and well polished with no breath of scandal to mar that image. It seemed evident to her that their subjects considered him a kind and upstanding king, who loved his queen and his son in spite of his son's handicap.

She knew better now, and so did two others. She was not alone.

8.

The Raven

Branwyn felt pleased. Her sojourn with Brenin had paid off handsomely. He was now her puppet, as were Blaidd, the Council of Ten, and Anfawl. They were all where she wanted them, and soon she would be the sole ruler of Ialana. She would have the mines, the crystal caves of Galon, and an unlimited supply of resources, and unlike Amrafalus, she knew what to do with them. She didn't need the Mu'A. Her own knowledge of the ancient arts far surpassed that of theirs, and she had long forgotten what the Mu'A had yet to learn about crystals. After all, she had been their teacher at one time. Like Irusan, she'd come from Agra'Tan to help the inhabitants of Ialana learn the ancient knowledge, and to act as a go-between and diplomat between the material world and the unseen Inner Worlds that co-existed with this one.

She was unstoppable, and she thirsted for revenge. The world of Agra'Tan would soon remember her and rue their hasty decision to remove her and confine her to the lower worlds. She had no plans to stop at this one either. She would take over the Inner Worlds, and from there the heavens were next. She had all of eternity to plan, and all of eternity to enjoy the fruits of her labor.

She thought of her first council meeting. It had gone well. She'd almost laughed aloud when Madfall announced her appointment to the Ten. The look on Udfa's face was priceless! He'd tried to disguise his dismay, but she was an expert at reading people. She knew he expected to be appointed himself. Oh well, poor Udfa— she would keep him for a while. He had his uses.

No one suspected who she really was, or how she travelled vast distances in an instant. Her raven body was not her only vehicle. She had another one, one that no human was aware of, and if she had her way, the humans would never gain this knowledge of her bubble of light. Knowledge in human hands was dangerous. They didn't know what to do with it, but she did. Oh yes, she did!

The Six and the Crystal Caves

The Six were escorted to the tower, and, after climbing a series of spiral stairs, they came to a large, partitioned room near the top. The Captain informed them that the room was for their living space, and the other smaller area behind a partition was where they could conduct their healing.

"I wonder how the lame and sick are supposed to climb the stairs," Tegan asked. The Captain shot her an ugly look and left, slamming, and then padlocking the heavy door behind him.

Overlooking the bay was a small window, though it was nothing more than a slit. They could see that the Keep perched precariously on the edge of the cliff, waves breaking and foaming against the rocky base of the cliff far below them.

"Even if we could squeeze through the window, the drop down the vertical cliff-face would deter even the most determined escapee," said Djana.

"There's only one way out, and that's the way we came," commented Tristan.

"And it's heavily guarded," said Adain.

"That hasn't stopped us before. We'll think of something," Tristan sighed.

"If I had my crystals," said Kex, "we could create a diversion, but I left them behind in the caverns below the Citadel."

Djana was concerned about her parents. "Do you think we could get a message to them?"

"I don't know, Djana ... we'll wait and see," Jarah replied. "We haven't been here long, and we need to see what's in store for us first before we make plans." But he felt that his words were not comforting to Djana, so he added, "Keep thinking though, and when the opportunity arises, we'll take it."

Djana shrugged, a doubtful look in her eyes, and Jarah could not blame her. He had no idea what to do or how long Ortzi would keep them here. Again, the responsibilities of being the leader weighed on him. Leaders were expected to find solutions, he thought, not hesitate and mumble platitudes or useless "we'll sees". He still had the Healing Crystal, though. He slept with it in its pouch and it never left his side for a moment. He wondered how it would cope with healing things it was never programmed to heal. He knew it would probably do its best, but if they failed, Ortzi would be furious. He seemed unpredictable; friendly one moment, and blowing up a storm the next, just like the weather in Aelfar.

The next few days saw a trickle of people coming to the Keep for healing. There were no lame or blind, but there were some, dressed in silks and furs, who came with various ailments that arose from too fine a living. Even a non-healer would have known how to deal with these: eating less at feasts would be a start, and walking up the hill to the Keep instead of being borne by servants in a litter—a comfortable sedan chair—would do more good than a crystal could. Nevertheless, they asked the Crystal to help these people, and they too did their best. There was no telling what the results would be, especially if the person went home and resumed their usual habits.

"Ortzi tricked us," said Adain, and they all nodded. They had already come to this conclusion, each on their own. "It appears that he only told the upper classes about our healing abilities, and that the poor will have to fend for themselves."

They passed a message to Ortzi through the guard. They asked if they could see more people who were actually lame or blind, regardless of their social status. They did not get a response, but they did notice a few more people that fit their request coming through the door. They felt the Crystal might actually work better for these people. If there was a distortion in their pattern that caused the lameness or blindness, it could work for them. They asked the people that if it did help them, to return and let them know.

They had been doing this for about a week when the door opened, and instead of another patient, the Captain of the Guard walked in.

"Ortzi wants to see you," he said. "Follow me." Puzzled, they followed the guard down the stairs and out into the courtyard. Waiting for them, was Ortzi, seated on a horse, a phalanx of guards on horseback, and six riderless horses.

"Oh no," said Djana. "I hate riding horses! I'd rather walk!" But Ortzi simply gestured imperiously for them to climb on.

"I have something to show you," was all he said to them.

They each climbed up onto a horse. Except for Tristan, none of them had been taught to ride. He was comfortable with horses. "Don't worry," he said. "We can go slowly, so hang on tight and don't show your fear. A horse can sense fear."

"Easy for you to say!" said Djana.

They walked their horses carefully out of the courtyard and down the steps, hanging on tightly, terrified at the drop down to the sea on their right. At last, they made it safely down the hill and continued through the city where the citizens of Abena gaped at them. Who were these people? Were these the healers they had heard so much about but were not allowed to see?

Jarah picked these thoughts up as they passed. The city gave way to residential, red-roofed palazzos built on hills that over-looked the city. They made their way over and around the hills, through green vineyards and olive groves. Tristan thought that everything here looked similar to Mernoc. He was from south Mernoc, and they too had olive groves and vineyards.

They continued moving northwest, stopping once or twice to give the horses a break and to eat and stretch. Ortzi told them he wasn't accustomed to moving this slow, but, he'd added, he didn't want *his* healers falling off a horse and being put out of action. They rode for several hours, and then the road, a mere track now, rose into rocky, barren hillsides. A lone umbrella pine provided the only shade for many leagues. The sun beat down on their bare heads mercilessly. They hoped that wherever they were going, it was not too much further.

After what seemed like the best part of a long, hot day, with the sun low on the horizon, they arrived at their destination: the foot of a jagged and broken cliff near the top of a hill. They dismounted from their steeds and Ortzi told them the final leg had to be navigated on foot. The soldiers removed rope, a sack, and an unlit torch from their horses' packs. They wound their way up a zigzag path that ascended a steep and rocky slope to the base of the cliff where a large, dark hole yawned in front of them. It was the entrance to a cave—a hole in the cliff that opened up into a sheer drop. They could not see the bottom hidden in its dark depths.

Ortzi nodded to his soldiers. One of them lit the torch with flint sparks and handed the flaming torch to him. One by one, they tied the rope under their arms with a secure knot and were lowered into the cave, Ortzi first, then each of the healers. The cave darkened even more as they descended into the pit, and Ortzi's small flame flickered far below. Jarah knew he had reached the bottom when he felt Ortzi guide him down to a level area. He untied the rope and it was pulled up for the next one.

When they all stood at the bottom of the cave, they looked up to see the small figures of the soldiers waiting for them at the entrance. "We must go," said Ortzi. "They will not accompany us. I do not wish for anyone except you and the members of my Cabinet, to know what these caves hold. All my soldiers know is that we're crazy and they have no idea why we are here."

They made their way deeper into the cave, their flickering light showing a path that had been cleared through rock rubble. The path took them to the back of the cave, and they scrambled over boulders the size of small houses to find another opening. They carefully clambered down more rocks and boulders before they found themselves in a downward spiraling tunnel.

They rounded the final bend, and it was then they understood what it was that Ortzi had brought them here for.

9.

The Crystals

They stood, awestruck, at the entrance to a chamber that surpassed any cave or grotto they had ever seen. They could not see its bottom, or end, and deep in the darkness below, enormous, translucent columns of crystal rose up to where they stood, touching the roof of the chamber. These crystals dwarfed the generator crystals of Mu'A and Rhiannon. Stone steps cut into the rock walls of the cavern descended from their ledge into the depths below. The steps were narrow, and they had to pick their way down gradually, until finally they reached what looked like the floor of the chamber. Now the crystal columns rose high into the darkness above them, but below them, by the light of the torch, a glittering array met their eyes. A crystalline bed formed the floor below their feet. They picked their way over and around the crystals, crystals ranging in size from small and palm-sized to the giants that towered above them.

"This is unbelievable!" said Jarah. "Can you feel their power?"

The Six nodded in agreement. The energy was palpable, immense, and their legs felt weak. They were standing in the energy field of a family—no, a community—of Crystal Beings.

Ortzi grinned. "I knew you'd be surprised," he said. "What can you tell me about them?"

"They have great power," said Tegan, ignoring Ortzi's sudden glare in her direction. She no longer felt afraid of him and spoke her mind without his permission. "I wonder if this is where the Basajaun found their crystals."

"Yes, I feel this is just one of the sources. Irusan told us there were others, but this one would be closer. The Basajaun dematerialized some of them from here and rematerialized them in—"

Jarah abruptly stopped, realizing that he didn't know what Ortzi wanted them to do with these crystals. Perhaps he should not give away too much of his knowledge. In addition, he had mentioned Irusan. He mentally kicked himself for saying too much.

"Who is this you speak of? *Irusan*?"

"*Um*, just a man we once knew from another land." Jarah hastily tried backtracking, but it was already too late.

"I am pleased that you would know what to do with these crystals. That is why I brought you here. Their power will serve my country. We will be *invincible* to attack."

"No, that is not what we do with crystals!" Tristan looked angry, and he gave Jarah a look of warning. He had already said too much. "We use smaller crystals, but only for healing. *Not* for weapons or self-defense."

"What about that man you spoke of? I can send my men out to search for him. I don't care if you take the smaller crystals too, as I am interested in the big ones only. I have heard the stories of the Basajaun, how they used them for protection and defense, but we can also use them to destroy our enemies, no?"

"Wrong," said Jarah, as he belatedly corrected his mistake. "We know nothing about using crystals in that way, and your men will never find this man."

"You lie." The way Ortzi stated this made Jarah feel suddenly cold. Ortzi's obsidian eyes glittered in the torchlight. "We will go back now. In the meantime, think of your future. Do you want to live, or do you want to die?"

They made their way silently back up the twisting stairs to the opening, and through the ascending tunnels, and into the cave where they had entered. They could see the soldiers looking down at them from the entrance. Ortzi shouted a command and the line snaked down towards them. Tying the rope under his armpits, he turned to them and as his soldiers pulled him up he shouted, "Reconsider! I'll return in a few days."

They looked at each other in horror. He wasn't going to leave them here, was he?

"He must mean *we'll* return," said Kex.

"No, I think he meant himself," said Adain. "Let's see if the rope comes back down." After Ortzi was pulled out of the cave, to their relief, the rope came down again, but this time there was something on the end of it—a bulging sack. They loosened the bag and held onto the end of the line, Jarah wrapping and tying it around Kex, but to their dismay, the rope fell from above, into a heap at their feet. Ortzi waved from the entrance.

"I'll be back," he yelled. "Think about what I want from you. I'm sure a few days here will help you decide. If not, I'll bring more food, and you'll find water in a spring at the back of the cave." He then disappeared.

"It's my fault," said Jarah. "If I hadn't opened my foolish mouth we'd be up there now."

"It's not your fault, Jarah," Tegan said, but she looked frightened. "I picked up his thoughts while we were climbing back. I felt that he had a plan to leave us here all along unless we agreed to his insane plan. I don't think it mattered at all what you said, or what any of us said." The others agreed.

"The reason he brought us here wasn't to find crystals to heal with but to see what we could do with these big ones, and to force us if we weren't willing to do what he wants." Djana bent down and opened the bag. "At least he's left us some food."

"And the torch," said Adain happily.

"But no sleeping blankets," Kex remarked.

"Well, since we're here," said Jarah, "we may as well go back to the crystals and see if we can communicate with them. Regardless of the outcome, it's an opportunity for us to learn what we can."

"Perhaps they'll even help us," said Tristan. They all heard the hope in his voice.

They made their way back through the cave and the tunnel, and stood on the ledge at the top of the cave.

"We don't need to go all the way down," said Djana. "We can reach this big one from here."

"Careful, don't slip."

They all carefully placed a hand on the nearest giant. It looked to be a six-sided crystal that terminated in a point just above their heads. They could not see all the way around it. They were startled by the jolt of energy they felt in their arms. This crystal was alive! They kept their hands firmly on it, and Jarah spoke.

"Greetings, Beloved. We come in peace. We have no evil intent, but we would like to find out more about you." He continued to speak, telling the crystal who they were, and each person added their story to his. Jarah stated it was only fair the crystal should understand who they were and why they were here. They told it of their history with crystals, their intent to co-create healing, and of Ortzi's plan.

To their delight, the crystal spoke back. They picked up its communication not in words, but in an understanding that went beyond words and pictures. It was a knowing that did not take the long, circuitous route used by human speech or thought. They all felt, instantly, what it wanted them to know and what it wanted them to do. They looked at each other and smiled. They wouldn't be here long at all.

Sorrow and Regret

Blaidd had his own reasons to find the Six Healers. He could no longer ignore the obvious, and he now knew what Amrafalus had done to him while he was unconscious during his session with the memory crystal. He had not only used the memory crystal on him in the cavern under the Citadel, but also his altering crystals, the ones that would change his pattern.

His awareness of the unspeakable horror that he experienced grew each day as his hands roamed obsessively over his nose, skull, and ears. He gazed at himself for hours in the mirror in his room, hoping that the evidence in front of his eyes was not real. He did not look like Blaidd anymore. He wasn't even Seryn, the respected teacher, anymore. Instead, he was turning into an animal-like ... thing.

He sobbed as the bull-face stared back at him. There was still much that was human there, but he knew it wouldn't be long before he too would become one of *them*—one of the Trueni. Amrafalus had done this deliberately, all the while soothing him with promises of how he would enjoy the rewards of his betrayal. He should have known.

He cried himself to sleep every night and stayed in his room during the day, too afraid and embarrassed to show himself in daylight. His days became a living nightmare that he could not be awakened from.

He wished that he was back in Meadowfield, back with his drunken father. He would even prefer a lifetime in the army to this. Not for the first time, Blaidd wondered why he had made the choices he had. Had he not learned as Seryn what happened to those who allied themselves with a reptile?

He no longer had any illusions about marrying Branwyn. The

Raven had betrayed him too, used him and then thrown him aside. She still allowed him in her house, but she too saw what he was becoming. He was of no more use to her as Blaidd, or even as a Trueni. He was only useful for his memories as Seryn, Teacher of Mu'A, and that version of Seryn was fast fading away.

He struggled to remember what he knew about crystals. He wrote copious notes on papyrus papers that he scavenged for in the house so that he would not forget. He begged Branwyn to heal him, but she only laughed and told him that when she found the Six, perhaps *they* could heal him.

"Or perhaps not, dear. It depends on how much they still dislike you. After all, you did betray them, did you not? Anyway, I have my own uses for them, and it doesn't involve healing. Oh, stop crying. You can be my slave! Isn't that what you always wanted?"

And she'd laugh—a cruel, gleeful sound that pierced his soul. She was cold in her clarity. She had no means, or wish, to heal him. No one in Rhiannon had that ability, and no one had any idea where the Six might be.

10.

Escape

The Six spent the night in the cave huddled together for warmth. They could see the stars and moon through the entrance far above them, and it gave them some comfort, even though they could not get out. They slept fitfully, each one going over in their minds what the Crystal Being had told them. It had linked them into the crystal generator in Mu'A, and that in turn linked into one in Agra'Tan. Since they couldn't sleep, they each shared their impressions, what they each learned from the enormous crystal.

"Irusan has been informed," said Tegan. "He'll be here soon."

"I felt the crystal link into the Healing Crystal around my neck," said Jarah. "There was a flow of information between them—almost like updates. The giant crystal told us about another development. Did any of you get that?"

"Yes," said Djana and Adain simultaneously.

"I did too," said Kex, and Tristan nodded to himself in the dark.

"It seems that Amrafalus is not dead," said Tristan. "He somehow managed to escape the Citadel, but no one knows he's alive. The crystals don't know what happened to him, but they do know he's not in Rhiannon anymore."

"But we are not safe from him," Djana said, "and there's another one we must be wary of. Maybe more, who are determined to find us and use us for their own ends."

"I saw a picture of a bird," said Tegan. "A raven. But that doesn't make any sense."

"I saw a king and a queen," said Adain.

"And Ortzi is not our problem, anymore," said Jarah. "The one they call 'the Raven' is. We'll have to wait and see. Perhaps it will all make sense later on."

They continued to discuss what the Crystal Being told them. It had been here for eons. The family it belonged to once ran energy throughout the entire planetary system, before the last great extinction, and before the reptiles ruled. It said that the world had faced many life-form extinctions, and humans were just one more chapter in the book of life. As a family, the crystals had made a choice: to remain dormant until a life form learned to use them in the way they were originally intended, to further peace and healing upon the planet instead of war and conflict. They chose the way they wished to be harnessed. If someone attempted to reprogram them, the attempt would not only be unsuccessful, but the consequences would be dire.

The future of the Six was to assist in healing the current planetary distortions as much as possible. The crystals would support those who desired to create in harmony with them and the universe. It told them that they had always been the embodied extensions of the consciousness of the crystals, and that is why they possessed the ability to program, understand, and utilize the crystals' power.

"Another thing I know," said Tegan, "is that we'll meet up with others soon who will help us and train us in our mission."

"We must proceed northwards," said Jarah, "towards the mountains. Not over them or through them as we did before, but towards a river that flows north. We will meet our helpers somewhere along this route."

"I don't know where or when either," said Tegan. "But our Healing Crystal will know."

"I didn't want to mention this," said Tristan, "but it does seem that since we're all getting the same thing it probably doesn't matter if I say it. We are to be pitted against impossible odds."

"Yes, even more frightening and dangerous creatures," said Kex. "I understood that too."

"Things that don't play by the rules," said Djana.

Everyone was quiet for a while. They all understood that their journey was just beginning, and they were poorly equipped. They had no weapons, and only a little food, which Ortzi had left them. Unknown people were still hunting them, and they had no idea of their destination or goal.

It would be a miracle if they made it as far as Aelfar, thought Jarah. "The crystals here have a plan," he said. "They will not allow themselves to be found again. They said we must let them know once we are out of the caves and at a safe distance, whatever that means."

The last thing the crystal being had said to them was to tell them to take a crystal with them. It directed them back down to the floor of the crystal cavern, and there they found a crystal that had detached itself voluntarily from its family. They were told that this crystal should not be used until the time was right, that the other beings they were to encounter were waiting for this crystal, and they were to keep it with the Healing Crystal at all times. They would also know when the time was right, and what its use would be.

The Six had much to think about and their minds were simply too active to sleep. Their torch died during the night and they sat, miserable and cold, in the dark. At last, dawn arrived. They ate a breakfast of dry bread, old bits of sausage, and a musty cheese. They swallowed it down with gulps of spring water. Ortzi had not left them much. It was as if he didn't want them to get too comfortable in the caves.

At midday, they noticed a large bird silhouetted against the sky, circling the entrance. They couldn't see what kind it was. Fearful that it was the Raven, they watched as it dropped into the pit. When it came closer, they could see it more clearly. It was an eagle.

"*Irusan!*" they exclaimed in unison, as the eagle dematerialized and reformed into the cat-man.

"I flew here as quickly as I could," he told them, although it was Tegan who spoke his thoughts. "I've been flying all night after coming through the nearest portal. I wasn't sure exactly where these caves were, but the crystals helped guide me. What have you found yourselves involved with now?"

They laughed and hugged him.

"We really did it this time," said Jarah. "Our *friend* Ortzi has some ambitious plans for us and the Crystal Beings." They sat down while Irusan rested and told him everything that had happened since he left them on the boat. Irusan already knew most of it, but they filled him in on the details. "The Crystal Being told us to let it know once we're out of the caves. It has plans of its own, and Ortzi won't be able to enter the caves again."

They wondered what the crystals were going to do, but they did know it would be dangerous to linger, so Irusan turned back into the eagle, picked up the rope in his talons, and flew up to the entrance. They could see his cat-man shape materialize above as the rope came back down, and one by one he effortlessly pulled them back up. It felt good to be out in the sunlight again.

They quickly descended the stairs down the cliff face, made their way down another slope, and then climbed back up to another ridge where they could still see the entrance to the cave.

They mentally sent a signal to the Crystal Beings in the cave of their location. They didn't have long to wait.

It started first as a rumble, and the ground shook beneath them. Holding on to each other as they tried to remain on their feet, they watched as a cloud of dust erupted from the cave entrance. The thunder grew and became a roar. Now it was difficult to stay on their feet, and even the trees around them shook and trembled. A strong wind roared overhead. Irusan shouted, through Tegan, to lie flat on the ground. He wasn't sure if there would be flying projectiles, so they all fell flat, covering their heads with their hands while trying to see exactly what was happening through the flying debris. They had heard of earthquakes, but none of them had actually been in one. They hoped that if this was an earthquake, they would never experience another one.

Loud explosions erupted around them, and they felt the rumbles and cracking of straining earth and rock under their bodies. They prayed that the earth they lay on would remain stable, and they would not all disappear into a gaping crevice, or under an avalanche of rocks and dirt.

The noises and heaving earth continued for what felt like, to them, an interminable length of time. It came in waves, and during one brief lull, they tried to stand up, but Irusan, through Jarah, commanded them to *stay down*, and then the shuddering would continue. Earth fell away in roaring landslides on either side of their ridge as trees swayed perilously overhead. Trees on the edges toppled over, away from where they lay, crashing and tumbling down the sides of the hill.

At last, it was over, and the noises slowly faded. Small tremors and aftershocks continued, but at least they could stand on their feet now. It took some time for the dust to settle, and they waited. They did not want to be caught descending a slope if it was not over. When the dust began to settle back to earth, they all stared, stupefied, at where the entrance in the cliff-face had once been.

It no longer existed. A pile of rock completely obliterated the entrance, and it didn't even look the same. The whole hill had changed shape. If anyone came there looking for the cave, they would not find the entrance under the enormous boulders and tree limbs piled one on top of another. They smiled as they thought of the look that would be on Ortzi's face when he returned.

"I'd give several moon's army pay to see his reaction when he gets here," said Tristan, and they all laughed.

"I wish we could wait for that. It would be almost worth it, but we have to keep moving," said Irusan, through Jarah. "He'll think you're all dead—no one inside the cave could survive that—so that means he won't be chasing us." It felt good to have one less person looking for them.

"Do you think we could head back to Ibai for a quick visit?" asked Djana. "I'm so worried about my parents."

"I'm afraid not," said Irusan. "That would not be wise. Someone would see us, and Ortzi would hear about it. I'll go back there myself in my human form when I leave you and look in on them. I'll tell them exactly what happened, and I'll make sure they are safe."

"Oh, thank you!" said Djana. She could now rest easy knowing that they would not once again be 'dead' to those who cared about them.

Jarah heaved a sigh of relief. He had felt tremendous guilt for his inability to help set Djana's mind at rest regarding her parents.

They told Irusan what the crystals had told them about Amrafalus; that he was not dead.

"I know. That is worrying. I have been looking for him too, but unable to locate him. He is not in Rhiannon, as you already know. It is strange that he did not stay in the city and reclaim his throne, even if it was buried under piles of rubble. Something must have happened to him." He stopped and thought for a while.

"The *Raven* ..." Irusan frowned as if recalling a long-forgotten memory. "I remember a shape-shifter, one of us, who favored the raven form, but she left Agra'Tan centuries ago. We asked her to reconsider, to work on self-healing, but she refused. Her thoughts and deeds were not in alignment with the Law of One, and the longer she stayed in her raven form, the worse things became. It became evident to the council that she much preferred to play the games of this world to the higher calling of Guardianship or Stewardship of other realities. She became much involved with the dramas out here, and soon her frequency dropped so much that she was unable to return to Agra'Tan even if she wanted to. Nothing could be done by anyone. She had made her choice. Last anyone heard, she called herself 'Branwyn' and took on the form of a human female. That is not her actual shape either. She is unable to return to her original form, and now she must shape-shift into forms that are akin to her frequency. I will put the word out to find her, and determine what, exactly, she is playing at."

They headed in a northwesterly direction, and after giving them more instructions, Irusan said he had to take his leave. They were safe now, for the time being, and he would head directly to Ibai and send a boat up the Garden River for them.

"I feel sure one of our friends—perhaps Askia—will be able to navigate a boat up the river. He can take you much further than you can go on foot, and it will be safer as well." He told them where they should rendezvous with the boat, and described the bend in the river with an island in its center. "It will take you about a day's walk to get to the river and to this bend. Just enough time for the boat to get there."

Irusan, without further ado, turned into his eagle form, and they watched as he soared aloft, turning in a southwesterly direction. He was heading towards Ibai.

Abban

There was only one thing to do, Blaidd told himself. He *must* find the Six without Branwyn knowing about it and he had to continue making notes. The notes were not just about the crystals. It was about who he was and what had happened to him. He knew what Amrafalus' crystals did to people. He knew that he would lose his ability to speak, and as a result, he would not be able to verbalize any of his past to anyone. He could not heal himself, as he didn't have crystals that were capable of doing so, such as the Healing Crystal of the Six. He knew that he must take steps now, or forever be lost to who he really was.

He sat in his room while he wrote so that Branwyn would not see. She wasn't there much anyway, and she never came into his room anymore. She spent most of her time plotting with Anfawl. He had no idea how the coup was going, or if it had even started, and he didn't really care. He also knew that he must protect himself now from her mind probes. If she probed him, she would know exactly what he was up to, so he pretended he was duller than he actually was. When she spoke to him—which was rare—he'd look at her stupidly and make his mind as blank as he could get it. That was becoming increasingly easier by the day, and he had to work fast.

She'd *tut-tut*, shake her head, and leave the room. He could still speak and string words together, but his vocal cords felt thick and unwieldy, so he didn't speak unless he had to.

One day, Marko, Branwyn's Trueni slave, came to his room. "Mistress say you go," he said, with a jerk of his massive head towards the door. Obediently, Blaidd packed the few things he had, making sure he placed his notes and some other items he had wrapped in his clothing into the bag he had been handed. Marko looked at him suspiciously. "You maybe one of us now?" he asked. Blaidd nodded. "You come with me, I take you Akelarre."

Blaidd followed him out of the house without a backward glance. It had been his plan to go to Akelarre all along. Marko found them a taxi-boat, and soon they arrived in the fishing village.

"Come, I take you friend," said Marko, and they made their way through the village to a shack on the edge of town. "This home for Abban." He knocked on the door and Abban stuck out a goat-like head.

"Marko! Come in." They entered, and Blaidd was surprised to find the shanty interior clean and well kept. Abban looked at him, but did not appear surprised.

"Please, you help Blaidd. He brother-friend now." Blaidd knew this meant they recognized him as one of their own kind, and he didn't know if that made him happy, or even sadder. He was surprised at Marko's generosity. He had not treated Marko well when he'd first arrived at Branwyn's house. He'd been imperious, ordering the slaves about and giving them things to do just so he could see how it felt to have power over another being. Now he felt ashamed.

"I won't be staying long," he promised. "Just a few days."

"You stay long if you need," said Marko, and Abban nodded. "I go now." With that, he turned and left and Blaidd stood there awkwardly with his sack. Abban gestured for him to sit on a wooden stool.

"I fisherman. If you like, you fish with me. I teach!"

Blaidd shook his head. "No, I do not wish to be a fisherman. But I do have a proposition for you."

"*Prop* ... ?"

"A *favor* to ask. I need a boat, and someone to take me somewhere." Abban looked curiously at him. "Where you go?"

"Galon. Can you or someone else take me there?"

Abban seemed stumped. "Galon? You run away. Amrafalus no here no more ... no have to run! Akelarre good fish!"

"Abban, I know some things you don't. Yes, Amrafalus is gone, but the people who are now ruling you are even worse. Slaves will be needed and the mines will continue. You are not free. You see Marko is still a slave—answer me. Has his mistress let him go? Does she pay him? *No.* She threatens her Trueni slaves with the mines if they object, but they don't. You are still Trueni. I am now one of you—a brother-friend—but I was not always a broth-er-friend. I did things ... ." He stopped. A tear fell and he wiped it away. "I am sorry for what I did, Abban. I don't expect forgiveness, but I will do what I can to help the Trueni. In order to do that, I must first help myself before I ... that is why I need to go to Galon, to find the people that can help."

Abban nodded slowly. He seemed to understand. He stood and thought for a while. "I know man who take you," he said. "Me."

"I can pay you well Abban." Blaidd opened up his sack, remov-ing a towel that he unwrapped. A pile of glittering jewels fell into his hand. He'd stolen them from a stash of Branwyn's that she'd un-wisely shown to him some time ago. She had most likely forgotten he knew where she kept her valuables, as well as the key. He didn't take all of them—he was done with being greedy—but he'd taken enough to finance what he thought he'd need for his escape.

"Me not need. If Rhiannon people not good, then I help. I not tell Marko. Marko tell mistress and she find us. We tell no one."

Blaidd agreed. He would still help the Trueni. He meant it. It would just have to be one day after he had healed his template and restored his old self. Well, not exactly the old self, but rather a new and improved self, he thought. He just could not do some things now.

They made their plans, and Abban gave him a fisherman's out-fit to wear. "We go now," he said.

Blaidd was surprised. He thought that it would take a few days for him to find a boat and someone willing to take him, but this was far better than he had expected. Yes, Abban was right. They must leave immediately. He didn't want the Raven to come looking for him, even though she had removed him. She might discover her jew-els gone, or she might have second thoughts. One just never knew.

The sooner they left the better.

11.

Three Rivers, Queen Catrin

Queen Catrin made an effort to speak daily with her husband. She no longer felt fear. Instead, a new lightness of being came over her. It amused her to play with him, and she had to ensure he did not suspect that she'd discovered his ugly secrets. She no longer tried to win his approval or validation. Her life, newly empowered, was joyful now compared to her earlier despair.

She observed Brenin with a different eye and a fresh awareness of who, and what, he really was. She realized too that her love for him had turned into loathing. His affairs, his mishandling of the kingdom, and his lack of character had never gone unnoticed by her. It had taken a threat to both her and her son to admit, even to herself, the reality of the situation, and depth of her feelings. It was only now that she could even acknowledge these thoughts. In the past, she'd mistaken possessiveness, and her own insecurities and dependence upon his good graces, for love. Her budding hatred now gave her the impetus to perfect her plans. The knowledge that Corrick and Callum were her undisputed allies and trusted confidantes buoyed her spirits, and they often met in secret.

"Milady, the king is planning to march on Galon with his army in the spring," said Callum. "They'll be moving through the villages of Meadowfield and Potters Hill. He does not wish to proceed with the capture of the Six before then due to winter weather, as it makes the roads impassable. He feels that the Six will remain in their respective villages until the winter is over. Branwyn will let him know when they arrive, and once he knows we will know too. How she knows, no one has any idea. Those who are aware of her existence are saying that she's a witch."

Catrin liked Callum. She was pleased to discover that he was perceptive and kind, much like her lady-in-waiting. She felt she had gained his loyalty. He and Corrick promised to listen carefully to any court talk and gossip.

"She's a witch, there's no doubt about that," said Catrin. "How can anyone—human that is—be in Rhiannon one week and Three Rivers the next? She has bewitched my husband, but there's no one alive more deserving of that!"

"The ladies of the court are saying they've fallen out of favor with the king," added Corrick with a laugh. "They're saying he does not call them to his bedchamber anymore."

"He's not been with Branwyn either," said Catrin. "I've not seen her for several weeks. The king walks around looking angry and sullen. He speaks to me, I make sure of that, but it is nothing of importance —the weather, the new cook who can't cook, and what Deryn is doing now with his tutor. I talk vapidly and continuously to him while carefully observing him. I see he is not interested in what I am saying, but stares off into the distance. I know of whom he thinks."

"We must be patient, and wait for the right moment," said Callum. "In the meanwhile we'll carefully make preparations to find the Six and bring them here. The king and his witch must not learn of our intentions. I'm fortunate to be one of the Witan and aware of the king's plans. The Witan fear both him and Branwyn, and none dares to oppose either of them. I'm less afraid, Your Majesty. Maybe it's my youth, but I am satisfied now that the king is not as invincible as he seems. I know many, both in the Witan and in the army, who would be happy to depose him and appoint you and Deryn rulers of Aelfar and Mernoc. Their fear and uncertainty hold them back, but if we have the right cards, we might stand a chance. These healers may hold the key. If Branwyn wants them then they must have power of some kind. It is our duty to find out exactly what it is, and use it for ourselves."

Catrin nodded. She felt better than she had in years. Not only was she going to find the healers before her husband, but also it was her intention, and that of Callum's, to be the catalysts of his downfall. Deryn would rule Aelfar and Mernoc, and she would never have to be afraid of her husband again. Callum was now the source of her information—he shared everything that occurred in the Witan assemblies with her and Corrick, and she now knew as much as her husband did. She rarely used the secret passage anymore. She was curious to know if Branwyn had returned, but the palace gossip indicated that she had not. She must finalize her own plans before spring thaw.

The Garden River

After Irusan had left, the Six made their way through the hills and down towards the Garden River plain. They still had their bag of food that was by now stale, rancid, and smellier than it had been the day before. They dug for brackish water in the dried streambeds they came across. The sun beat down from a cloudless sky, and they were relieved when night fell. It was difficult sleeping on the stony ground, so they rose long before sunrise to continue their walk with only faint starlight to light their way. Dark shapes scuttled away as they approached, things with many legs and eyes, but nothing that looked larger than a small rabbit.

They were thankful, at midday, to reach the strip of green that marked the river plain where fresh water was plentiful and where there was shade from the sun. They rested for a while and continued down the banks towards the bend with the small island in the middle that Irusan had described. A man hailed them. He stood on a solidly built papyrus raft with a square sail, laden with supplies. The raft was moored on the Galon side of the riverbank, and as they drew nearer the man began to look more familiar.

"Askia!"

"I am glad you escaped Ortzi," said Askia. "We were all worried about you, but Irusan told us about what had happened."

Askia was a different person to the one they had left. The Healing Crystal's work had continued to heal even after the sessions had ended, and now he was fully human: a distinguished man of forty-plus years. His speech was on a level of sophistication that matched their own, and Djana felt that her mother had done an excellent job. She knew from their training, that once the pathways in the brain had been healed, language would continue to improve, and that the Trueni were as intelligent as they were, but their neural pathways for speech had been disturbed by Amrafalus' crystals. They'd remembered learning about the brains of humans and animals in Mu'A during their past lives on the island. It was the knowledge that had once been taught in Ialana, but had been lost with the fall of Rhiannon, and the scattering of the Basajaun.

As they sailed up the Garden River, Askia told them that many Trueni had been healed, and some were still in the process of healing. They knew now that even a few sessions with the

Crystal would be enough, and felt relief that their absence had not stopped the process. Askia said that many of the Trueni, who had been against the healing at first, were now wishing they had not listened to Mikel. He was still convinced the Six were sorcerers.

"Ortzi is displeased too with the healing of the Trueni. He's afraid we'll revolt, and that is a real possibility. Many former Trueni now understand how they were used as cheap labor and not helped in their basic needs by those who have always been fully human. It suited the Galonese to use Amrafalus' creations, and even though they did not enslave us, they did not improve our living conditions or pay us living wages. The Trueni in Ibai lived in almost as much poverty as those in Akelarre. Education was not a part of their plan. I am afraid for your parents, Djana."

Djana looked concerned again. "Why did my parents not come with you, Askia? They could have traveled back with us to Aelfar!"

"I asked them to, and Irusan said they should come with me too, but they refused. They both wanted to stay and help the Trueni. They've opened up a school in Ibai for the children. They said if they leave now, then Ortzi will win."

"That sounds like my parents," said Djana. "As stubborn as donkeys."

She was silent then, and no one knew what to say. She had lost her parents once before. Now it was going to happen all over again and there wasn't anything anyone could do about it. At last, she spoke again.

"Do you think I should go back with Askia, Jarah?"

"What are you going to do, Djana? You can't stop Ortzi or the Galonese from whatever it is they are going to do, and you will also give away the fact that we escaped from the crystal cave. Ortzi may send a battalion of men after us. I think it will just make things worse."

"And how can we heal with just five?" said Tegan. "We really need the six of us to sing to the Crystal. We don't know what effects may occur with one of us absent."

"I would like you to go back if there was something you could accomplish in Ibai, Djana," Tristan added, "but I agree with Jarah. There's nothing to gain by going back and everything to lose. We could all choose to go back, but Ortzi will certainly capture us again and find another way to use us, or even kill us. He's not a rational man."

"Mikel, and those who are still brother-friend with him will betray you," said Askia. They all nodded, and Djana reluctantly admitted, again, that going back was not a good idea.

Askia had brought plenty of food, and they heaved what was left in Ortzi's sack overboard, before they ate their fill of real food. They took turns resting and helping Askia sail when conditions were right, or in the absence of wind or tide, using a long pole to propel the raft through the water. It was light and easy to navigate.

"I got the raft from my neighbor—a river fisherman," Askia said. "My boat's a sea-boat and not suitable for this river. I'll return the raft to him when I get back."

He said he could take them as far as Lake Yorath. Irusan had given him as much information about the navigability of the river as he could. Lake Yorath bordered Galon, Mannanon and Mernoc, and the Esti River flowed from Yorath to the east coast of Ialana. The unnavigable northern tributary of the Garden River flowed south, from its source in the Osgoi range in Aelfar into Yorath, and out again to the coast. Askia would have to leave them at Yorath and return to Ibai.

They tied the raft up at night and slept on the riverbank. They saw few signs of habitation on either side of the river, but at night, they noticed mysterious lights bobbing around in the forests. They also heard an occasional howl that froze the blood in their veins. Askia said that Mannanon had a bad reputation among the people in Ibai. It was a wild and untamed land, and the few people who lived there were savage and barely human.

"Not Trueni like us," he said, "But strange creatures without reason or understanding. They come from the mountains and kill all. They are big and strong and the people of Ibai stay away from the Mannanon side of the river." It was then he told them what else Irusan had said to him before leaving. "He said you must go to the Mannanon side of the river and go north from there."

"Why?" asked Tristan. "That doesn't seem like a wise thing to do if there are fearsome creatures who will kill us!"

"He said there is something, or someone there you must find. That is all I know."

They looked at each other, bafflement on their faces.

"The Crystal Being told us we would need to find some other beings and give them the crystal we found in the cave. Maybe it meant they're not *all* evil on that side," said Jarah. "We'll do as he says. He hasn't steered us wrong yet."

They all agreed. They would go to Mannanon.

12.

Night of Fear

The weather became colder as they alternately punted or sailed northwards. Gone was the balmy air of the tropics, and instead the bare branches of winter began to appear on the riverbanks. Far on the horizon to their west, they could see the cloud-shrouded peaks of the Osgoi Range, but the river swung back to the northeast again, and they lost sight of the mountains. It took them a full eight days to reach Yorath, and they sailed into a beautiful, late-winter sunset on a placid lake that stretched north and east as far as the eye could see.

That night they moored the raft on the western shore. Askia said it was safer to stay close to shore, but not too close. He had been warned about the dangerous and unknown creatures both in the lake and onshore. They all slept huddled close together for warmth. They woke up after only a few hours of sleep as their raft rocked gently in the wake of something bulky passing them by in the water. They could hear cries, grunts, and the snapping of large branches from the forest. The noises kept them awake until, exhausted, they closed their eyes and drifted off.

Splashing sounds nearby jerked them awake again. Something, or someone on the shore was throwing rocks at them, but they fell well short of the raft. The next morning found them all tired and jumpy from lack of sleep.

"Did you see the eyes?" asked Tegan. "They were watching us."

"Glowing, red eyes," said Kex. "Did you notice how far apart they were? Whatever they were—they were enormous."

"I hope it doesn't get much worse," said Djana. "This area is even scarier than the mountains!"

Jarah wondered, aloud, how they were going to make their way on foot north when unknown things on shore waited for them. Would it have been any better on the Mernoc shore?

"I don't think so," said Tristan. "I know of that part of Mernoc, and have heard the rumors of wild beasts near the lake. We must be careful when we begin our journey on foot." His hand drifted to where he used to keep his sword. He no longer had the comforting weapon at his waist. It had been lost in the ocean when the sea monster many moons ago attacked them. He wished he had another one, but since all they possessed now were small utility knives that Ortzi had not taken away from them, he felt even more vulnerable than ever.

"Askia, you need to drop us off soon and make your way back," said Jarah. "I don't like the thought of you returning alone."

"I will be safe," he replied. "Even if you were with me, what could any of us do against these monsters? I know how to survive. I'll make it back."

They hoped he would. All too soon, they found the northern branch of the Garden River where it emptied into the lake. They spent another night moored near the shore, and in the morning, at first light, Askia helped them carry their supplies to the shore before he bade them goodbye and quickly set sail in the direction they had come.

"I think we'll be safe if we travel by day," said Tristan. "Those things seem to prefer the dark, just like in the mountains. We'll find a spot to sleep at night that can be defended."

"I really miss my bow and arrows," said Kex. "If we had time I could make myself something, but it's probably better to keep moving. Those creatures will come back here tonight, and without the raft we have no place to sleep."

They each picked up a bundle of their supplies and began to walk. They weren't sure where, exactly, they were going, but they kept the riverbank to their right. Irusan had told them to follow the river north.

They were heading into the thick forest now. The trees were no longer the stunted pines of the south Garden River plain. These pines seemed to tower over them. The bare branches of oaks, elm, and maple laced overhead and dry leaves crunched underfoot. It felt as if they were getting smaller as the trees rose higher and higher above them. The river's current flowed faster towards the lake. Irusan was right; the river was not navigable here. It narrowed further upstream as the banks rose steeply on either side. Below them, they could hear the roar of the water that tumbled helter-skelter over rocks and through narrow channels. The Garden River's source was still many leagues ahead, to the northeast in the Osgoi Range, but they felt as if they were already climbing uphill and had to stop frequently to rest.

A few hours before darkness set in, they looked for a place to sleep, somewhere where they could see what was approaching from as many directions as possible. They left the riverbank and walked west, up an incline. The sun was sinking below the tops of the trees and the shadows lengthened into darkness as they climbed. The slope, which at first was gradual, became steeper, and as the last rays of the sun disappeared, they found themselves standing on a flat rock that jutted out from the top of a small hill.

The sky above was clear, with a full moon rising behind the

trees. The trees dropped sharply away on either side. This looked like a good place to spend the night, and they gratefully put down their bags, making their beds on the still-warm rock. It was perfect.

"I'll stand first watch," said Tristan, "while the rest of you sleep." They ate, and exhausted by their lack of sleep the night before, along with the day's long trek, they all fell asleep quickly.

Tristan climbed a stunted tree that had pushed its way through the smaller rocks nearby. It gave him a better eye-view of the surrounding area. He was used to keeping watch at night, and even if the moon had not been full as it was tonight, he would have no problem adjusting his eyes to penetrate the dark shadows of the forest.

The moon slowly rose until it was almost directly overhead. It lit up the rock and the surrounding forest like daylight, and Tristan felt uncomfortable. Something wasn't right. The forest was silent. Too silent. He felt the hairs prickling up on his neck and arms. He took his knife out and scanned the forest below. Was that a movement? He wasn't sure.

Suddenly, he heard a howl. It was like the one they had heard last night near the lake. It sent chills up his spine, and it was close! A bolt of fear pierced him like a sharp knife.

The others were awake. They had heard it too.

"What is it?" asked Tegan, her eyes round with terror. The others looked no less frightened, and they crept closer to each other as Tristan came down from his tree and stood on the rock, still looking down into the forest below, in the direction the howl had come from.

"I don't know, Tegan. *Quiet!*"

The howl came again, but this time from behind them. Tristan spun around. It was closer. Then, another howl, from another direction—and another. They were surrounded.

They leapt up from their beds. Now everyone was scanning the forest below, but still they could not see anything. Tristan wondered if they should run for it—get off the rock. The howls came closer, from every direction now. They were approaching the rock they were on. The shadows in the forest moved, and it was then that they saw the eyes. Eyes that glowed redly. Eyes that had seen them.

It was too late to run. They could see that now. They'd led themselves into a trap. If they fled, they'd run straight into these creatures on every side. All they could do was watch, helpless, as the dark shapes crept towards them.

Departure, Blaidd

They left Rhiannon before sun-up. Their fishing boat glided silently out of the bay, with no torch light to light their way. No one challenged them, or even saw them, but it wasn't until they rounded the southern headland and headed east, into the Sea of Alania, that Blaidd began to relax. Abban's boat was small, and Blaidd hoped they would enjoy fair weather. He'd not paid much attention to sailing before, leaving it up to others, but now he wanted to learn. It felt to him that he wanted to develop any skill he could. It would help keep his brain active, and, perhaps, delay the onset of the change that was occurring in his body.

Daily, he recognized the progression of the template structure that Amrafalus had imposed upon him with his crystals. He recognized it as mostly that of a bull; a beast revered and worshipped by many cults over time for its strength. Amrafalus, he now realized, did not intend to share power with him.

After he had used him to activate the generator crystals under the Citadel—as he thought—he once again was ready to dispose of him. Only this time, it was not through death, but through slavery. What exactly Amrafalus had had in mind for him was not clear. He knew that his body was becoming gigantic. His muscles had developed so fast that he had to teach himself how to move without hurting himself or breaking everything around him. The horns on his head were now clearly horns, and their sharp tips lengthened daily.

As the light rose in the sky, he noticed Abban observing him carefully. Was that fear in his face? He wasn't sure. He tried to smile at Abban but his lips pulled back from his teeth in a snarl. Abban shrunk back and turned his head. Blaidd knew it must be difficult to look at him.

"I not hurt you, Abban," he said, trying to sound reassuring. What came out instead was a thick, growly voice. Was he even saying it right? He didn't know.

Abban nodded his head and continued to sail. Blaidd sank down on the deck and cried. His sobs sounded like moans, like that of a sick cow. He had never heard anything like it, and with that thought, his moans became even louder.

13.

The Gardeners

The moon bathed the Six in a spectral light. It reflected coldly off the approaching eyes, eyes that now approached them slowly and quietly as they stood back to back on the flat rock. In the bright moonlight, the shapes stood out clearly. They were tall, at least twice Tristan's height—he was the taller of the group—and stood, manlike, on two hind legs. But there was nothing else remotely human about these creatures. The closest resemblance to any animal was that of a wolf, but they had never seen any wolves as large as these. They had wolf-like heads and snouts, and fangs that glistened in the moonlight. Muscles rippled under grey fur as they crept up the hill. It looked as if they were approaching cautiously, but Jarah knew that as soon as they were in range they would pounce, and it would be fast. The creatures were holding back now because they didn't know what defenses the Six had. If they knew how little they had, they would have been torn to pieces already.

"When they come close enough to us," said Tristan, his voice trembling, "run. Try to break through their line. I will keep them occupied with my knife."

"Not good enough, Tristan," said Jarah. His voice shook too. "I will stay. The girls must run."

"And me too," said Adain. "Three of us can hold some of them off while the girls run for the forest."

"You must be joking," said Kex. "They'd only chase after us. We can't outrun them. I'm staying."

"Same here," agreed Djana.

"Could we use our Crystal?" Tegan asked. "It worked for the Arrach—"

"Holy mother of Idris, why didn't I think of the Crystal?" said Jarah, quickly taking it out of the pouch still around his neck. It had become so much a part of him that he barely thought about it anymore. He wanted to slap himself. "*Tone!*" he commanded.

Tremulously, they all began to tone. Waves of light from the Crystal rippled the air around them. They toned louder. The waves slowly spread out, and to their immense relief the wolves stopped their approach, but they did not retreat. Jarah realized their mistake almost as soon as it happened. They should have waited until the wolves were in range. Instead, the wolves could now wait, just out of range of the Crystal's light and sound field, which is exactly what they did. They snarled and growled, snapping at the air around them, but they knew that the healing power of the Crystal could not touch them if they did not come closer. These were intelligent creatures, thought Jarah. A mere beast would have continued their approach and experienced the consequences of the Crystal's power.

They looked at each other but continued to tone. They all knew what Jarah was thinking. They must keep toning, all night if necessary. He wondered if they could keep it up—and for how long. All the wolves needed were a second's hesitation, a single break in the field around them, and they would rush them before they could recover. They needed to tone as their lives depended on it.

The moon reached its zenith in the sky and still they toned. Jarah wondered how long they had already toned. His voice cracked with exhaustion, and he was sure they would not be able to keep this up indefinitely. The wolves were doing their best to distract them by running in circles around the edge of the Crystal's field, setting up a howling and snarling that would wake the dead while their jaws snapped at the air around them. Even though they were out of range, it couldn't have been pleasant for them either. They felt the frequencies of the Crystal and it angered them. They worked themselves up into a frothy rage that was even more frightening than the howls and growls.

They kept toning.

The moon was now disappearing once more into the western tree line behind them, and they were losing even its cold light. Soon the darkness would overtake them and so would exhaustion. They lost all sense of time as they toned, and now the Crystal's light was all that they could see. They could hear the wolves at its rim, and they could see dark shapes moving beyond, but nothing else.

Just as Jarah thought he couldn't get another sound out, he noticed something out of the corner of his eye, far out into the forest. What was it? Perhaps his eyes were playing tricks. He thought he had seen a light. He continued toning and turned his head, looking around, but saw nothing. He had imagined it.

But there it was again! It was a light. Were the wolves bringing in reinforcements? He hoped not. Now Tristan had seen it too. His head jerked around towards the direction where Jarah looked.

I see it too, Jarah! It was a thought from Tegan. *There is not only one, but several lights. I've been watching them. They appeared a few moments ago.*

They flashed, like fireflies, in the distance. They came from the west, and they were getting closer to their hill. Now the wolves had seen them too. They stopped their running and growled as they looked towards the lights.

Jarah felt that this was not another wolf attack. They obviously were as surprised by the appearance of the lights as the Six were. The larger of the wolves howled what appeared to be a command as he took a step back. The other wolves all followed suit, and as the lights came even closer, they could hear something.

It sounded like a chorus of voices, a trilling with deeper bass tones, accompanied by the high-spirited tempo of fiddles. Not sure what they should do, they continued with their now-faint toning, but watched carefully. The wolves crouched on the ground on all fours, and instead of surrounding the hill, they huddled together in one area. One of them whimpered. The music grew louder. The wolves snarled and whined as they slowly retreated backwards.

"Stop toning," said Jarah. "Let's see what happens." They stopped, their throats raw, and the light from the Crystal vanished. "Be ready to start again, just in case." They all nodded.

The lights, fiddles, and singing were almost at the base of the hill when there was a flash of sudden fire, like that of a lightning bolt, and an earsplitting crack rang out. The wolves all howled, turned tail, and fled into the forest so quickly that they were in front of them for one heartbeat and gone the next. Some of the lights took off in the same direction as the wolves, and they could hear and see crashing bolts of blue flame, and the yelps and howls of the wolves as they leapt away through the trees far below them. The other half of the lights began to move up the hill towards them. Jarah wished he could see what was coming, but all he could see were the lights, not what was carrying them.

"They say to follow them," said Tegan, and they all looked at her.

"Are you sure?" asked Tristan.

"Have I ever lied to you or been wrong before? We need to go with them—*now!*"

Without further hesitation, they bolted down the hill toward the lights. The lights moved back from them, into the forest heading west through the trees. They were some distance away from the hill before they realized that they had left their supplies of food and blankets on the rock, but they didn't want to lose the lights. They could worry about their supplies later.

The lights moved silently and rapidly away from them, and it was difficult to keep up, especially since they couldn't see in the dark. The ground was uneven, and they tripped and fell several times, but they stood up, and kept running. It seemed the lights were losing them now, getting further and further away. Jarah wondered where they would end up. *Is this the legendary fairy-lights that led unwary travelers astray?* Perhaps, by following, they were getting themselves deeper into trouble instead of out of it, although he couldn't think of a worse situation than the one they had just escaped from.

And then, a moment later, they lost the lights completely. They were in the middle of the forest. It was as black as a tinker's pot around them, and they had no supplies and no idea where they were.

They slowly came to a stop, panting and gasping for air. The trees around them were even bigger than those they had just left behind, and they grew so densely together it was difficult to see the path or way through. They could hear sounds, but they were the noises of the forest, and not the fairy chorus they had heard earlier.

"I think we've just followed the mischievous woodland sprites of the old legends," said Jarah.

"Whatever they were, they saved us from the wolves, but what have they brought us to?" asked Tristan. They shook their heads. No one had any idea of what to do now.

Then they heard the sound that brought back the raw terror they had felt earlier. A long roar, almost next to them that shook the ground, and a loud snap as if something had uprooted a tree, or snapped it in half like a matchstick. They were paralyzed by fear, their feet rooted to the ground.

"Well, are you going to take all night or would you like to meet the owner of that roar?" asked a voice nearby.

Startled, they jumped and looked around. They could see nothing.

"Over here! Come on! I don't have all night." They spun around again. All they could see were tree trunks. Then a small shadow, about half their height, detached itself from one of the trunks and snapped its fingers. A flame, a few inches high, appeared in the palm of its hand. They could see, beneath a mop of carroty hair, bright eyes that twinkled in the light of the fire. The little man wore the wool and leather clothing of the Aelfar region, and his beard hung to his waist. "C'mon, *move!*"

The Six did not need further encouragement. They followed him through a gap in the tree trunks that they had not noticed in the dark. He led them through the trees until they came to one so large they could not see around its trunk. To their astonishment, they saw a small door in the tree trunk. He opened the door, and they all ducked down and stepped through before he closed it behind them.

"The creatures out there can't get in. They can't even see it, so there's no need for concern," he said. They found themselves in a small room or vestibule in the tree. On the other side was another door as small as the one they had just walked through. He opened this door, and they bent down again, followed him out, and stopped to stare into a world of light and sound that made the dark forest and the night behind them seem like a bad dream from a long time ago.

14.

Ibai

Abban sailed into the Bay of Abena. The whole trip had taken them seven days, but the weather had held, and their passage was uneventful. Abban was no longer afraid of Blaidd. He'd kept his word, and he had not harmed Abban.

As they stepped off the boat and onto the crowded dock in Ibai, nearby fishermen scattered in fear. They'd never seen another Trueni quite like Blaidd. He towered over both Trueni and human. As they walked through the streets, mothers pulled their children into houses while men melted away into alleyways and buildings.

They did not know what they were looking for, but Blaidd wanted to find someone he recognized. Someone like Holgar or Adne, or Yared and Askia. He looked closely at every face that did not recoil or shrink away from him—there weren't many—but didn't see anyone he knew.

What if he'd made a mistake by coming here? Perhaps the Six

had not come this way at all. Abban knocked on doors, but they weren't opened. He stopped those in the street who did not flee quickly enough, but they pulled away and ran before he could question them. They had no choice but to keep walking.

After walking for what seemed like most of the rest of the day, they came to a group of houses on the banks of the river. Word had reached this area of the frightening creature that prowled their village, and the streets were deserted. Ibai was now a ghost town. Only the dogs that roamed Ibai didn't seem concerned by the stranger who stalked their alleyways. Finally, Blaidd stopped. He had to do something different. This was not working. He placed his claw-like hands around his mouth and bellowed.

"*Holgar! Adne! Come out! I need talk.*" He kept on doing this as they walked down each street and narrow alley. "*I no harm you, please, come out!*"

Just as he was about to turn around and go down another street, he heard a creak nearby. A door cracked opened. Someone was watching him. He stood quietly and waited. Finally, the door opened a bit further, and a head peered cautiously around the door. It was Holgar!

"Who are you and what do you want with us?" Holgar asked.

"Please come out, Holgar. I know you. I explain it all to you. I promise you not be hurt."

Holgar slowly stepped out from behind the door, indicating to someone inside they should remain where they were. He stepped out into the street and walked towards Blaidd.

"You say you know me? How?"

Blaidd lowered himself down onto the ground, right in the middle of the street. He had to appear as unthreatening as possible. He knelt. He remembered a time when Holgar had knelt in front of him. He wished, more than anything, that he could undo the past.

People were slowly coming out of their houses, drawn to this spectacle of a monster abasing itself in front of their teacher, Holgar.

Their curiosity overcame their fear, and it helped that Blaidd was now kneeling with head bowed and hands where they could see them.

Abban stepped forward. "He friend-brother," he said. "Blaidd no hurt—"

"Blaidd ... *Blaidd*?" Holgar interrupted. "How can this be?" He looked incredulously at the kneeling monster in front of him.

"It indeed I," said Blaidd. "I change, because Amrafalus ... I not boy anymore, but monster. Please, help, Holgar!" He bent over and sobbed, appalled at the low mooing growls that came from deep within his throat. The curious crowd fell back in fear.

Holgar just stared. It was too much to take in. How could a person change this quickly? He had seen quick healing from the Crystal, but this ... *this* was unbelievable. Could it be true?

He made up his mind. He grasped Blaidd by a horn and indicated he should get up.

"Follow me." He walked back to the house he had just come out of, Abban and Blaidd behind him. He opened the door and they stepped into the cool interior. Blaidd ducked his head down, but his horns still scraped the rafters. As Blaidd's eyes adjusted to the dim light inside, a woman stepped forward. It was Adne.

"What—who ..." she asked, eyes wide with fear.

"He won't hurt us, Adne. This is Blaidd."

"Blaidd!?" She too looked at him in disbelief. Blaidd was still moo sobbing, and clutching the pouch around his neck. Wordlessly, he lifted it from his neck and handed it to her. Adne looked at him uncomprehendingly.

"Open it," he said. "It yours."

She opened the pouch, and the glittering gems tumbled out into her hand. She looked again at him. "What is this, Blaidd? What am I to do with this?"

"Use to help Trueni," he said. "I sorry for all past mistakes. I be warned, but I not listen. Now here to heal. I look for Six Healers. You know?"

"Oh Blaidd, I am really sorry." Adne looked as if she meant it, her eyes tearing up. "The Six are not here anymore. They were taken away by Ortzi—the leader of Galon. They ..." She stopped and looked at Holgar. She didn't know if she should go on. Could they trust this Blaidd? Nothing he had ever done in the past had earned their trust, and what if all this was a trap—a trap to find the Six for reasons of his own?

The primary reason seemed obvious; it crouched in front of her in all its hideousness. But, would he betray them again after being healed, assuming he ever could regain his health? Holgar interrupted her thoughts.

"We can't tell you where the Six are because we don't know."

Blaidd had so hoped ... but he must continue. Surely, *someone* would know something. He wanted to say something, but what came out was "*Mmmoooo*" and he fell onto the floor, covering his head with his massive, clawed hands.

He wanted to kill himself. He raked at his face with his long claws and blood dripped from his wounds. The hopelessness he felt was like nothing he'd ever experienced before, even in his worst moments, and he continued to *Mmmoooo* as Holgar, Abban and Adne looked on in horror.

"*Stop!*" cried Adne. "We'll help you, Blaidd. Just stop." She went towards him and clasped his enormous claws in her own delicate hands, forgetting that he could disembowel her with a single swipe. Holgar and Abban pulled her away.

"Get up, Blaidd," said Holgar. "Adne is right, we *can* help you. Just because we don't know where the Six are at the moment, it doesn't mean it's hopeless."

Blaidd stopped moaning and stood up, but then had to sit down again on the floor. It was too uncomfortable for him in this small space. He was almost eye level with them now.

At that moment, the door flung open with a crash, and Yared rushed in, a large knife in one hand.

"*Where is he ... ?*" Astonished, he stopped as he saw the monstrosity crouching on the floor.

"It's all right, Yared. Please put the knife down," said Holgar. Yared slowly lowered his knife, but he didn't put it down. "This is Blaidd. He's been altered by Amrafalus' crystals and is seeking help from us."

"*Help*? I should kill him ... what he did to us," said Yared, panting, his face flushed with anger. He'd run non-stop to Holgar and Adne's home as soon as he'd heard the news about the monster who'd called them out.

"Yes, I understand," said Holgar. "I wanted to kill him too, but look at him ... don't you think he's suffered enough?"

"Maybe, maybe not," said Yared. "Let's give him to Ortzi. He can decide what to do with him."

"No!" Adne held up her hand. "This is not time for revenge. Yared, I understand how you feel, but we must use our heads instead of our emotions. Holgar is right. He's suffered terribly and he's remorseful about what he has done—"

"He's sorry that he's getting repayment for his lies and deceit," Yared argued.

"Maybe. But that doesn't give us the right to judge him. I feel sure the Six can help him and," she looked at Holgar, "I believe it is safe to tell him what we do know."

Holgar thought for a while. He trusted Adne's judgment like no other. She'd been right about his business partner, the man who'd betrayed them to Amrafalus, and he trusted her judgment now. Djana had inherited much of her mother's sixth sense when it came to people, and he needed to know when to take a back seat to his wife. He felt that Djana would have agreed with her mother if she were here.

"We will help you, Blaidd."

Blaidd's eyes shone with a newfound hope. "You not sorry this time, Holgar," he said. "I do anything, anything at all. Me your servant, forever."

"Not necessary, Blaidd. We'll do what we can." Holgar hoped they could do something about the situation, but he didn't think so. He wished his daughter and her friends were still here. They would know what to do.

The Raven

Blaidd was right. Branwyn did have second thoughts about letting him go. She sent Marko back to Akelarre a few days after Blaidd had left, and when he returned to say his friend had gone, along with Blaidd, she brought up her Merkaba and flew across the bay in the invisible bubble of light to look for him.

She felt he would be hard to miss. He was already so misshapen and distorted that he would stand out even from the Trueni. Her search took her over Akelarre and into the marketplace. She listened, unseen, to conversations. She was sure that rumors would spread quickly about the enormous beast who had arrived in their midst, but there was nothing.

She flew over the bay again, heading south. They might have gone fishing. Marko said his friend, Abban, was a fisherman, but there was no sign of them on the bay. She would continue her search. They must be somewhere.

She wondered why she had let him go. She had felt that he could no longer be useful to her with his brain deteriorating and all his knowledge of crystals gone, but then she realized she might just have another use for him, one that did not involve intellect. He was turning into a monster, yes, and she could use that. Fear was a great motivator, and Blaidd now inspired fear in any beholder. She *would* find him, of that, she was certain.

She was also certain that Blaidd was, just like her, searching for the six healers. Perhaps it was good that she had let him go. He would lead her straight to them. He was motivated to find them, and she would find Blaidd.

She smiled. A beast that size couldn't hide from her for long.

15.

Ardvale

"**M**y name is Finn," said the little man. No one noticed him. The Six stared open-mouthed at the world around them. They had stepped out from the darkness of night into warm daylight. A golden light filtered through the green leaves above, dappling the ground in front of them. The grass was springtime fresh, and flowers bloomed in a meadow nearby. The lights they had seen in the dark forest were here, softly glowing as they drifted, spun, and bounced in playful delight. The tinkling chorus of tiny voices, accompanied by the musical notes that they'd heard in the forest, were here too, and now they could hear that it originated from the glowing spheres.

As their eyes adjusted to the unexpected radiance, they saw that the "lights" were actually glowing orbs of many colors and sizes.

Finn cleared his throat. "I am Finn," he said again, and the Six looked at him apologetically.

"Oh, I'm so sorry," said Jarah, as he introduced himself. The others introduced themselves too. "We're just a little surprised at where we are. By the way, where, exactly, *are* we?"

Finn smiled. "I do understand. You weren't expecting this, even though Irusan warned you. Our world is rather different to yours, and it will take some getting used to."

"So you know Irusan?" asked Tristan.

"Yes, he's a dear friend. We work with him a lot. You might even see him while you're here. He's able to stay longer in our world than yours, as ours is close to Agra'Tan in frequency. As to where you are ... *hmm* ... well, let me see. That is rather hard to explain. Let's just call it Ardvale. That's not its real name, but we don't give out its real name to anyone." Finn gestured at the world around them. "We request you do not speak of us once you leave. If it weren't for Irusan requesting our help for you ..." He stopped, and they understood that humans did not regularly visit this place.

"You already understand the dimensional worlds, so it won't be too difficult to proceed from what you already know," he continued. "Let's just say that we are in a world that is in-between worlds—in-between dimensions, actually. We operate on a different frequency level and angular rotation of spin to yours. We are not a 'where', but a '*when*.' Our time is different to yours. Some, a very few, of your people may enter Ardvale without harm, while others ... well ... to others, even if they had the means to enter, it would quickly become extremely inhospitable for them. We are safe here. We are the gardeners of your world. We take care of life-forms such as trees, plants, and animals. We control many of the elements that make up your world, but not all."

Finn looked at them, his once-cheerful countenance now grave.

"We do not control the dangerous beasts that attacked you. They have their gardeners too, but they are not like us, and I don't think you'd want to meet those gardeners!" He paused a moment, then winked and smiled again, and indicated they should follow him.

They walked down a path through the tall trees, accompanied by the excited but incomprehensible chatter of the orbs, who stopped singing just long enough to satisfy their curiosity about the new-comers. They touched them lightly as they chattered and laughed.

"Ignore them, they'll go away once they understand your composition," said Finn. "They don't see many life forms like yours."

Tegan held out her hand, and one alit on her palm like a butterfly. It felt gentle, like a soap bubble. She laughed, and the orb floated away with a giggle.

As they walked, Finn continued to speak. "I want to be sure you understand. You may think you're here because *we* wished to save you from the wolf-creatures. Nothing could be further from the truth. We do not save random travelers who are unwise enough to enter these forests. We would have left you to your own devices had not Irusan not informed us you would be entering these forests. We knew you were coming by the Crystal you carry." He nodded towards Jarah. "When you began your singing to the Crystal, we knew you were here. We realized those creatures had cornered you, and others were on their way. You would have made a feast for the many creatures that roam those forests." He frowned. "You couldn't have picked a worse place to sleep."

"Why?" asked Tegan.

"That flat rock is where the wolf-creatures go to howl at the full moon!" His frown disappeared, and he laughed heartily, wiping tears from his eyes as his beard shook with mirth. "*Yoiks!* They must have been infuriated to see humans desecrating their special spot!"

Jarah shuddered. What if Tegan had not remembered the Crystal? They would all be dead by now. "What are those wolf-things?" he asked. "Who made them?"

"Not us, that's for sure!" Finn gave another belly laugh, and then looked serious again. "They were created in a time so long ago that even we have forgotten. There have been, and still are, many otherworldly races out there that have used your world as a playground. What you see as the current inhabitants are the new-comers. What is out there is older than you can imagine, and that part of the forest is theirs. They don't take kindly to interlopers. But I was going to tell you why you are here," he said. "You are here to continue your education. There are things we can teach you that you were not able to learn in Mu'A. Conditions here are better than those in Mu'A. Irusan will be teaching you as well."

The Six were pleased that they would be seeing more of Irusan. They were now walking down a road bordered on each side by privet hedges. A meadow was on one side, and they were approaching a building that looked like a house on their left.

Jarah patted his Crystal and realized that he was carrying another one, the one that they had removed from the Crystal Cave and had been told to give to someone they would meet later. Surely, that someone was ...?

"I almost forgot," he said as he took the crystal out of the pouch that hung from his neck. "We were told to give this crystal to you." He handed it to Finn, who looked at it, then handed it back.

"Keep it," he said. "It is not for me, but for someone you will meet later. She will ask for it, so there won't be any doubt."

"Will you tell us more about yourself, about the orbs?" asked Djana.

"All in good time. Now, here is your home." They stopped in front of a house. Tegan felt her heart lift. All her life she had wanted a house like this. It was as if someone had read her mind. She had dreamed of this house for years and now it was here, in front of her! It was a cottage with a thatch roof and low-hanging eaves, a picket fence, and a beautiful garden.

Kex gasped too. She had longed for this home, while on the road; a permanent structure instead of animal hide tents. It was made of stout logs with a turf roof. Smoke came from the chimney, and there were chickens in the wood-fenced yard.

Djana looked astounded. How had someone known what she had always wanted? A sturdy stone structure stood in front of her.

The roof was clay-shingled, and there were balconies that over-looked the lake on the other side of the lane.

The men also saw what they would have preferred: Jarah, a small log cabin with log roof. Tristan, a comfortable house that he'd always admired in the port city of Anjou, and Adain, an un-pretentious cottage with just enough room for a small kitchen, bed, and a table with chairs. He had never placed much impor-tance in dwelling places, and if he could design his own place, this would have been it.

"You will come to realize that each of you will live separately," said Finn. Your space will not intrude upon anyone else's, unless both parties agree, so you each live in a different home, but in the same space. That is how all our worlds co-exist with each other. You will also find that you have each created your own space al-ready. Ardvale allows instantaneous creation, so be careful of what you think!"

With that, Finn disappeared in a small flash of light. They each walked through the gate, each to their own house.

Askia

Askia had lied when he told the Six he would be just fine to return to Ibai by himself. He was frightened. He had not been this frightened since the destruction of his boat and almost his life by the sea-monster. He set sail back down the lake and tried not to glance towards the shoreline. Every ripple under his boat or log in the water set his heart racing. He dreaded nightfall. He wondered if he should just continue to sail on through the night, but realized that would have been rash. He could not see what was in the water ahead of him, and he could not use flame to light his way.

His first night on the water, moored near the bank, but not

too close, was sleepless. The forest sounds and rock throwing continued, but he knew he was safe from these beasts as long as he stayed on the raft. He may as well have continued to sail on, he thought, but the fear of what could be waiting in the water scared him more. He set sail again at the first light and didn't stop until he reached the Garden River.

It didn't take much effort to make good time down the river as he was headed downstream. He felt safer mooring the boat on the Mernoc side of the river at night. The worst of the creatures seemed to be on the western bank. He heard less howling from the eastern bank, but he ventured as little as possible off the boat until he arrived in Ibai. His joy at arriving home safely was tempered by the news he received from Yared, who met him at the docks.

"Blaidd is back," said Yared, with a grim look on his face.

"What? How did this happen?"

Yared filled him in about Blaidd's arrival and appearance. He had arrived yesterday, and Adne and Holgar were housing him. They did not want anyone to talk of this, in fear that it would reach Ortzi's ears. A special town meeting was held last night when Holgar and Adne pleaded with the people of Ibai to not reveal his presence. They had all wanted to turn him over to Ortzi's army, but since the townsfolk held Holgar and Adne in such high esteem, they acquiesced to their request and decided not to turn him in.

"What about Mikel?" asked Askia. "He will turn him in."

Askia was right. Mikel would betray Blaidd in a heartbeat.

"We have appointed a delegation of our strongest to visit Mikel," said Yared. "He will be '*persuaded*.'"

Askia smiled. He knew what that meant. He decided to go with Yared straight to Holgar and Adne's home. Even though Yared had prepared him for what to expect, he stopped and stared in shock at his first sight of Blaidd. This was even worse than he could have imagined.

This creature could have stood his ground with the creatures of the forests of the north—perhaps even defeating many of them.

He hoped he was really was as friendly as Yared said he was, although it was obvious that Yared still had his doubts. The memory of the betrayal still lingered in Yared's mind, and it would take a lot for him to trust Blaidd again. It looked to Askia that Blaidd was part bull, part human, and part ... unknown. It was bull, yes, but the hands were talons and the teeth—he didn't even want to look at the teeth—fangs. He had never seen a monster like this before. Blaidd was a walking weapon.

"We're glad you made it back safely, Askia," said Adne. "Please sit and give us the news about our Six." He sat, ignoring Blaidd, who didn't look at him. Blaidd sat in a corner of the room, looking down at his feet. He seemed lost in a world of his own. Abban was there, and he sat close to Blaidd as if protecting him. Abban said he was leaving to return to Rhiannon in the morning.

Askia told them about the journey, that he'd had to leave the Six on the banks of the northern branch of the Garden River and that he had no idea what had become of them. He tried to downplay the experiences with strange creatures in the forest while they were on the raft, but Adne looked worried.

"I understand there was nothing else you could do, Askia. Irusan told us they would be all right. He said they had the ability to protect themselves from ... what is up that way."

Askia nodded. "He said too they would be met by ... others. I trust that they were, and all is well." That is all they could hope for.

Blaidd looked up. "I go there," he said suddenly. "I find Six." They all looked at him, astonished. "I not afraid of monsters."

"Well, Blaidd, if you must go and look for them, then we won't stop you," said Holgar. "Maybe it's better that way than waiting for Mikel to betray you, as he eventually will, although that would be rough justice. When do you want to go?"

"Now," said Blaidd, rising as Askia gaped. He looked at Askia. "You take, *now*."

16.

Anfawl, City of Rhiannon

It hadn't taken long for Anfawl to gain support amongst the troops that were once the Army of Amrafalus, who were forced to swear allegiance to Madfall. Anfawl was relieved that Udfa was not put in charge of his army as well as the navy. To a man, they all resented Udfa. He was not one of them, and his navy was a joke. He had proved himself unworthy when he'd lost the six children he'd been hunting down on the sea. They had apparently fooled him quite easily.

Anfawl was the highest-ranking officer of Madfall's army now. He knew that his pledge of fealty to Madfall was not worth the illegible mark he'd made on the papyrus oath. He lay low, not allowing a breath of rumor to reach Madfall's ears about where his loyalties really lay—to himself. Branwyn had schooled him well. To all intents, he appeared to be a loyal officer and council member, but behind the scenes, he plotted with Branwyn.

He thanked Idris every day for Branwyn. She was the best thing that had ever happened to him. She understood his real potential and knew he was capable of strong leadership. He would be proud to have her by his side on the throne of ... well; they didn't have a throne anymore as the golden throne of Amrafalus was now lying under a pile of rubble and stone blocks that still defied all attempts to remove it. He wished that the Citadel still stood, although he was grateful that it had squashed Amrafalus like the cockroach he was. Fortunately, he had escaped himself, but so had Madfall and Udfa, and no one had seen the little piece of excrement, Blaidd— or Seryn, whatever he called himself. Anfawl assumed he was also buried, and his body still lay under the large chunks of stone.

After the fall of the Citadel, Headquarters were set up in the interior rooms of the wall that still surrounded the rubble that had once been the Citadel. At least the walls had not fallen. Slaves were in the process of removing the debris in the center, but it was slow, and he was sure it would take years to complete. Branwyn's plans were to rebuild a palace on the site, one that would make the old Citadel look like a child's construction. If it kept her busy, he was fine with it. Women liked that sort of thing, and it would leave him free to run the country, which in his opinion, was a man's job. He hadn't decided yet if he'd crown himself king, or if he should be an emperor. Both sounded acceptable. He'd sleep on it.

Branwyn had recently returned from a trip to visit her family in Ak-Gala, across the bay, she said. It hadn't taken her long, and he'd asked her why she hadn't spent more time there. She replied that she didn't like her family much, and the less time she spent with them, the better. When he asked why she didn't bring them here, she replied that he wouldn't like them either. She added that she might need to visit them regularly since her father was sick, but she would never stay too long. He was glad that Branwyn did not appear too interested in family or politics. She chattered brightly about her trip, and the clothes and baubles she had found. Occasionally she made a suggestion to him about how to talk to the troops and gain their trust and loyalty. He found this useful, since it was usually something he hadn't thought of himself, and her advice always seemed to work.

He was delighted when, at last, Branwyn invited him to visit her home. He had never seen it before. She always came to see him at his home, and he felt his modest dwelling was not suited to entertain a woman of her stature and breeding.

He thought her home the most beautiful place he had ever seen. She was truly a woman of taste and refinement. She would do an excellent job in rebuilding the Citadel. He spent many hours out on her terrace, overlooking the bay. Soon, everything he saw would be his. His troops were ready.

Blaidd was as good as his word. He left that same night. Before leaving Blaidd handed his satchel to Holgar.

"There something in there for Healers," he said. "I not take with me. Too dangerous if fall into wrong hands. You see later, you give."

Holgar looked surprised. What could Blaidd possess that was so dangerous? After Blaidd and Askia left for the river, he and Adne looked inside the satchel.

A bundle of papyrus papers wrapped in an item of clothing with small, close-together writing and diagrams were inside. It must be important. They stowed the satchel on top of a rafter where it would be difficult to see. It would be safe there, and they'd give it to their daughter next time they saw her.

The River

The night was dark, with no moon to guide their way. Askia

and Blaidd crept down to the river dock. When they reached the raft, Askia covered Blaidd with an old sail cloth and poled the raft north, up the Garden River. Holgar had advised Blaidd to conceal himself since he didn't want the town gossips, or Mikel, to know in which direction he had gone. He would merely disappear.

Askia said he could go a-ways upstream, and then they would anchor for the night in a quiet spot before leaving again in the morning. Blaidd was in a hurry to leave, but even he saw the sense in not going too far at night.

It was in the morning when Askia and Blaidd had an argument.

"You not go with me, Askia. You go back!"

Askia refused. "I will go with you Blaidd. I know the river better than you, and you are no sailor."

"I can work raft. One pole."

"It's not as easy as it looks. The river can be treacherous and—"

"You go!" Blaidd growled. The argument went back and forth for a while, but unsurprisingly, Blaidd had his way. Askia reluctantly handed the pole over and stepped off the raft and onto the riverbank. He would not have far to walk to get back to Ibai. He didn't want to admit it, even to himself, but he was relieved Blaidd didn't want him to go. He had not looked forward to returning to what would be waiting for them upstream.

He looked back, and the sight of the hulking beast poling his raft upstream was one he would never forget. He watched until Blaidd rounded the bend and disappeared into the early morning mist.

17.

The Water Sprites

The Six slept in comfortable beds for the first time since leaving Mu'A. When they awoke, it was daylight outside and they had no idea what time it was, or how long they had slept. It felt as though they had slept for days, but when Finn arrived at the garden gate, he said he hadn't been gone for long. "There's no time here as you experience it in your world," he said. "When you sleep, you go into another time dimension until your body has repaired itself from your world's wear and tear. You come back here at almost the same time you left." They all looked at each other in confusion. It was difficult understanding this time stuff. "You are all hungry, right?" They nodded. "I realize you have to eat. We don't eat as you do, but you should not leave your house until you've eaten."

"But we don't have food in the house," Kex protested.

"Yes, you do."

"No, I looked," she insisted.

"Stop arguing. Didn't I tell you to be careful what you thought about? You think you don't have food when in fact you do. Go back, and don't return here until you've eaten!"

Feeling like children again, they walked back into their individual houses. To their amazement, where there was an empty larder before, the cupboards were now filled with food. Each one quickly ate their fill, and when they were done, they noticed Finn still standing, waiting, at the gate.

"We can begin your education," he said as he danced down the lane ahead of them. Piping music came from somewhere, but they couldn't see its source. They wondered if they should dance too, but they decided they would feel foolish, so they left the dancing to Finn. He led them into the surrounding forest, to a shady stream surrounded by mossy rocks and ferns. The water tinkled and gurgled, sounding almost like a song. Tegan began to hum along. Finn looked pleased. "You have heard the water elementals, or Undines," said Finn. "We are all elementals here, and I'm an earth elemental. I adopted this form as something you would more readily understand than my actual form. You may call me a *Cluricaun*, though we're generally known as the leprechauns in your part of the world. But this is not about me. Today, we will learn about Water Command. Your lessons here will be how to use the elements in a way that honors and respects them. If you show elements respect, you will earn their trust, and they, in turn, will help you, provided you used them *honorably*. If you were a dark magician, for example, you would not use us, but instead the dark elementals who have no honor, and who only know how to destroy."

"Like the wolf-men?" asked Jarah.

"Yes, exactly. The wolf-men are the creations of long ago by those who were inspired by elemental forces—the forces that were twisted and reversed by those who use your world as their playground. They use mankind to assist in creating their distorted life forms and pit their creations against each other and mankind. Their only goal is to destroy mankind because a force that embodies love created them. They do not understand love, or anything else that is good in your world, so it must be eradicated."

"Why are there both forces existing in our world? Can we not just have one—the loving and good?" asked Djana.

"Your world is polarized, a world of duality. So is this one, to an extent and even Agra'Tan. All of the manifest creation in the lower worlds experience duality: 'good' and 'evil.' Those words you and I use are labels, but in reality, there is no better or worse, simply choices. If one chooses to experience the dark force, then one will experience whatever those forces have to offer. The consequences are there, and so are the results of choosing the light. Which do you prefer? Death over life? One expands and the other contracts. I don't have to tell you which is which."

They looked at each other and nodded.

"If you choose the expanding creation, you will develop along with it and expand back into your original form in the higher worlds from where you originated. You may even decide to leave polarity altogether and never experience the worlds of free will choice again. That is up to you. Some prefer to choose the contracting path, and contract until they are reduced to nothing—the tiniest particles in the universe—without memory or form. But they are all still a part of the Original Source, and they will return and start again if they wish. They will never not be a part of that Source, since nothing can ever leave it, but Source will not allow itself to be out of balance. The universe is always in perfect balance, and nothing is ever lost."

"It really gives me a better perspective on why there are such bad things happening around us," said Jarah. "I always wondered why a loving God would allow its creations to suffer so much."

"It's about free will then?" Kex asked. "Source wanted to experience the ability to choose?"

Finn nodded. "In a manner of speaking. Now it's time to say hello to Arlyn and Nerina."

The water in the stream next to them where Tegan had been dangling her fingers suddenly came to life and rose up towards them. The silvery form took shape as a small figure that detached itself from the stream. It sat down on a rock on the bank. Another column of water shot up as it too became a shape, sitting down next to the first one.

"I am Arlyn," said the first shape in a voice that sounded like water flowing over gravelly rocks.

"And I'm Nerina," said the second shape. Its voice sounded lighter, like rain splashing into a tin cup. Nerina looked feminine, thought Jarah. She had softer features, while Arlyn seemed to be male.

The Six introduced themselves, and Finn gave a little bow and said, "I'll be back for you later." He disappeared, not in a flash, but he was there one beat and gone the next.

They did not know how much time they spent with the Undines. Time seemed to pass quickly, but it also felt as if they had experienced a month's worth of lessons. The Undines described their composition to their eager students, how they connected to waters everywhere, and how even water could experience free will choice.

"Water is a Conscious Being, just like you," said Nerina, in her tinkling voice. "We Undines are a small part of her consciousness. Our role is to allow her to experience her being-ness fully. We have free will choice as part of the water consciousness field, although we are not individuals as you are. We are subject to the laws of physics in the outer worlds, and the will of the greater consciousness. We can be reabsorbed into the greater consciousness and be continually recreated. We recreated ourselves here as you connected with us, and chose to appear in the forms you are most familiar with."

"We have many names, and we chose the names you might be more comfortable with as well," said Arlyn. "You see us as male and female, and that is merely how our polarity appears to you. When we combine ... " as he said this, the two forms merged into a single form that continued to speak, "we become a unified Being that is neither male nor female, but embodies the qualities of both." The Six perceived how the voice had changed, sounding now like water flowing over smooth stones. They separated again and became two.

"During our lesson today, one of you will feel more of a connection with us than the others. That is normal. Each of you will feel more connected with one element than the other. You may find more of an affinity with water, or with earth or crystal, than say, another. Some of you may feel an affinity with more than one element. Your partner may or may not be the same element as you. Don't worry though. You all have roles to play in elemental command."

"Now you may join us with your own consciousness," said Nerina. She instructed them to lie down on the soft, mossy bank and close their eyes as she led them in their mind's eye into the water. She told them how to separate a part of their own consciousness, turning it into water forms like themselves.

"Your bodies are made up primarily of us," she explained. "You can connect with this part of us through your physical bodies. You *are* water."

To their astonishment, it was not a difficult thing to do. They each felt themselves in the same forms as Arlyn and Nerina, and following them, they merged with the stream, becoming one with it. They flowed with the stream as it tumbled over rocks, splashing, dancing, and singing a song that they all became part of. They sang, danced, and felt the exhilaration of falling over cliffs in a free fall tumble to a quiet pool below. They swam through crystal-clear water, weaving around jewel-colored lilies and through forests of slimy weeds. They caressed the smooth scales of fish, played with tadpoles, splashed startled frogs sunning themselves on rocks, and then merged into a larger river.

As they gathered speed, they turned into frothing foam that leapt skywards over boulders and fallen logs, singing a roaring song of delight as they fell back into the river. They continued downstream until they reached the sea. They maneuvered around sandbanks until the water felt salty and they reached the waves—waves which were them. They rose and curled over as they delightedly rushed towards the shore, doing the same thing repeatedly—until Arlyn and Nerina tugged impatiently at them.

"C'mon, we need to keep moving!"

They found themselves in deeper water. Tangles of seaweed floated around them, and they swam laughingly between the thick stems and leaves as aquamarine sunlight scintillated from above. Rising to the surface, they skipped over the waves into the open sea. The water turned a brilliant, but darker blue around them as dolphins and other fish gamboled playfully with them. Once again, Nerina had to pull them away, saying there was much more to see and learn.

As they rode on top of the large swells, they noticed a disturbance in the water ahead that looked like an approaching school of flying fish. The splashing came closer, and the Six realized it was not fish at all, at least, not in the usual sense. These sea-creatures were half human, half fish. They were smaller than the average sized person was, but not as small as the Undines. They had fish tails, and their top half was human, but with fins on the backs of their webbed hands, and a large fin on their back.

"We are the Sea-Gypsies," one of them said. They did not move their mouths, but they could understand them as if they were speaking.

"I've always wanted to see a Sea-Gypsy!" Tegan exclaimed. "Ever since you saved us from the sea monster."

"We remember you," the one who introduced himself as Saraid said. Another one said she was Shan. "You are the six healers the Mu'A were looking for." They followed Saraid and Shan as they leaped over the swells, and the rest of the Sea-Gypsies followed.

They must have looked exactly like flying fish to any observers, thought Jarah. The sense of flight over the water was exhilarating, and he could see how they sparkled in the sunlight as they splashed and flew over the deep troughs. All too soon, Nerina and Arlyn indicated they must return.

"You can spend more time here later," said Nerina. "We still have much to learn."

They turned and headed back the way they came. The Sea-Gypsies accompanied them back to the mouth of the river where they bid them farewell. They all felt sorry to be leaving these happy beings, but it was comforting to know they could return at any time.

As they returned to the stream, they realized that it was now nightfall in Ardvale. Their bodies lay silently on the mossy ground, looking almost as if they were in death.

"Don't worry," said Arlyn. "Your bodies are fine. Just intend to rejoin them."

They blinked, and they were back. Finn was there waiting for them. They slowly rose to their feet and stretched. It felt as if they'd had a long sleep. Their bodies felt slightly stiff, as if they had not moved at all during the time they had been away. Nerina and Arlyn were no longer there.

"Come with me," said Finn. "Your education has begun."

18.

The Coup

Madfall, Lord of Rhiannon, woke up one morning unaware that this was the day his life would change once again. It had started out as a normal day. He sat down for his usual hearty breakfast, and then left for the barracks so he could inspect his troops. Anfawl was there, as he usually was. Madfall had three of his most loyal men with him. He did not think it necessary to have a personal bodyguard, but he was a cautious man, and he made a habit of never going anywhere alone.

As he walked into the barrack courtyard, the men were already assembled in line formation, their weapons lowered. The platoon sergeant began the count-off.

"Open ranks! *March!*"

As was also usual, the front row of the squad took two steps forward, their swords remaining in their sheaths. The second rank took one step forward, their battle-axes lowered, and the third rank remained fast, their crossbows also lowered. The three remaining ranks took steps backwards, their weapons pointed down. Madfall, with his three guards behind him, began the inspection. As he went from row to row, he felt a sense of pride welling up in his chest.

His army was battle-ready, their weapons in perfect condition. He nodded and smiled to himself as he began to walk down the center row. These soldiers were the cream of the crop. They carried falxes: weapons that looked like a hybrid of both sword and scimitar. At close range, they were deadly; the point could pierce helmets, and their blades easily split heavy shields with one blow.

It was then that Madfall felt a pang of fear and confusion. The falx-wielding row, against all regulations, raised their weapons. At a command from the platoon sergeant, the row behind him turned and raised their crossbows. It all happened so quickly that Madfall, who was not a military man, did not realize initially that his companion's throats had been slit from ear to ear and that he was now surrounded by his own troops.

Anfawl stepped forward, a self-satisfied smirk on his face. "Madfall, you are no longer leader of this land. I hereby proclaim you an enemy of the state, and you will be escorted to the brig to await trial and sentencing."

Madfall sneered. "I suppose *you* are taking over, now?"

"Wrong, *we* are taking over."

Madfall whirled. Branwyn had walked into the courtyard, and now stood next to Anfawl. She was compelling. Her honeyed voice would make a man do anything, anything at all. He had to fight himself to not look her in the eye and dwell on her seductive face.

Why had he not anticipated this? He had felt so secure. He should have known that there was no such thing as security with the kingdom in flux. He should have been better prepared. Udfa had warned him about her, but it was too late for recriminations now. He was up against sorcery—for he felt sure this woman was a witch—and there was no defense against that.

Nain

Ten days after Askia returned on foot to Ibai, a stranger walked into the town and asked to see Holgar. The woman was a Trueni. She looked in amazement at those who were now fully human.

"Me want heal too!" she stated. "Take me to Holgar. He help."

She gave her name as Nain, which meant "grandmother." She was indeed old. Her hide was nearly white and she had no teeth, which made understanding her difficult.

"Where did you come from?" asked Holgar. He wondered how an old lady like her could have walked unaided into Ibai.

"Me come from Abena. Granddaughter bring me, but she leave. She has work in Abena."

"So you want to heal? It may be possible, yet, but our healers are not here. We do not know where they are."

Nain hung her head and tears spilled down her wrinkled, porcine snout. Adne put her arms around Nain and tried to comfort her. "Don't worry," she said, "we'll try to help. You may stay with us until we hear something from our healers."

She hoped the old lady would live long enough for the healers to return. Later, she and Holgar, out of earshot of Nain, discussed the situation.

"We don't *really* know who she is," said Holgar. "She could be a spy for Ortzi."

"I find that ridiculous," Adne argued, peeved. "She's an old lady, not a spy. Surely, he would pick a spy who was younger!"

"No, he'd pick one less obvious. Be careful what you say to her, Adne. She won't benefit from knowing the whereabouts of our daughter and her companions, so why tell her?"

"I'm not that stupid, Holgar. I haven't said a word, and anyway, other than the direction they went in, we have no idea at all where they are now, either."

Nain was the perfect guest, helping Adne around the house, cluck clucking when Adne seemed to work too hard, and generally making herself useful and endearing to all. After a few days, Adne wondered how she had ever managed without Nain. She enjoyed her company, and Nain felt like her own grandmother. She wanted to help her, but she didn't know how.

Many people in Ibai felt the same way about Nain. They all wanted to help, to provide her with a support system and family life. Apparently, her grandchildren didn't care about her. What kind of people would drop off their aged grandmother in a strange place?

It didn't take long before someone talked. They told her about the healers who had been here and healed them, that Ortzi had removed them and that after that no one knew where they had gone. They just knew they were no longer in Abena. They also told her about the terrifying monster that had recently appeared in their town. Some had known that Askia had taken it upriver, and then he had returned the next day, without the raft.

The next day, Nain was gone.

Blaidd, Garden River

Blaidd poled the raft up the Garden River. As the sun rose to his right, the morning mist dissolved into ragged ribbons, the water ahead glistening brightly. It was a beautiful day, but Blaidd was frightened. He had never felt so abandoned. Even though he had told Askia to leave, a part of him had wanted him to stay.

But Askia was gone, and now it was just him alone in a vast wilderness. He missed the Six and wondered why he had never appreciated their company before. He realized that he was still capable of reason. His mind had not suffered the damage of his body. It was only expressing his ideas—turning his thoughts into speech—that frustrated him.

Now that he was alone, he had a lot of time to mull over what had happened to him since that day so long ago, when he left his sot of a father in Meadowfield to go with Jarah and Adain. It had been fate. Everything that had happened to him and the Six had been rooted in the past, their shared past, five hundred years ago. They were reliving the original mission, but this time it had turned out differently.

He realized that Irusan was right. He'd had the opportunity to make different choices, and he'd made the same choices as Seryn, thinking things would turn out differently this time. Well, he hadn't thought at all—that was the problem. He hadn't remembered how bad his past choices had been.

Now he knew, but it was too late. He couldn't change the past.

Before leaving, Askia warned him of the perils upstream. When Blaidd thought about what he might yet encounter, he wished he could just command his heart to stop. He wished he could find a place to lie down and go to sleep. Forever. He didn't want to have to deal with the outcome of his choices. He didn't want to encounter ferocious beasts and the unknown. It was too much, but something—call it a will to survive—kept him going. One movement at a time.

He decided to stay in the moment and not anticipate anything. It was how he would conquer his fear, and survive. He kept poling upstream. If he had been on a picnic trip with the Six, he would have enjoyed the rafting and the scenery. He imagined that they were on board with him, and how they laughed and talked as they pointed out the prettier sites along the river banks. Kex would argue with Tristan about the best picnic spot, and Tegan would be making peace by saying both were beautiful. Adain would be complaining that he was hungry, and they'd better find a spot to eat soon or he would pick one, and he wouldn't care if it were beautiful, shady, or sunny.

He did this all day, and when the sun began to sink into the west, he pulled over to the bank and tied the raft up. He fell asleep quickly. It would take several nights before he encountered any dangerous beasts, and he needed as much sleep as he could get while he still could.

By day he fished with the net Askia had left him. He found that he now enjoyed his food more raw than cooked. He barely bothered with fires, as he chewed the fish whole. They tasted better that way, he thought. He would save his flints for later, for the colder weather up north. He needed a lot of food. The fish did not really satisfy his appetite, and one day, shaking with hunger, he spotted a deer on the bank. Before he could even think about it, he had leapt off the raft with a single bound and gave chase to the startled stag. The raft floated, unattended, downstream in the direction it had come from.

Blaidd was amazed at the speed he now had. To think that he could outrun a stag—it would once have been ludicrous. Now he caught it with ease, and with a single snap broke its neck. He effortlessly slung the deer over his shoulder and made his way back to the raft.

It was gone. With all his supplies. He shrugged, and, placing the deer down on the bank, he began to gorge.

19.

Fire and Earth

Jarah and Tegan left the water elementals reluctantly. They both felt they could have stayed with them forever. The others all agreed that it was an enjoyable lesson, but they were looking forward now to becoming acquainted with the other elementals.

"I think we're both water elements, Tegan," said Jarah. She nodded, smiling.

"I already know I'm fire," said Kex.

Adain laughed. "I can see it in you clearly, Kex!"

They didn't have long to wait for their next lesson. After a refreshing sleep, they found Finn in his usual spot at the gate. "I can see you're already getting used to this place," he said, with a chuckle. "How is the manifesting coming along?"

"Well, we're not starving," said Djana. "I manifested a breakfast this morning I haven't had in years!" They all laughed and talked at the same time, telling Finn what they were manifesting for themselves.

"I had a bad experience with that this morning," said Tegan. "I flashed back to my village—it was burning, and I could hear the screams—then I had to put the fire out in my house. Fortunately, I was able to manifest a bucket of water just in time!"

Finn chuckled. "It's just as easy to create unpleasant manifestations," he said, "as it is to create wonderful ones. Here in Ardvale, creating is instantaneous. It doesn't happen in your world. Usually, one must to wait a while for the thought to manifest, but manifest it does. You have to work at it a little harder, and there are all other kinds of factors involved—other's free will choices and creations, laws of physics, for example. But here, you do not have that. It seems magical, but it is because we have not created barriers to our manifesting abilities. We're able to take these abilities out there with us, to your worlds, in order to assist the life forms we represent. That is what we are teaching you. To remove those barriers, and become your own masters.

"Your lessons with each element will still take time, but fortunately, here in Ardvale, time does not exist. Yesterday was a start, and today is another beginning, but we must start somewhere. And here we are!"

They had arrived at a cave opening in a rock wall. Finn led them through the cave and they made their way, by the light of the flame in his palm, through tunnels, deep into the earth. It began to get warmer, and they soon found out why. Ahead of them a reddish-orange glow appeared. It looked like a small river of ... they stopped, perplexed. Melted rock?

"It's called lava," said Finn. "And now, I'll leave you with our fire-friends." He did his disappearing trick again, and they sat down and waited.

They waited for a while. Nothing happened. The cave was silent, dark, and empty. They looked at each other, wondering aloud if they should just get up and leave.

"If you did," came a hissing voice from the fire-rock, "you'd miss the best part!" A bubble burst up from the lava, and it was joined by another, and then another. The bubbles sprayed out fiery particles of lava, and Jarah and Tegan found themselves cringing, pulling back in fear. "I see we have some water elementals here," the voice said. "We promise not to turn you into steam!" It laughed, a bubbly gurgle, and the spraying drops coagulated into two shapes. The shapes looked vaguely human, but they were small, just like the Undines. "We are Topaz and Uri. It doesn't matter which is which. We both look the same. Now, we will go on a journey. I sense fear from a few of you. We are the most fearful of all the elements according to some, but once you know us, we're kitty-cats. You'll never be able to command our element if you still have fear. Today, we will lose that fear!"

Topaz and Uri told them to lie down and make themselves comfortable. They all felt a sense of warmth, as if they'd been wrapped in warm blankets and lying in a comfortable bed. It made them sleepy too, but they kept listening to the voices of the fire elementals.

"You are lying now in front of a hearth with crackling logs. It is cold outside, and you are warm and safe. You can see the flames dancing and blazing in the fireplace. Step into the fireplace and become the flame."

Kex became the flame almost immediately. She opened her eyes and she was in the hearth. She could feel herself moving as she consumed the wood, turning it into ash. She felt as if she was transmuting the wood into energy and releasing it back into the ethers. She felt the gratitude of the wood as it rejoined the consciousness it had come from, ready to return as a sapling once again. She looked around at Adain. He was in the fire with her, and she knew he felt what she felt. The others were more hesitant, but one by one, they stepped cautiously into the hearth, as if they were putting their feet into icy water.

Jarah could not ignore the fear he felt. He was convinced the fire would burn him. He slowly put his hand out, feeling the heat from the flame.

"Become the flame!" Topaz commanded. "You should not fear yourself."

Jarah took a deep breath and stepped all the way in. It felt pleasant; no burning, no pain. He felt the purpose of the flame: to transmute and burn away what was not needed anymore. Tegan, Tristan, and Djana also stepped in, and now there were eight flames in the hearth. They shot up the chimney as sparks, falling back again and becoming the flames once more. After they had played at being sparks for a while, Topaz and Uri told them they could now join them as lava. They saw themselves back in the cave again and plunged into the lava. They flowed back down into the rock and became a river that flowed down into the earth. After flowing for what felt like a long time, they joined another river of lava and then another, and soon they realized they were deep in the earth. They became one in consciousness with the earth itself. They were her life force, and they kept her alive. They assisted her to reform herself into mountains and island chains. Without fire, there would be no soil, no life, only a dead planet.

They went from lava oceans deep under the earth, spewing back up through crevices and mountains, becoming forest fires where they swept away old growth so that new growth could take root. They were campfires for the weary traveler, pyres that transformed bodies in death back into their spirit matter. The process was hygienic and transformative. In their material world, they could be used for good or evil, and they did not judge or refuse to burn, no matter what the circumstances. They knew that those who understood their element could work with them if they knew how.

They felt transformed themselves, as if the fire had burned away all their fear of the unknown. They realized that they were the consciousness of the whole earth, and they could rejoin this consciousness any time they chose. Finn was waiting for them as they opened their eyes and found themselves back in the cave.

"Looks like you are finding your elements," he said. "Now, let's go to another one. Djana, I think you are going to like this one!"

He didn't take them back to their homes to rest. Instead, he continued down the tunnels until they came to a cave much like the one they had left behind in Galon: the Crystal Cave. This one was not as large and the crystals not near as massive as those had been, but they were impressive.

"Did you ever wonder why you were able to find your way through those tunnels under the mountains, Djana?"

"Well, yes, I did," she responded. "I still don't understand it!"

"You have an affinity with earth and crystal—and rock. A part of you was in constant communication with the rock and the mountains. They knew where you were at all times, and when you thought you were lost, you were, in fact, being guided. That is why no one else will ever be able to find their way completely through those tunnels in the Osgoi Range. The rock itself will block all attempts to find exits or entrances. You were all coded to open the access doors, but Djana was the only one who could find the way."

They all nodded in surprise. They had also wondered how Djana was the only one of them who knew her way through the mountains.

"You are all coded for crystal communication, so we will sit here and talk to our crystal friends. They don't choose to change forms like the Undines and fire-elements, but if you just sit here and join them in their consciousness, you will *feel* their thoughts. I will come back for you later."

The Six were getting used to his sudden appearances and disappearances, so they didn't think anything of it when he vanished once more.

They sat, not moving, even though the crystal beings seemed to be in less of a hurry than the fire elementals. After a long while, they sensed a quiet voice.

"I am Eirnin. I am an earth elemental, speaking through our higher, crystal form. We come in many forms, and we are made up of the substance of the earth itself. We are your bodies, along with fire and water, and we work cooperatively together. I work with Topaz and Uri to transform the earth. Sit with me for a while, and we'll go on a journey."

They felt themselves drawn into the surrounding rock. Veins of ore were their blood, crystal was their brain, and the rest was their body. They felt the emotional pain of ore extraction from the mines. It felt as if something was eating them alive, but they understood that their substance was useful and provided protection and comfort to many. They would work with the fire to bring more to the surface so that their body would not be depleted. Eirnin told them that the earth could recover from this if it was not abused, but, unfortunately, that had not been the case. Amrafalus' mines were almost depleted, and it wouldn't be long before the ravagers of resources would be moving on to deplete yet another area.

They moved into the mountains where they became the giants of the earth who looked to the sky. "Here, we work with the elements of air," said Eirnin. "The wind also shapes us and brings much-needed water to our slopes. We cooperate with the air to bring weather to certain areas."

They felt the tunnels they had traversed so long ago; tunnels formed by lava flows and man. From here, they moved on into the agricultural areas, becoming united with the soil and learning of the areas that needed different crop rotation, and where over-grazing had become a problem.

"Here, we work with the water elements too," said Eirnin. "Without our cooperative methods, you would all starve. Life on earth would become extinct. We work with the plant and animal kingdom, and even the insect life to sustain the eco-systems. If one element in this chain does not cooperate, or if the balance between us is shifted even slightly by man, life will become extinct. Take bees, for example. A small life form, and one that is not usually noticed, unless one is harvesting their honey, or is stung by one. If this life form were not here, the whole chain would fall. We all depend on each other. Never forget that."

Their journey over, they returned to Finn and the cave. Finn led them out, and this time everyone was silent. They had a lot to think about.

They had always taken their food for granted. Their ability to live on the earth was assumed that it was their birthright. They never gave a moment's thought to what it took to make this possible; that all life was connected and nature did not tolerate ignorance, greed, or ingratitude.

20.

The Raven Follows

Branwyn, as Nain, left early before sunrise to walk away from the town and into a small grove of palms, where she shape-shifted into the raven form. Sometimes she preferred her bird form. It gave her a sense of flight and freedom, and made a change from the invisibility of her Merkaba vehicle. Her Merkaba was often too quick, and she noticed lately that it was getting more and more difficult to control, and she missed things on the ground.

She pushed the little flicker of fear she briefly felt from her mind. She would never lose her Merkaba, or any of her abilities. It wasn't possible, she thought. She just wasn't staying in practice.

The raven flew northwards, following the river. She flew all day without seeing any sign of Blaidd. It wasn't until the next day that she found the raft. It was caught in a thicket of overhanging brambles and brush on the bank, and she had been lucky to notice it at all.

Descending to the river, she perched on a tree limb and surveyed the raft. All of Blaidd's supplies were still on board. Everything he would need to survive. It didn't make sense. Why would he leave all his supplies and the raft? It could only mean something had happened to him.

She continued to fly north, sometimes in her Merkaba vehicle, sometimes in her raven form. Now she would have to search either for a floating body or for his remains on the riverbank.

Perhaps he had encountered one of the inhabitants of Mannanon. She knew of these creatures. The old inhabitants of Rhiannon had formed them long ago. Long before Rhiannon had learned from its mistakes, crystals, along with the black arts, were used as means to change one's body form without the benefit of the knowledge of shape shifting. The physical DNA had been altered, spliced, and mutated until nothing even remotely human was left. The monsters had been released—no one could control them—and they had gone over the mountains and into Mannanon, mingling and breeding with other, even darker, elemental forms. Some remained in the mountains, but many had found a home in the sparsely populated areas across the Osgoi Range. Those humans who had settled there quickly left. If they did not, they became food for the beasts. Now little besides mutant beasts roamed here, and they were able to reproduce. Lack of food kept them at lower numbers than they could have been, but they were resourceful, and made raids into neighboring areas to obtain meat. They didn't particularly care what kind of meat. Anything would do, even that of their own kind.

She didn't know how well Blaidd would fare if he had run into one of these creatures. The last time she saw him he was already formidable, but against a pack of these creatures, he stood little chance.

Towards the end of the day, her raven eyes picked out a disturbance in the long grass, close to the riverbank. She flew down and surveyed the area. She could see where the grass was flattened and speckled with blood. Her sense of smell led her to the carcass of a stag that had been dragged under a bush. The horns had not been disturbed, so she knew it did not meet its death at the hands of humans. This was either another predator, one of the beasts, or Blaidd. She could see the sharp teeth marks that had torn into the flesh, claw marks, and bones scattered around. It had eaten most of the carcass. Whatever it was, it had been hungry.

Rising up into the air, she let out a squawk of triumph. She was on the right track. She would find him, or whatever was left of him, soon.

Three Rivers, Aelfar

Callum, Corrick, and the queen sat on the terrace overlooking the River Mair. It was an unusually warm day for that time of year. The spring thaw was not due for several weeks yet, but it gave Catrin hope—hope that she could carry out her own plans sooner than anticipated.

"The king's army is almost ready for battle, milady," said Callum. "The king desires that we march south towards Galon at the first thaw, which is in a few weeks. At the same time, our navy will leave the port city of Anjou for Galon. It's important that they both reach Abena at the same time. Branwyn will place her navy in the Bay of Abena at that time too, so the Galonese will face a formidable force from sea and land. The king will accompany the army southwards, leaving the Witan here to keep an eye on his kingdom while he is gone. The Witan is loyal to the king, milady, with the exception of myself.

"I have concocted a story that will explain my own absence, and that of Corrick's. We are to be married, and wish to be married on the sunny shores of Mernoc. The king and the Witan will not find this an unreasonable request, since they feel I'm a junior member and not important to the function of the kingdom anyway."

Catrin smiled. "I want to go too, Callum. Both Deryn and myself. I could say to the king that I wish to attend your wedding. He won't think it an unusual request either."

"Milady, it's too dangerous!" said Corrick, aghast. "You should leave this up to Callum and me. We'll bring the healers back here through the secret passage. It will be safer, that way."

"I agree with Corrick," said Callum. "You must stay here. We'll be racing against the king's men. He'll have dispatched a whole troop whose primary function is to capture the healers, and we must get there before they do. If you excuse my words, milady, we cannot have a child and ... ." Here he stopped and cleared his throat.

"Yes, yes—I know," said Catrin. "You don't want to be weighed down with extra baggage. A queen who is not used to fast and rough riding, and her son who is not strong. I understand. However, it will cut down on the time since we don't need to bring them all the way back here. We can find a safe place, closer to their village, where they can heal my son."

"There *is* no safe place, milady. The danger is great that we will be discovered, and the king's men will recognize you immediately. If Corrick and I are captured, you can always say you had no knowledge of the plan."

"You must stay," Corrick said forcefully. "We can't take the chance that you will be discovered. We promise to bring the healers back here safely. Callum and I have explored the passage and discovered another branch that leads to a small room. That is where we'll keep them. The walls are thick stone, and they will not be heard by anyone in the palace. It is better that we stay with our original plan."

Catrin thought for a while, soon understanding that they were right. She couldn't afford to be discovered; her plans would unravel. She must think of what was best for Deryn. It was not about what *she* wanted.

She realized it was her impatience that drove her desire to travel to Meadowfield. She couldn't wait for the healing to begin, but she must not make any mistakes now. If Callum and Corrick were caught interfering in the king's plans it would be *their* heads, not hers. If anything happened to her, she could not help her son.

21.

Discovery

It was difficult making good time on foot. Without the raft, Blaidd had to wade through swamps and over difficult terrain. His size helped him, and he didn't think he would have been able to make it through the swamps if he had still been his normal size. Some of the swamps were deep, but for him that meant chin-level. He also found plenty to eat in the swamps. A large and scaly reptile tried to make breakfast out of his leg, but found itself becoming breakfast, instead. There was also waterfowl that he managed to sneak up on, with his horns and eyes barely visible above the waterline.

When he came out of the swamp, he found wild turkey, and to his delight, large sloths hanging from trees. It was like picking fruit in an orchard. His hunger no longer gnawed at him and he felt himself becoming bigger and stronger each day. He hadn't really needed his supplies after all.

For the first time in his life, he was not weak. He was powerful and self-sufficient. He wished the Six could see him now. Wouldn't they be surprised! A part of him wanted to show them what he was capable of, that he was not to be pitied and that he was capable of great things. Another part of him did not want them to see him. He thought they'd be disgusted, and would find him frightening, that they would blame him for what he had become. That thought made him sad, and sometimes he'd still shed tears as he mooed, looking up at the lonely moon from his bed of leaves, hides, and feathers.

He thought about Branwyn too. Some of the tears were for her, for what he had once thought she was, for what he wanted her to be. His illusions were gone. He would never find a partner. As far as he could tell, he was one of a kind.

He didn't know how long it took before he left the swamps behind him. Days and nights ran into each other—he didn't keep count. The warm weather was also a thing of the past, but he found that his long, razor claws were easily able to skin the animals he caught. He also noticed that the fur that covered his body was growing longer and thicker. There was no longer any sign of human skin showing.

It was just as well. He didn't want to freeze to death at night.

One day, as he walked along the riverbank—he had found it again—he thought he saw shadows in the forest around him, but when he looked again, there was nothing to be seen. He realized he must be on his guard. Askia had warned him about this area. It wasn't until nightfall that he heard the bays and howls in the distance. Sometimes he heard loud wood knocks that would be answered by bone-chilling screams. He instinctively knew that this was a form of communication: a passing along of information. He would need to learn what they meant, and how to avoid being ambushed by any of these predators. He preferred to travel by night, now, although he chose to keep moving during the daytime as well. He found the sunlight harsh on his eyes.

The day he found Lake Yorath became the most frightening

day of his entire life. It was even worse than the encounter with the mountain Arrach—the scorpion-beast—or the day he realized he was changing into a monster. The lake opened out suddenly in front of him, and he blinked, his sensitive eyes recoiling at the water that glistened and flashed in the early morning sunlight. It looked serene, though, and he wished he could plunge into it and bathe the stink of dead animals and dirt off his hide, but he kept walking, keeping well in the shade of the forest. He knew that Askia had dropped the Six off on the northern shore. It was the last place they had been seen. He thought that they would stay on the banks of the Garden River as it flowed down from its source in the mountain range, so he continued to walk along the western shore.

He looked up. A bird circled high above him. Was that Branwyn? Could it be? Was she even looking for him? He couldn't tell if it was a raven or a hawk, so he kept on walking, deciding to remain concealed in the forest instead of taking to the open lake shore. He walked all day, and as night fell, he felt the familiar hunger returning. He must find food.

Food this far north was becoming scarcer to find. An uncomfortable feeling in the pit of his stomach, that wasn't hunger pangs, told him that it was not merely the cold that caused the scarcity of deer, turkey, and rabbit, but it was because they were already over-hunted by something else. Several days had passed by without finding anything substantial; a few rabbits, some squirrel, and an unwary snake sunning itself on a rock, but nothing more than that. He was reduced to digging for roots, which he hated, and they did nothing to satisfy his raging hunger.

The now familiar howls, screams, and knocks began, and he avoided the areas from which they came. He was just about to dig in for the remainder of the night in a hollow in the middle of a glade, when out of the corner of his eye he caught a glimpse of movement.

It darted silently to his left. Then he saw another on his right. He slowly turned, a sinking feeling—a pulse of fear. More shadows—a gleam of red, first one, then two. Eyes. Now he knew. They had found him.

The Raven

Branwyn picked up Blaidd's trail again while flying over the swamps. She did not let him out of her sight, and if he disappeared into thick vegetation or cypress stands, she'd circle the area until she caught sight of his bulk wading through the next bog.

She noticed, too, that he travelled more at night now. She thought he slept during the midday hours, waiting until the strong sunlight began to fade into twilight before setting off on his quest again.

She wished Blaidd had kept the raft since he would have progressed much faster, but she couldn't hurry back to Rhiannon now. Anfawl would have to govern the kingdom by himself. While she didn't think he was a truly capable person, she felt that his army supported him, and she did have Udfa's support with the navy. There wasn't too much that could go wrong now. She would talk with Blaidd once she thought the time was right to do so. Maybe she could use his brute strength as well. She felt he would help her find the Six. He hated them, didn't he? He had betrayed them so many times she was certain that he wouldn't hesitate to betray them again. If they couldn't heal him—and she thought they either could not or would not—his rage would explode, and she would have to contain him before he hurt them, but he'd find them. She knew he would. In the meanwhile, she was satisfied with just following him and biding her time.

The day would come when she would be the sole ruler of the land, and she could move her plans forward to marry Brenin. Alas, he'd suffer a similar fate as Anfawl, but such was life; here one day and gone the next.

She chuckled a raven chuckle as she waited, perching on a tree limb, for Blaidd to emerge from yet another swamp.

22.

Air—Ilma and Amun

The Six sat on a high mountain peak. Strangely, they did not feel cold, even though they were surrounded by snow and ice and they found they could breathe easily. Their guide, Finn was not with them.

"How did we get up here?" asked Djana, looking around her in surprise.

"Do you mean you're still surprised by what happens in Ardvale?" Kex asked, smiling.

"No, not really. I like to know, that's all."

"We are the air around you—you are now us." The voice was breathy and it might have been the wind, but they all turned to see where it had come from. There was no one else up here with them.

"I'm Ilma." They heard it clearly now. "You can't see us, but you can feel us." A gust of wind buffeted them. "That was Amun!" said Ilma. "I am warmer and softer, and I stay mainly in the valleys.

Amun prefers it up here. We had an argument about where to meet you, and he had his way, as usual."

They all jumped, startled, as a roar of the wind hurtled over the peak, dislodging icy particles that stung like needles on their faces.

"That's enough, Amun. We should leave here before he gets too enthusiastic. Follow us!"

"What are you saying? How will we get down this mountain?" asked Jarah. They all looked alarmed. They were on the edge of a precipice, and even with a rope, they would have found it impossible to get down.

Amun roared, "You haven't been listening. You *are* the wind! You came up here the same way we did—you blew. Now get off your hindquarters and fly!"

"Amun, you are too harsh. Follow me," Ilma's gentle voice eased their fears. "I'll make myself visible if it helps you, but don't expect me to do it all the time." They looked around and something darted across their vision. It darted back again, hovering in front of them, its wings vibrating like that of a small dragonfly. "I'm a Sylph. I'll keep this form until you get used to being the wind. If it makes you feel any more secure, imagine you have wings, too."

To their surprise, they each felt the vibration of gauzy wings on their backs. They practiced moving their wings, rising up, and then setting themselves gently down again. Ilma joined them, encouraging them to go higher while Amun gusted impatiently around the peak. Once they felt more comfortable, Ilma led them off the cliff, and they soared down the mountain. Amun buffeted them forcefully from below until they again rose above the peaks of the mountains. Pulling away suddenly, they fell like stones, plummeting through the clouds until they found their wings again and they levelled off. Jarah thought that this was even more frightening than the fire element. His heart skipped beats as he looked down at the ground far below. He felt dizzy. He could tell that everyone else, except for Tristan, was terrified. Tristan seemed to be enjoying this. He roared alongside Amun, and together they rose up again and again. Plummeting back to the earth, they'd pull up and away seconds before reaching the ground.

Ilma shook her head. "Show-offs!" Jarah thought he couldn't agree more. "Come on, I'll show you my favorite sport!"

She beckoned to Tristan, and he reluctantly left Amun to follow them. Below them was a wooded area next to a lake. "I love trees. They are my friends and they play with me." She had lost her Sylph form, but they knew she was still there. They could feel her as a mild breeze. "You don't need your wings," she said. "Feel yourselves as the breeze now."

They flew with her through the tree-tops. It was exhilarating, and the trees responded to them with a rustle of leaves. They could feel the living force that emanated from their tops. It felt as if they could do this forever, but Ilma took them towards the lake, and they skipped over the surface of the smooth water, ruffling it, causing little ripples to lap softly on the shore.

"Enough of this," said Amun after a while. "I have other things to show you. Follow me." He led them across the landscape, soaring over fields, forests, and mountains, until they came to a vast plain. "You'll like this, Tristan!" The others felt their fear rising again.

"You'll be fine," said Ilma. "It's not my idea of fun either, but remember, it can't hurt you." They all wondered what *it* was. Towering clouds, white and puffy, soared far above them. They were so thick they almost looked solid. It was as if one could bounce on them like a child playing on a feather bed. Amun and Ilma led them into the thick wall of the cloud, and they immediately felt themselves lifted up, as if pulled by a giant hand. Large chunks of ice flew around them, but they felt nothing, and the chunks passed harmlessly through their forms.

"*Down!*" shouted Amun, but they couldn't tell what was "down" now, and what was "up." "*Follow me!*"

They felt Amun's breath on their faces as they tumbled through the cloud with him. They came out of the bottom of the cloud and looked up. All they could see was darkness, and at first, they thought night had fallen, but then a bright flash of light filled the sky and simultaneously a tremendous crash reverberated around them. They all shrieked in fear. "It's only lightning and thunder!" Amun laughed, his breath a chuffing wind, as they shakily flew through the storm. Ilma was quiet. They felt her presence, but she didn't say anything. They wondered if she was frightened too.

Then they heard her soft laughter. "This is nothing, just wait."

Still trembling, they flew under the cloud cover as lightning flashed and thunder roared around them. They tried hard not to show fear, but if they'd had skins they would have jumped out of them a long time ago.

Up ahead, a strange black cloud extended a finger to the earth. Swooping down towards it, they could see what looked like a dust cloud swirling at its base. As they came closer, dirt, branches, and debris spun angrily around them until they could barely see in front of them, but Amun still led them on—into the finger itself. To their amazement, they felt themselves twisting around and around until they felt dizzy and disorientated. They closed their eyes and heard Amun shout, "*Be* the tornado!"

As they adjusted their consciousness to embody the form of the cloud, they felt themselves shift into a place where they were no longer buffeted and whirled around uncontrollably. Instead, they were in a dance; a dance that led them skipping and hopping over the ground below, touching down light as a feather and lifting up again, over and over. After a while, the cloud form dissipated. The landscape below showed their path, a swath of destruction that carved through forest and field. The storm moved away, into the distance, and the sun shone brightly above.

"Phew!" said Ilma. "I'm always glad when that's over."

"You may think that I'm not an enjoyable element," said Amun as they blew, gently now, over the landscape. "But I am the mixer, or the regulator, of the earth's temperature. Without me, some areas would be too hot while others would be too cold. I come in, mix them up, and distribute the energy. When these air masses collide, I become a tornado. Sometimes, I become a hurricane. That happens over the ocean."

"Is that what we experienced before?" asked Jarah.

"It is. I remember you well. You were hunkered down in a little boat that looked like a small cork bobbing below."

"Why did you do that to us?" Kex asked.

"I wasn't *doing* it to you at all! You were in the way. If I hadn't mixed up the temperatures in that spot, many life forms would have perished from overheated water. It had to be done."

As they flew back to the mountaintop, Jarah realized that humans were not as important as he'd always imagined they were. *We are only one more life form here*, he thought. *Nothing stops just because we're doing important business, and the elements all have a job to do, with or without us.* It was humbling, and he felt he now had a wider appreciation of the inter-connectedness of everything.

"Now that we know you," said Amun, "we'll teach you how to communicate with us in the appropriate way, so that if there is a next time when you are in our way we'll be a little more careful around you."

"You mean simply talking to you won't work?" asked Tristan.

"Not in your human speech," said Ilma. "You think you are speaking to us in your human language, but in reality we are communicating in our language. It sounds normal to you because you learned it a long time ago, but you don't remember."

"So how are we remembering to speak it now?" asked Adain.

"There is a part of you that remembers. It needs to be re-awakened, and you will remember it consciously again. We and the other elements speak and communicate in mathematical code that translates into human speech. If, for instance, you call on us to 'stop blowing,' we won't understand that."

"But," said Amun, "We do understand certain requests, which you will be taught, in both movement and sound—"

"Oh! Do you mean the same as we do for the crystals?" Jarah felt as if something in his mind clicked into place, and he understood.

"It is similar, except we have our own sounds that we recognize and that go along with certain movements. These sounds and movements set up a mathematical code—our language—that means something to us, and we will then decide if it is for the greater good to do it or not."

"It doesn't mean we and the other elements are now your willing slaves though," said Ilma. "That is what those who choose the dark magic do. They enslave us and command us to do things. Parts of our consciousness have chosen to experience that, and work with the dark forces, but there are parts of us who do not choose this. We hope that you will always work with the elements respectfully, in full understanding that it is not always your wishes and desires that are for the greater good."

They found their mountain top, and as the Sylphs bade them goodbye, they asked how they would get back to their homes.

"The same way you came here," was their parting shot.

Jarah was going to ask them again, how they would do that, when he opened his eyes and he realized he was in his house in Ardvale—back in his comfortable bed. It felt like a dream, but he knew it was not. He arose, made himself breakfast, and sat down to eat. As he finished, he looked out his window. Finn was waiting.

They all gathered by the gate, and Finn asked them how they had enjoyed their experience as air sylphs.

"One of the best," said Tristan. "I really felt a connection with that one." No one else agreed with him, but they all laughed as they told Finn about their fear in the tornado.

"If the earth was a little less tilted we may not even need tornados," Finn said. "Right now, our sphere is tilted off-center and we get the extremes of temperature. It is not like this in all worlds, but this one has been damaged."

"By whom?" they asked.

"The same ones that made it possible to use crystals in a way that goes against nature. The same Beings who ... but don't get me started." He looked, for the first time since they'd met him, unhappy. "Without going into detail, I will only say that we have Guardians at other levels who care about this planet and its life forms, and who would like to see things restored to balance again. But there are those Beings who feel it more important, for reasons of their own, to alter the original design of not just this planet, but many of its life forms. They have had unlimited access here for a long time, and they are advanced enough so that they are able to make these alterations. It is up to us, as elements, to do what we can to keep the balance so that life does not become extinct here."

"Why would anyone want to do that—to alter what was not broken?" asked Adain.

"Because they can. And because it might make things here a little more hospitable for their own life forms, or because they simply hate. These beings do not care about the life here. If they had to reduce this planet to a dead cinder, they would. They would then move on to another planet in the universe. There are many playgrounds for them, much food out there for them to siphon as energy, and this is one of the many places they have chosen to express themselves in."

"Why would a Supreme Being allow this?" asked Tristan. They all nodded since they'd all been thinking exactly the same thing.

"Here is someone who can answer that question," said Finn, and they looked up. They'd been too busy talking to notice someone standing next to them.

"Irusan!"

They hugged him in delight. Irusan waved his hand, and they looked around. They were each standing inside a sphere of light. Finn, unsurprisingly, was gone.

23.

Ether

"I will answer your question about the Supreme Being because it ties in with our next lesson," said Irusan. To their surprise, they could all hear him, even though he was still communicating telepathically and Tegan and Jarah no longer needed to translate. "There is a misperception in the human belief that a Supreme Being is a man-like Being with a body, but with a longer life-span. In a way, this is correct, but it is also wrong in so many ways.

"It is correct in the sense that we are all part of this Supreme—I don't call it a 'Being', since that is a limiting word—but I will call it 'Source.' It is the Source of everything that exists now, will exist, and has existed. There is nothing outside of it. Everything, down to the smallest particle, is a part of this Source. You can say with the greatest confidence that each one of you and myself are this Source." Irusan stopped and thought for a bit.

They were moving, in their bubbles that Irusan called Merkabas, over the landscape. They felt as if they were the wind again, but their bubbles kept them confined.

Irusan continued. "As Source, we stepped down from the higher frequency worlds to this world. We fragmented ourselves. If we hadn't, our frequency would destroy the worlds we created. The suns, planets, and everything on them are a part of this experience. All are Beings in their own right, with their own free will. Not all of them experience consciousness as you do, but all of them, including you, will return to our Source one day. I am you, and you are me, and we are everything down there."

He pointed down towards the rivers, fields, and forests.

"We are the Ether. We are always the Ether, but we sometimes forget. The Ether is you and all the elements combined. It is the life force, or *Chi*, as it is called in other places, that bind us together and keeps us connected to our Source. It is the tiniest particle, and it is also the largest universe. It is not always visible, and we often are unable to measure it using our standard measures, but it is there. It is a unified field of consciousness. We can sense it sometimes because it is who we are. It is how I communicate with you telepathically. It is how I shape-shift. I use this field to alter my pattern and my particles, and I do this with a precision that does not allow for mistakes.

"The mutant beasts out there were experimental. Created by those with a basic, but flawed, understanding of the laws of the universe. Mistakes were made. Their patterns were indelibly altered, and their fate, if not healed, is to de-evolve and contract until they become the smallest particles once more. Only then will they be able to return to their Source."

"It doesn't sound like something I would choose," said Tegan. "How can we prevent this from happening to us?"

"Be careful of the choices you make," said Irusan. "One does not need to be a mutant beast to de-evolve or contract over time. One's personal template will determine whether your choice to evolve—expand and grow—or to shrink, is manifested. You cannot fool your template. No amount of lies, sweet-talk, or ignorance will alter your path if you make the wrong choices."

"Who is 'Idris,' then," asked Jarah. "My parents worship him as a God. They make sacrifices and try to earn his favor."

"I know. There will always be myriads of gods and godlets worshipped by those who have forgotten who they really are. Idris, and others like him, are among those who have caused all the problems here to begin with. They have many names, and they come from different worlds, but they're all the same in that they want to create a world favorable to their own competing agendas. That is why we have wars and ignorance. Keeping humankind in ignorance and always fighting each other suits them just fine.

"Man, and woman, have forgotten that no one can save them from themselves. They are the only ones who are able to do that. Understanding your origins, understanding who the players out there really are, and not viewing them through childish eyes or wishes or from a disempowered stance is the only way to ensure you make progress on your chosen path. *You* are the architect of your fate. It is what you chose to do when you accepted the assignment to heal the mutants. You chose to heal yourselves first, to return to your contract from the same ignorant place that everyone else is now in, so that you could prove it is possible to re-learn and to remember.

"It would mean nothing for me—for example—to come here and try to heal others. It would be pointless because I have not experienced what they have. I would be placing myself 'above' others and putting them in a disempowered place. You, on the other hand, have the advantage of healing yourselves first."

"But we have already started healing with the Crystal," Djana said. "What does that mean? Are we disempowering those we've healed?"

"No, you are giving them the same chance they should have had—the same chance that every human here has. Their patterns were damaged, their evolution was interrupted, and they were unable to grow until their original patterns were restored. You volunteered to do that, but it doesn't mean you don't need to work on yourselves. You have also suffered impairment as a result of planetary damage, and part of that damage manifested in forgetting who you really are."

The sun was setting over the western horizon. Irusan waved his hand and the light in their Merkaba spheres dimmed. They floated, silently, over the hilly landscape below. It was as if they were sitting in large, glass bubbles, and they could see a herd of deer below them. The deer did not react or look up. They felt invisible, and Irusan confirmed that they were.

"What is this Merkaba thing?" asked Kex. "How does it work?"

"You will learn more about it when we return. You each have one, as you can see, but at first, they are often difficult to control. You all have had lessons in Merkaba control in other lifetimes, and you are now accessing a broader part of who you are that remembers how to do that. If you used your current mind, as it presently understands little, you might crash, but you all agreed to hand over the Merkaba controls to the part of yourselves that understand how to use it. We can travel slowly, or instantaneously, just by thought alone. Oh, I might add, the Raven also has one. Remember that. And she knows how to use it. Don't think you can outrun her without your Merkaba."

As it grew darker, Irusan said, "I want to show you something. We are briefly going to leave the safety of Ardvale."

Their Merkabas flashed, and they found themselves over a dark forest.

"I took you to a portal. We are now in your world."

They floated over a river, recognizing it as the northern branch of the Garden River. It was close to where they had been surrounded by the wolf-men. They descended slowly towards a glade in the forest. The glade was not empty. Someone—or something—stood in the center as a group wolf-men circled it. The central figure was twice the size of the wolf-men. It had long, pointed horns that curved outwards like scimitars. Its teeth—or fangs—curved over a bovine mouth. They could see rippling muscles under the long, black hair, and long legs that ended in hoofs. It had claw-like hands, and its eyes glowed red in the moonlight. Irusan allowed the sphere to alight softly on a nearby rock.

"Why did you bring us back here?" asked Tristan. "These are the creatures that nearly killed us!"

"And what is that—*thing*—in the middle?" asked Adain.

"You will soon understand why I brought you here," said Irusan. "Don't worry, I won't leave you here! We're safe—they can't sense us. I want to show you two things. One of them is the one in the middle of the circle, and the other one is up there." He nodded to a nearby tree.

They looked up, and for the first time noticed an enormous raven sitting on the topmost branch.

"It's ... it's her!" Kex gasped, as did the others.

"Yes, it is. And the other one is Blaidd."

"It can't be!" said Jarah.

"Oh, but unfortunately, it *is*."

Blaidd and the Wolf-men

Blaidd circled, trying to keep the creatures in his sight, but they outnumbered him. They were fast, even if smaller than he was. He was not sure that he could defend himself against so many. The wolf-like creatures ringed him, grunting, growling, and yipping, their jaws dripping with slather. They must have been as hungry as he was.

He felt the all-too-familiar fear rising in his throat. It mattered little to him that he was the most fearsome beast of all. He still saw himself as young Blaidd, a boy from Meadowfield. He wanted to cry, but he choked back the tears and fear. A part of him realized he could not show his terror. It would be his death. He had to pretend he was brave and strong.

He took a deep breath and let out a roar.

The ground under his hoofs vibrated, and the wolf-creatures stopped circling and looked at him in amazement. Birds flew out of the trees, squawking and chirping. All but one: a raven that sat on a branch and stared down at him. He knew who it was. He let out another roar and decided that he wouldn't wait for these creatures to attack—he'd make the first move.

He singled out one of the beasts, the largest and the ugliest. It was taller than the rest, and scarred from old battles. It was the one who didn't seem fazed by his ear-shattering roars.

He would think of it as his prey. He was hungry, and he needed food. This one would do.

All fear evaporated as Blaidd lowered his head and charged, his horns meeting wolf-flesh with a speed that surprised even him. With a toss of his head, he threw the beast into the trees, guts and blood spewing from its open belly. He turned as he felt something impacting him from behind, and with another roar, his knife-like claws ripped the creature's throat open. A fountain of red blood gushed from the half-severed head. One more came at him, but the rest began backing away. He kicked at it, and, yelping, it rolled away.

The wolf-men stopped. The circle had opened up. They appeared disorganized.

The blood lust was in him now, and his eyes glowed. He was ready for more. No, he *welcomed* more. "Come on, you cowards!" he yelled, but it came out as another roar. *Come*, he thought, instead. *I need to eat tonight. Your flesh is probably as tasteless as it looks, but it's better than nothing.*

We will obey you, master.

He stopped. *What? Who was that?* He looked around.

Master do not kill us. We are your subjects. One by one, the wolf-men knelt, whimpering and growling. Their mouths had not moved. He realized, astonished, that he had communicated with them telepathically! He had never been telepathic before. It must be another one of his new abilities.

He roared, and the pack trembled visibly.

I *will be your master*, he said. *But you will obey me. Those who do not will lose their guts, just like your previous leader there*, he said, nodding towards the dripping carcass. This was more fun that he could imagine.

The raven cawed once and flew away.

24.

Irusan

The Six were stunned. They rose up from the trees below, and Irusan gave them some time to process what they had just witnessed. He realized they felt sorrow, a sense of loss for their old friend, Blaidd, who would probably never again be the boy they once knew. Even if they had never trusted him, he had been human. He had been one of them. They had picked up his thoughts and that of the pack. They all noticed the Raven leaving. She flew northeast, and Irusan said it would be better not to follow her.

"She does not know we're here, but we can't take the chance of her picking us up with her senses. She still possesses many abilities, even though she's damaged."

"Is she able to shape-shift into different forms, just like you?" asked Kex, "Or is the raven her only shape other than human?"

"Good question. I have never seen her in any other form other than those two. It is possible she is still able to use another form, but

I wonder if her lengthy stay here in this world has damaged her so that she is unable to choose a variety of them anymore. I'm fairly certain that may the case. If so, it would be logical to say that the longer she stays, the less proficient she'll become in her shape-shifting. It will be interesting to see what her final form will be."

"Why is she interested in Blaidd?" asked Jarah.

"She is after *you*, not Blaidd. She feels he'll lead her to you. That is why I showed you what we've just seen. I feel you will meet up with Blaidd again, and you should be aware that he is being watched. Now let us return to Ardvale. We have a lot of work to do."

Catrin

Catrin was alone. She still had Deryn, but Corrick and Callum had left a week ago for western Aelfar, while Brenin had left today with his army, heading south. She usually loved this time of year, the season of renewal.

She stared out of the window, not noticing the soft green that blanketed the forest, or the flowering peach trees below her. She thought of how, last night, she had gone again to the grate in the secret passage. She wasn't sure why she had gone, she only knew that its pull was irresistible. Maybe it was a sixth sense that told her to go, but she wasn't sure if she believed in that. Whatever it was, she was glad she had listened to her instincts.

Yesterday had been a busy day for Brenin, and he was tired. He'd gone to his chambers early last night. She didn't think she'd hear much, if anything at all, but she was taken aback when she heard voices coming from the grate. It was Brenin and that woman. She was here! At first, it was inconsequential chatter, mostly Brenin talking about his preparations for his army: how much food had to be taken with them, the cost of horses, the problems with training conscripts, and so on until she thought she'd fallen asleep. Her attention refocused suddenly, with a start, when Branwyn interrupted his monologue.

"I think I know their approximate location."

She'd located the Six? Catrin hardly dared breathe.

Brenin didn't seem much interested, but he said, "Oh? How?"

"Don't worry your handsome head about how, darling. Let's just say I have my ways."

Brenin laughed. "Don't I know it. Where are they?"

"They are somewhere in the forests of Mannanon. How they escaped the—" She stopped suddenly and then continued, her voice changing into a silken whisper that Catlin had to strain to hear. "Well, I know they're there because one of my spies told me. We must head south, darling, to Galon through Mannanon. We can intercept them as they continue northwards to their village."

Brenin sat up. "Do you mean to tell me I must lead my army through the most dangerous part of the south-lands to find six children? You must be out of your mind."

"Beloved, how do you think your army will cross two large and wide border rivers, and arid, hilly terrain? There is another way that makes more sense. To approach Galon from its western side, south of Lake Yorath. This way, you'll only need to cross one river, and the land is more hospitable to an army. As far as the danger in Mannanon is concerned, you're listening to old legends and myth. I have travelled through that region myself. How do you think I get here? It's safe, I tell you."

"Yes, how *do* you get to visit me so often—from Rhiannon? That would be impossible. You would have to be a bird!" He laughed again, but his voice had an edge to it. "Tell me, my sweet, what sorcery do you use to come all that way in a few weeks? Or are you lying to me, and you're not from Rhiannon at all?"

"*Shh*, my love. Do not speak of sorcery. It frightens me!" Her voice changed pitch again to that of a much younger woman. "I use horses, and have many stops along the way with steeds that run like the wind without stopping. I change horses many times, and I do the same thing going back. I am a master rider and—"

"I have never known a horse that can ride all day without stopping," said Brenin. He sounded even more suspicious now, and Catrin thought it was about time. She too found Branwyn's story unbelievable. Riding north from Galon would mean weeks journey for most, but only for those who used the fastest horses. She had last been here about a month ago, and something just didn't add up. She knew Brenin felt the same way, but the fool was too besotted with her to ask any hard questions.

Branwyn stroked his face as she purred sweet-nothings into his ear. It wasn't long before Catrin heard the familiar sound of Brenin snoring. She turned away from the grate. There'd be no more information tonight.

She had been unable to sleep, options running through her mind like sheep herded by monkeys. Finally, when morning arrived, she had settled on a plan. Earlier today, Brenin, along with Branwyn, had left for Galon, and she knew she must act swiftly. Turning from the window, she summoned her Equerry. When he arrived, she commanded him to prepare two horses for her and Deryn's daily ride.

"Have the horses waiting for us by the River Mair. We both wish to take a walk first before we ride, and tell the groom to leave the horses tied to a tree and to immediately return to his duties."

"But, milady, the horses may be stolen if the groom does not remain with them."

"I will take responsibility for that. Just make sure my orders are obeyed to the letter."

"Yes, milady." The Equerry bowed and left, still looking puzzled.

She knew the Equerry would probably wonder what she was up to, but she had to take that chance. She couldn't afford to allow anyone to see them leave. She wondered if she was making a colossal mistake, not just for herself, but for Deryn too. But the more she thought about it, the more she realized this was her only option. She had to get Deryn to the Healers before ...

She walked down the palace stairs to the kitchen and told the cook that she wanted to be sure her husband had taken enough food. She doubted his ability to take care of himself sometimes, and she *tsk-tsk-ed*. She would send a rider after him with a good supply, and she was to prepare food that would keep well in this warm weather. She specified what was needed: salted meat, hard tack, cheese, bread, and dried fruit. She also demanded sturdy flasks for water. She went to her chambers and gathered some things she knew she would need, and then crept, as if a thief, to her husband's chambers, making sure no one saw her. To her relief, no one was there, and she quietly gathered some items of clothing and a stiletto knife from his weapons collection before she returned to her own chamber.

She used the stiletto, which was nice and sharp, to cut her hair almost to its roots. She placed her beautiful, long locks into a bag and hid it under her mattress. She didn't want anyone discovering what her plan was.

She changed into her husband's clothes. The outfit she had found was one he'd scarcely worn. He'd only used it for rough riding; it was well past its prime, and she looked like a farm hand in it. She donned a pair of his boots that were strong and would last for a while, and finally added an old cloak that his manservant had put aside for mending. She then pulled the hood up and looked at herself in her mirror.

She hardly recognized herself. The hood effectively shielded her face, and when she lowered it, she looked like a young lad whose whiskers had not yet sprouted. She placed the stiletto into its sheath and stowed it in her boot.

She then made her way to Deryn's room where he was supposed to be studying for a test with his tutor later in the day. She slipped quickly into his room, thankful no one had seen her, and that Deryn's room was close to hers. Deryn looked up, startled. He was just about to say something when Catrin put her finger to her lips.

"*Shhh* ... it is I—your mother!"

"Mother! What ... ?"

"Don't say anything. Come with me and be quiet!" She took the puzzled Deryn back to her room, and, taking the bedrolls, satchel, and a lit candle, she awkwardly maneuvered herself and a surprised Deryn into the secret passage, trying to pull the armoire over the open panel behind her. It was difficult, but she managed to draw it closer to where she thought it would take an observant eye to notice it was slightly out of place, and closed the panel behind them. She picked the bedrolls up, handed one to Deryn, and, taking the satchel, she indicated that he should remain silent. They made their way down the passage until they reached the door in the outer palace wall.

The horses were waiting, exactly as she had ordered, and she tied the bedrolls and satchels to their saddles.

"We can talk now," she said. Deryn climbed onto his horse, with her help, and his expression told her that he thought his mother had lost her mind. "Deryn, we must go on a journey that no one else can know about. It's important that we do not tell anyone who we are. My name will be Roland, and yours is Brohan. I am your brother."

"Why are we doing this, mother? Why can't we just stay home ... I don't want to go on a journey!"

"I don't, either, *Brohan*, and remember to call me *Roland*, but we must. I can't tell you right this moment why we are doing this. Please, just trust me, and maybe things will become clearer one day. You will understand. Speak as little as possible so you will not give yourself away. I will do all the talking."

Deryn was used to obeying his mother, so he quietly allowed her to lead their horses through the forest alongside the riverbank until they picked up the road that headed east, away from Three Rivers and everything he knew.

25.

Branwyn

Branwyn knew she'd overstepped her mark with Brenin when he became suspicious of her unexplained ability to know where the Six were and the incomprehensible distances she covered over short periods. She'd managed to smooth things over and set his mind on other things, but she knew it was only a temporary respite. She couldn't afford to lose his trust now.

She had guessed at the whereabouts of the Six the night Blaidd was attacked by the wolf-men. She knew, thanks to what she'd picked up in Ibai, that the Six had disembarked at the northern shore of Lake Yorath. From there she had no more knowledge of their journey, but she also knew they must have encountered, at the very least, the wolf-men. They could not have survived an encounter with the inhabitants of Mannanon. If somehow they had escaped what was a certain death, someone must be helping them.

Irusan came to mind, and then she rejected that possibility. He would have been with them, and she knew that, through talk in Ibai, a strange man who fit the description of one of Irusan's shape-shifting forms visited with Holgar and Adne while the Six were traveling up the river with Askia. She also knew Irusan never stayed long in this world's reality. She sniffed. He was too afraid he'd suffer template damage. Well, that was a possibility—for her as well—but she didn't have a choice. That was why she had to make the most of her life here, and she may as well do what she could to seize power and make it all worthwhile. It was a choice between controlling, or being controlled.

As one of the erstwhile Guardians of this planet, she also knew the approximate locations of the portals to the world of the Gardeners, as the elementals liked to call themselves. There was one close to where Blaidd had encountered the wolf-men. She could not access it anymore, but she knew where it was—the old tree— yes, that was it! She was certain. All she must do now is to place her spies nearby and wait for them to emerge. They would, eventually, and she and Brenin would have them.

She couldn't do anything about her frequent disappearances though. Brenin would remain suspicious even though she often used her powers of persuasion on him to lull his senses, but it wasn't like telling Anfawl stories about her family in Ak-Gala. She must rely now on Brenin's infatuation with her, and her ability to soothe him and redirect his attention to other things. When he left for Mannanon with his army, she told him she must go home.

"But I'll be with you in spirit, my love!"

She smiled to herself. Little did he know how true that statement was—the Raven was her spirit body. It had the power to morph her template into its chosen form. It had been a long time since she'd been in her true form, and to tell the truth she didn't even know what that would look like anymore. Irusan's true form was that of a cat-man, but hers—well, it could have changed over the centuries. She hadn't returned to it for so many years now because she preferred being a beautiful woman. She had her way more often.

Brenin had objected. "I want you to ride with me, Branwyn. Show me how you travel back and forth." His mouth formed an ugly pout, and he looked to her like a three-year-old child.

"Look at me," she ordered. Brenin lifted his hurting eyes to her face. She waved her hand in front of him, snapped her fingers, and his chin dropped to his chest, eyes closed. "You will never ask me to travel with you again, or how I travel. You will only remember we agreed to travel separately, for reasons you will no longer remember, or question." She snapped her fingers again, and Brenin's face jerked upwards, his eyes snapping open.

"Well, goodbye my love," he said, smiling, as he kissed her cheek. "See you later!" He turned towards the door without a backward glance, leaving Branwyn sitting alone in his chambers.

Branwyn left the palace as she usually did, walking out into the bustling city of Three Rivers, and finding a deserted alley where she could safely activate her Merkaba. Soaring over the city, she set her course south. She must go to Mannanon and ensure the Six did not leave the portal unseen, but just in case they did, she'd have Brenin send some of his men to Meadowfield as well. She wondered what they were learning in Ardvale. Would they pose a challenge for her? Maybe, but not for long. She had something they did not have: years of experience in elemental command. She also had friends, and ones who would be happy to assist. She must go see them first.

She wasn't concerned about the inhabitants of Mannanon either. Now that Blaidd commanded the wolf-men, by extension, they were hers to command as well. Blaidd would ensure that she had either their cooperation while Brenin's army traversed their territory, or perhaps, and she smiled again as the thought occurred to her, they would even help with fighting the Galonese. The Galonese, although fierce and with a well-deserved reputation for bravery, would not stand long against the hordes from the north.

Catrin and Deryn

Catrin and Deryn rode hard the first day. They stopped often to rest so that Deryn and horses could eat, drink, and cool down, but then, they'd mount and ride until their horses were in sweat again and could not go any further.

Cresting a small hill, she noticed the vanguard of her husband's army not too far down the road. She had caught up with them.

"Father!" exclaimed Deryn, smiling in delight. "We are going to battle with Father!" Catrin sighed. She knew this would be a true test of her disguise and whether Deryn would obey orders or not. She stopped their horses and pulled Deryn's hood on his cloak up around his head. Hers was already up.

"Do not remove your cloak, and *do not* talk to anyone! Even your father—*especially* your father!"

"Why?"

"I'll explain later. Right now, we don't have time. We must pass the army as quickly as we can. If anyone tries to stop us, we must … ." She stopped. She had no idea what they should do if they were stopped. "Just leave it up to me. Don't talk, and don't take your hood down."

They galloped past the rear guard and no one stopped them. It took them quite some time to pass the columns of marching men, but they remained unchallenged at any point. The soldiers seemed to pay them no mind as they averted their faces and spurred their horses past the phalanxes of troops, wagons with supplies, horses, and finally, her husband at the forefront with his generals. She could see him clearly, and she was now frightened—no, terrified—that Deryn would shout out or that Brenin would recognize them both as they passed, but Deryn stayed silent and Brenin didn't even glance their way. She did not slow down as they pulled out in front of the marching men. She indicated to Deryn that they must gallop until they were well ahead of the columns. At last, they were leagues in front of her husband, and she slowed the panting, sweating horses down to a walk. Once she determined it safe, they stopped to rest in a small forest by a stream where the horses could drink.

Deryn looked sad, and she didn't know what to say to him. They ate in silence, and they mounted their horses again and set off at a steady, but sedate pace down the road.

They encountered a few travelers, mostly farmers carrying produce to market in their carts. Their haste discouraged any exchange of greetings. They kept their cloak hoods up and did not look directly at anyone. She felt a little more relaxed now that she had left her husband and his army behind. They would get to Meadowfield long before any army troops arrived there. They were slow, and she and Deryn could move fast, unencumbered by wagons and supplies.

She told Deryn as much as she could, without giving away his father's secrets. She told him that she had heard of six healers from western Aelfar, where they were now headed, and that she needed to find the healers.

"Why do we need healers, mother?"

"I want you to be well and strong, my sweet. I have heard these healers can heal anything, and I have tried all the healers in Three Rivers to no avail."

"But why must father not know of our journey?"

"Because he felt it was too dangerous for us to go, and he had other things on his mind, such as the war, so he couldn't come with us. I have disobeyed your father, but once he sees you healed, he will forgive us." Deryn seemed to accept this explanation. She knew his greatest desire was to please his father, and if that meant that the only way to accomplish that was to heal his withered legs, he would do it.

Their first night out in the open, alone, was more terrifying than she had anticipated. They left the road and found shelter in a small copse. She hoped bandits were not on the prowl, but the night was thankfully uneventful. Encouraged, she rode their horses less hard the next day and when they stopped to rest, she always went off the road and made sure no one could see them.

They needed to find more food. The stocks from the palace kitchen were getting low. By the end of the third day, she noticed a small farm not too far from the road. They cautiously approached the farmhouse. A woman emerged, dressed in the peasant-clothing common to the area.

"May I help you, sir?" she asked.

Catrin was not used to being called *sir*, but she was glad that her disguise was convincing. "I'm looking to buy some food from you, mistress, if you are able to help me. I would be grateful."

The woman seemed pleasant, and she invited them in.

"I see you are both just lads," she said. "Where are you travelling from?"

"My brother Brohan and I were visiting family in Three Rivers. We are now heading back to our village near the mountains. My name is Roland."

The lie seemed to satisfy the motherly woman, who told them her name was Genove. She began to prepare food for them.

"Well, be careful, Roland. There are many dangers on that road, as I'm sure you well know. Bandits and thieves abound. My husband heard that two travelers were robbed and murdered yesterday! Why don't you and your brother stay here tonight and leave in the morning? My husband Angus will be home soon. He'll put your horses in the barn with the others. They look tuckered out. Probably each needs a good bag of oats too."

Catrin didn't require convincing. She felt safe at this farm, and it was better than sleeping out in the open. The farmer was home by sundown from his work in the fields, and he welcomed "Roland and Brohan." Catrin went out to the barn with him while Deryn remained inside with Genove. She hoped that he wouldn't say anything that would make the woman suspicious about them. They unsaddled the horses, and Angus gathered some oats and hay mix that he placed in feedbags. She felt touched by the hospitality of these people. They didn't have much, but what they had they were willing to share with them, two strangers.

"I have not told your kindly wife about this yet," she said. "But on the road I passed the king's Army headed west. Please warn as many people as you can that they're coming, and spread the word. I know he may still gather conscripts as they pass through villages, and they will need food, so they will raid farms and villages enroute."

Angus spat. "I did hear rumors about that, too. There is talk of another war, this time with Galon, but I thought it was just talk. I will pass the word along immediately." They went back inside, and Angus whispered to Genove, who nodded. He went outside again, towards the barn.

"He will use what we call the farm-alarm. He'll ride to the next farm who will ride to the next, and so on, until as many people as possible have been warned," said Genove. "We well remember the last time the king's army passed through here gathering young boys and supplies. We've still not recovered from that. Angus and I lost a son in battle to the army some years ago ..." She stopped, her face becoming tearful.

Catrin wondered how she would feel, losing Deryn. She couldn't imagine what it must be like.

Genove continued. "He was our only son. We have no one to leave the farm to, no one to help us ... ."

She had to stop again. She collected herself and bustled around the kitchen, trying to look busy.

"We're supposed to love our king," she said. "But what he's done to the people of this land is—" She looked at Catrin, gauging her reaction. It was not safe to criticize the king. One could lose one's life or freedom talking to the wrong person.

Catrin looked at Deryn. "It's time for you to be in bed, brother. I promised our mother he would go to bed early every night."

"Of course! Of course! Here, let me put him in my son's room tonight. There's plenty of room for you both in there. It's been a while since I did this." Together they tucked Deryn into the straw bed. Catrin thought she'd sleep on the floor in her blanket tonight. It was important for Deryn to rest comfortably after the hard riding of the past few days. When they were done, they returned to the kitchen. Catrin looked Genove in the eye before speaking.

"I'm sorry I interrupted you," she said, "But my s— brother should not hear us speak. He has trouble keeping a secret."

"I understand," said Genove. "I should have been more careful. Talking to strangers these days can be dangerous. We were talking about the king, and people have lost their heads for less."

"I know. That's why I warned you. He's an evil man, and he runs his kingdom as if it existed for his personal convenience. Don't worry about me. I have no illusions about this king anymore."

Genove continued, her face etched with relief. "Neither do we. He's brought the farmers to their knees. His army comes regularly to demand supplies, among other things. They raid the farms and villages, and if they don't like what they get, they burn them down. Sometimes we don't have enough food to get us through the winter. Many have died in harsh winters while their livestock is plundered. They take horses, and most of our winter hay, so many of our own livestock are left to die with no food."

Catrin felt appalled at what she was hearing. She knew things were bad, but to hear of it firsthand from her husband's subjects left her dizzy with shock. She felt ill. As if a levee had burst, the words began to pour out of Genove, and Catrin sat silently at the rough-hewn kitchen table, listening. She knew Genove had a need to talk. She had felt the same way once.

Genove told her how hard it was for them as farmers to make a living wage with all the new taxes. "We live too far from Three Rivers to sell our livestock and vegetables there, so we have to sell locally, and yet we are taxed the same as those who have the larger markets available to them. The king's tax collectors don't wait to be paid either. They arrive without warning, and we must have the money ready or they burn down your house."

Catrin knew something that Genove did not know: Brenin did not tax the rich noblemen. He taxed his poorer citizens, and the money went into the palace coffers to keep the noblemen in luxury and ... yes, even herself. She too had profited off people like these simple farmers. She fingered the pouch she wore hidden in her waistband. It bulged with money and gems.

The next day, before they left, Catrin placed a large amount of money—much more than the food and lodging warranted—on the bed Deryn had slept in. She knew the farmer's wife would discover it after she had already left. She felt they were proud people, and would not accept charity. They did not want to be paid for their hospitality, and they had treated her and Deryn as if they were their own sons.

She felt bad for them, knowing that Brenin was leading his army into a war that was both unnecessary and dangerous. She wanted to cry as they galloped out of the farmyard and towards the road, and wondered how else she could help people like these; people who were the backbone of the kingdom and who deserved better treatment. She felt she could help the situation by ensuring that her son became the next ruler of the Aelfar and Mernoc kingdom. She would see to it that he was taught how to be a fair king, one who genuinely cared for his people instead of lining his own pockets and those of his nobility.

The sky was grey. It was going to rain. She hoped the army would get bogged down in the mud. She prayed to the Gods to get herself and Deryn safely and quickly to Meadowfield, as the first raindrops splashed onto the dusty road. The farmers needed the rain, but the army did not. Her prayers to Idris were already being answered.

26.

The Six, Ardvale

Life in Ardvale settled into a routine of lessons and apprenticeship. After their introduction to the elements, they realized that they had a lot to learn. They divided into three teams, each one apprenticing with a different element until they were proficient enough to move on to the next.

Tegan and Jarah agreed to combine their home as one, and so did the other teams. They all felt as if they were life-partners, and Tristan and Djana, and Adain and Kex, shared the idea.

They had no idea how much time had passed since their arrival in Ardvale. They measured time by the successful mastery of their lessons. They also measured time by Tegan's pregnancy and subsequent birth of her and Jarah's first child.

To no-one's surprise, the baby was a girl. Tegan said she had felt the feminine spirit in her womb and had already decided on a name: Anwyn. Finn was delighted, as a grandfather would be with his first grandchild. The elementals assisted at birth while Djana acted as midwife.

Jarah's happiness was now complete. He felt that no matter what happened to them from now on, nothing could ever take away from the moment of his first child's birth. If he died tomorrow, he would be a happy man. He wondered if his own parents had felt this way at his birth. He wondered what they must have been feeling now, to lose him to the unknown. He re-evaluated his treatment of them while still in Meadowfield and felt shame and sorrow. How could he have known what it was like to be a parent? He would have been much kinder, and tried to love and help them more. Now, it was too late, but he resolved to correct that whenever the opportunity arose. They still intended to visit their families once they left Ardvale.

He wondered too how they would travel through the still-dangerous lands outside Ardvale with a baby, or small child. He shared his concerns with Finn, who looked concerned as well. Finn held discussions with the other elemental beings and returned to Jarah and Tegan's home with a proposal.

"We will be happy to keep baby Anwyn here when you leave. It is up to you, though. She can remain here and undergo training as a healer and adept in Elemental Command. Humanity needs more people who are able to learn these skills and teach them to others." Noticing the looks of dismay on Tegan and Jarah's faces, he hastily added, "But of course, she is *your* child, and if you do not wish this we will concur. I also want you to know that you will be able to visit with her, as she will be able to visit with you when conditions are right. We have many portals to the outside world, and we can always keep track of where you are and arrange for brief visits. Your crystals will guide you to the nearest portal, and you will see your daughter often."

Jarah and Tegan discussed Finn's proposal for a while, then came to a decision.

"We agree," said Jarah. "It's what is best for the child, not what is best for us. And it will allay our fears for her in the outside world to know that she is safe and secure here."

Tegan cried for a while, and Jarah felt sadness, but they were both determined to enjoy their daughter as much as possible before leaving. They did not know how much time they'd have with her. It would depend on how ready they felt to leave once their lessons were done.

"Anwyn can be returned to you, permanently, once you feel it is safe for us to do so," said Finn. "We will not keep her any longer than we need to."

Tegan was able to take care of Anwyn as well as focus on her lessons with help from the elementals. They loved taking care of the baby if Tegan needed to be alone to study or practice. The other members of the Six also took turns with caring for the baby, and they all enjoyed her. Djana said she wanted a child too, but she and Tristan would wait. She felt she really needed all her energies for her studies, and Tristan agreed. Kex and Adain said they weren't ready yet either, but they would have fun with Anwyn and hand her back to her parents when baby-sitting became too tiresome for them.

Each of the Six discovered a particular field of healing and elemental command that they were drawn to, and each one began their apprenticeships in these fields. Jarah wanted to learn how to make a diagnosis, how to recognize imbalance and how to treat it in humans. Tegan was more concerned about animals. She worked with the animal elementals who taught her everything they knew about anatomy in various species, and with herbal elements. Each one of them worked with the flora elementals, but Tegan found herself quickly becoming the expert on herbal medicines and salves. She and Jarah both worked with the water elementals as well, learning how they affected the bodies of animals and humans, and the body of the earth.

Djana and Tristan worked mainly with the earth and air

elementals, in programming crystals, learning how to communicate with them, and how to gain their cooperation in healing imbalances. Planetary healing was part of their study, and they learned about growing plants, crops, and the stewardship of natural resources. While studying with Eirnin, the earth element, it asked them for the crystal they were given in the Crystal Cave in Galon.

"It is now time," Eirnin stated, "for us to learn what this crystal can do in healing. It is not like the Healing Crystal Jarah carries. It is rather something to use to heal the earth and its elements. You may use it for healing for wounds, along with the fire element, and for general imbalances in humans and animals. I will show you how to use it, and the two of you will become its keepers."

Kex and Adain commanded the fire element. They learned how to use it in cleansing of wounds, and balancing the fire elements in the planetary, human, and animal kingdom bodies.

They all studied the all-important ether element: the chi essence of every living thing. Irusan made appearances as their teacher in this element. He stressed the importance of self-healing, and they conducted many sessions on themselves, healing distortions and imbalances in their own bodies.

"If you do not heal yourselves first," he warned, "you will transfer your own distortions to others and cause more problems than you heal." He also told them that picking up other's distortions and imbalances was not acceptable. They had to learn how to protect their fields and template from these distortions that were always looking for receptive and unhealed areas to latch onto. "Think of yourselves as not only transmitters of energy, but as receivers as well. You want to transmit only pure energy, and you do not want to receive anything that you will need to clear and transmute again. This is how the well meaning, who understand virtually nothing about chi, find themselves becoming sick. Even sicker than their patients. They learn the consequences of improper shielding and self-healing the hard way."

The protocols of healing were strict. Irusan was a difficult taskmaster; he presented them often with hypothetical situations where they would determine if it were appropriate to heal, and what the outcomes would be if they did or did not. They began to understand more about free-will choices. If, for example, they encountered a life form that was unhealed, but it did not wish to heal for any reason, they were to respect that and leave it alone. One never imposed healing on another, and one never requested healing for another unless they had requested it and all the appropriate shielding and protective techniques were in place. They would be expected to discipline themselves, cleansing and healing their own templates on a daily basis, and applying protections. If not, consequences could be dire in the outer world.

They would be held to higher standards of behavior than most people would. Harming others, even in self-defense, was not acceptable. They had other choices to protect themselves now, and they were expected to use those methods first. If they had to lose their lives rather than kill, then they would do so, but Irusan said they would be trained well and would not need to sacrifice their physical bodies.

"You will learn self-defense. You will do what is necessary to discourage and repel attack, but deliberate killing is not what we aim for. Leave that to the unenlightened. They simply don't have the choices you now have."

He also trained them in control and activation of their Merkabas. "Bringing up your Merkaba in the outer world is not going to be easy," he warned. "It is much easier here, but conditions in the outer world will make it difficult to impossible. That is not your fault. Understand that it will take you many years out there to learn how to use your vehicles, but you will use them the same way as you do here, so you will have the basic training. It will become easier as time goes by with much practice. Just keep plugging away!"

They were so busy that they barely noticed the passage of time.

Anwyn was no longer a baby. She began to walk, and to their amazement, her motor-skills and speech abilities developed at a rate they had never seen before. Babies, in the outer world, usually developed more slowly, and were at least three years old before they began to speak in anything resembling sentences, then at six years they may begin to sound like little adults. Anwyn, at two years old, spoke in full sentences, and her vocabulary was that of a much older child. She began to sit in on their lessons, and spent less and less time with her baby-sitters.

It wasn't long before Finn said she was ready for "school", and she began her training. "I also feel that you Six are all ready for the outside world," he said.

They looked at him in dismay.

"We ... No! Not already!" cried Tegan, and the others felt her pain.

"We'd like to stay longer," said Jarah. "But if it is time for us to go, we must go."

He clenched his jaw. He wasn't going to cry too. His heart felt as if it would break, and he knew they would all be happy to stay here forever, to never return to the outside world. But they had a job to do. It was not over. It was time to go.

Irusan understood the reluctance of the Six to leave Ardvale and the child. His heart ached for them, but he knew they all understood what their mission required. Personal desires did not take precedence. Self-mastery was not easy. He, of all people, understood that. He too had once lived in the outer world and undergone his own apprenticeship. He too once had a family and ...

But that had been a long time ago. It had been another world, long before mankind had been created. His people no longer existed on this world.

The awful day dawned, and the Six followed Finn and Irusan down the lane for the last time. The elemental orbs lined up along the pathway to say goodbye, singing in their tinselly voices and touching them softly on their cheeks. They did not seem sad, and they knew that to them they would never be "gone". Irusan told them that the elements would always be aware of their consciousness because they were all one, and they would never be alone, even if they could not see the elementals with their physical eyes.

"You are an indelible part of us, now," said Finn. "This is not goodbye. This is yet another stage of your training. You must now apply yourselves in the outer world and learn how the laws of physics work there. Here, you have not been subjected to the laws of the outer worlds, but you will be there. It is surmountable. You now have the skills and knowledge needed to overcome the obstacles."

They sighed, and all knew that things were going to feel ten times more difficult "out there" as they now thought of their world of origin. It would take a lot of adjustment.

They reached the portal—the tree—with its doorway into their world. They each hugged Finn and Irusan, and kissed the child one last time, then tearfully stepped through the door and out into the forest.

They turned for one last look, but the door had gone. It was now just a tree.

27.

King Brenin

Brenin was not happy. He'd already flogged three of his generals for dereliction of duties. In turn, they'd flogged their underling officers, and so it went down the ranks. Everyone was blaming everyone else. It was incomprehensible to him why they could not find enough supplies at the farms they stopped at. They all appeared to be deserted, and most of the horses, except for a few lame or ancient nags, had gone. The carts that were left had missing wheels or looked as if they would fall apart in no time at all. It was obvious that someone had put out the word of his approaching army, but who? He had kept his troop movements secret, and not even his generals were aware of the day they would leave, or their route.

They'd burned down a few farmhouses just to set an example, but that did not solve the problem of finding enough food and supplies for their months-long march. Perhaps the farms further west and south would not have been alerted, and he hoped that they'd find food and horses there. They could not ride their own horses until they were lame; they needed constant, fresh supplies.

It was still early spring and the crops had not produced much in the way of food. Maize was still ankle-high, wheat had not yet ripened, and there were few vegetables available. His men had to slaughter cattle and sheep to stay fed, but even those were gone. He began to doubt his decision to leave at this time of the year. Perhaps he should have waited until summer, but Branwyn had said—

Branwyn! Where *was* she? She didn't have the problems he had. All she had to do was go back to Rhiannon and her navy would do the rest. She seemed to trust her admiral—what was his name again? Oh, yes, Udfa. He hoped this Udfa was reliable. Their whole strategy depended upon him placing his navy in the right place at the right time. Brenin knew his navy was already preparing to leave, and it wouldn't take them long to sail south to Galon. They would leave when they thought he and his army must have been getting close to their destination. They'd already worked out how long it should take his army to march southwards, planning the attack down to the last detail.

Now Branwyn wanted him to find six healers. He couldn't be less interested. Healers were charlatans as far as he was concerned. Why did she need these particular ones? He could have produced hundreds of them, all in Three Rivers. Didn't they have any of them in Rhiannon?

But, he thought, he would do anything Branwyn asked of him, even if it didn't make sense to him. A few days ago, by Branwyn's request, he'd sent a troop of ten men onwards ahead of them towards Meadowfield, their task to find these kids. *What a colossal waste of men and time*, he thought.

And today, as if things weren't bad enough, the road was a river of mud. It had been raining for three days and the wagons were bogged down. There was mud everywhere. The march was progressing too slowly, and they'd never make it to Abena in time, no matter how many of his generals he flogged.

But he thought he'd flog them anyway. It relieved his stress.

Branwyn Plots

Since leaving Three Rivers, Branwyn had made more plans. She guided her Merkaba to the Osgoi. She remembered Blaidd telling her about the Arrach, how frightening and formidable they were. She knew of the Arrach, things created under the direction of demonic forces. They were hideous creatures, and completely uncontrollable by man, but she was no human.

She located the pass, and then the gorge where the Six had almost been trapped by the Arrach army, then simply disappeared. *The exit or entrance to the tunnels must be located somewhere along this gorge*, she thought.

She flew along the cliff wall where the river narrowed and where Blaidd said they'd found the entrance. She could see nothing, but this is where she would bring the Six once she found them. They would show her exactly where it was and they would open it. Then they would guide her through the caverns and tunnels created by the Basajaun to the other side of the mountains. She'd leave signposts and marks so that, in the future, her army could find their way through. It would be easy.

She decided to wait until dark to look for the Arrach. They were nocturnal creatures, so it wasn't until the moon rose in the sky that she located them. She could hear their hissing and clicking as they approached. She knew they were not able to speak or understand the human tongue, but she'd have no trouble communicating with them. All creatures had an unspoken language, and she knew them all. It was once part of her own training, training that she'd put to good use here. She found it useful for mind probing as well as communication. Unless one knew how to shield oneself from her probes, she could gather any information she needed. It was not possible to lie to her.

She could now see the horde as they scurried over and down the cliff-face, their scorpion-like tails and appendages waving in the moonlight. They were foraging for food, and anything that moved became their prey. Staying safely in her Merkaba, she approached them unseen, and when she had located their leader, an enormous horror twice as large as the rest, she stepped out of her vehicle in a flash of light. The large Arrach reared up and hissed, covering its eyes with a claw as big as her body. The remainder of the Arrach cringed from the light, and she realized there was little time left before they attacked. She didn't have all night to waste, so she immediately sent a telepathic communication.

"*Peace*! I come in peace, to talk. I have a proposal for you."

"Who dares to approach us in this way?" the large Arrach demanded. "Prepare for death!"

The horde began to approach again, their claws raised in attack.

Branwyn let loose with another flash of light and they once more retreated, covering their eyes. "I am but a small snack," she said, "but I have information for you that will lead you to more food than you've ever dreamed of."

This focused their attention. The large Arrach stepped forward.

"Speak, now. First, who are you that you know and understand our tongue?"

"I am Branwyn, also known as the Raven. I know many tongues, and I know many things. It would do you well to listen."

"You may call me Golzark," the large one said. "We will listen, but not for long."

"Golzark, there is an army that approaches these mountains ..."

Golzark and the Arrach excitedly began to click amongst themselves. Branwyn picked up their thoughts. They liked armies. It was a moving feast for them. She smiled and continued.

"But they are not coming through these mountains." The clicking died down. "They will not be your food." They began clicking again, this time, angrily. "*Wait*! I am not finished. There is another army. They will be fatter, and better fed than the army coming from the north. This is the army I intend to make your meal. But you must come south when I give the word, and you must leave the northern army alone. You must not take Galon. Galon will be mine. Your prize is a territory that runs alongside the mountains, and is more to your liking. It is called Mannanon. Join in our fight, and you may take as much land as you wish in Mannanon. I do not think you will be disappointed."

Golzark and the Arrach clicked noisily again, and Branwyn knew they were debating whether she was telling them the truth. Golzark was suspicious. He wanted to eat her then and there, and forget the whole thing, but another Arrach came forward and said her proposal should be considered.

"We have little food left here," she said.

"We haven't had a good meal in months," said another.

"My young go hungry every night I come back empty-handed," another one pleaded.

At last, their discussion was over. "We accept your proposal," said Golzark. "This area is becoming less able to feed us, and we must move to new lands where there is more food. If this Mannanon is indeed a rich area, it will suit us well. We'll help your army, but they must vacate the land as soon as the battle is won."

Branwyn nodded. She would deal with the Arrach later. She'd agree to anything if they helped Brenin's army against the Galonese. She knew of ways she could get rid of the Arrach, or at least confine them, once they'd served their purpose.

"I'll be back in a month to let you know when to start moving south," she promised. "It's important to coordinate the convergence of the armies, since we don't want any killing until it's time. Oh," she said, as an afterthought, "and if you see the Six Healers who escaped you last year, I want them. Alive."

Golzark hissed. "They killed our last leader! I have a bounty on their heads!"

"Well, I don't care, but just make sure you bring them to me—alive—or our deal is over. Don't underestimate my abilities."

With that, she pulled up her Merkaba once more and disappeared. Part two of her plan must now be put into effect.

The night was still young and the rising moon full. She shape-shifted into her raven form and continued flying south. She could see dark tree shapes and long moon-shadows below her as she sped over the foothills of the mountains. She enjoyed experiencing the beauty of this world through the feeling of flight. It was why she'd chosen her raven form as her favorite. Even though her Merkaba was faster—instantaneous—the feeling of wind in her feathers and in her face gave her a sense of freedom that the Merkaba could not. Her raven form was slower, but so much more enjoyable.

After flying for hours, she approached the area where she'd last seen Blaidd, and she slowed down even more, circling and straining to catch sight of movement in the forest. She could hear the baying of the wolves. *Of course!* They would be at their baying rock on the hilltop. She descended towards the hill, just in front of her, and ... yes!

There they were. They stood on the flat rock, staring up at the moon, and in their midst stood the enormous bulk of Blaidd. He too howled and bayed, his deep voice almost drowning out the higher pitch of the wolf-men.

She laughed to herself. He must really be taking his job as leader seriously. She perched on a nearby tree and watched as the moon slowly sank towards the west. Finally, it was over, and the pack was about to descend from the rock when she made her appearance. Surrounding herself in a ring of fire, she changed into her human form in a flash of light. The wolf-men drew back, yipping and snarling, but Blaidd stood his ground.

"What *you* want?" he demanded. He wasn't pleased to see her at all. He'd hoped she'd given up looking for him and leave him alone.

"That's no way to greet an old friend, and one who saved your life," she responded. "But since you've asked so nicely, I have a proposal for you."

"I know you not ask hand in marriage. What you want?"

"Call off your wolves, and I'll tell you," she said. "It's a little difficult keeping this ring of fire around me while I talk."

Blaidd gestured towards the pack, and they pulled back even further and crouched, ready to spring should he give the word. The ring of fire disappeared with a few sparks, and all that was left was a black circle on the rock. "I can bring this up again anytime I want to," she warned, "so don't even think about attacking me." She continued to stand inside the black circle as she spoke. "I need your help."

"Why you think I help you?" he asked. "I not feel I owe you anything. Maybe you save my life, but—"

Branwyn adopted her most honeyed voice. "I know," she said. "You don't owe me your life. I understand that. But I also understand that you deeply regret the way you treated your erstwhile compatriots—the Six." She looked carefully at Blaidd, and to her satisfaction, she noticed she had hit a painful spot with her guess. He flinched. "Perhaps you owe *them* something?"

"What you mean?"

"The Six will be coming through a certain portal at some point. There will be many dangers waiting for them on this side of the portal as they emerge. I wish, as you do, to see them survive. The Six are needed in this world. They're needed for many things. They are talented and knowledgeable, and I can use their healing powers as much as you can. I know this is the reason you came up here after your change—to find them and heal. Am I right?"

Blaidd's massive head did not move to indicate agreement or disagreement, but Branwyn knew she was right.

"If you do find them, hold on to them. Do not allow your pack to destroy them." She turned to the pack, and, using her telepathic abilities, she said, *You all deserve better than this forsaken land. Your food sources are dwindling, and you compete with many other life forms to survive. If I can promise you all the food you can eat south of here, will you join my army to help defeat the southlands?*

"No talk to my pack!" Blaidd roared, and the forest trembled. "I only talk." He turned to his pack, and his thoughts went out to them. *You have heard what this woman has said. Now I leave it to you to decide what you want to do.*

One of the pack cautiously crept forward, crouched low on its haunches, towards Blaidd. *Master, we do need food. We have gone hungry many days now. Food is no longer plentiful in our land.*

Yes, master, said another. *We all wish to find more meat. If this woman can lead us to meat, we are willing.*

Blaidd turned to Branwyn, and using his thoughts, since he didn't want to be misunderstood and he wanted his pack to understand, he said, *We agree. What do you require?*

Branwyn felt pleased. This had gone a lot easier than she had expected. Hunger was a powerful motivator.

"When you see Brenin's army coming through your territory, you will allow them safe passage. Follow the army south, towards Galon. Bring the Six with you, or hand them over to either the king or me. Do not tell them anything, and once we get to Galon, your pack will find as much food as they can eat. It is a land of plenty."

Blaidd nodded and Branwyn pulled up her Merkaba. She needed to move fast now. She must return to Rhiannon and make sure all her plans were in place.

28.

Amrafalus

The enormous reptile slithered out of its cave and into the sunlight. The mountain peaks gleamed a bright white in front of him and he blinked his eyes. The sun felt strong, and he knew that it would be safe to cross the mountains now. He had spent too much time here, on the western flanks of the Osgoi, but he'd regained his strength and his leg was now healed completely. His clothing was lost a long time ago, but it didn't matter. His scales protected him well. He remembered that he used to walk upright, on two legs, but now he found it easier to slither and crawl. It also gave him the advantage of being able to creep up to his prey, unseen.

While building his strength in the cave there was time to reflect, and to remember. His memory was slowly returning, and he now knew his name: Amrafalus. He remembered that he was once someone of importance, but that he had been betrayed. Now he must find the betrayers and the person responsible for this betrayal.

He remembered this person, what he looked like, and even his name, as he ran out of the crystal cavern while the Citadel above collapsed. His name was Blaidd, and this Blaidd had left him to die as the cavern collapsed around them. It was important to Amrafalus that Blaidd must pay with his life. He remembered that he came from a place over the mountains, and that, like a homing pigeon, he would return there. Amrafalus would be waiting for him.

It took him many days to find a way through the mountains over the passes, but he eventually found a route that avoided the snowy peaks. He followed many snow-melt rivers that tumbled and roared down from the high peaks. He was comfortable in the water, and the strong currents did not slow him down. There were also plenty of fish for him to catch.

He lay in the sun on the bank after each immersion and allowed his body to lose the chill of the river, and then he'd continue. When he couldn't find streams or rivers, he'd climb rock faces and work his way down sheer descents like an ant on a wall. His strong claws easily found the smallest cracks in the rock, and there was little that stopped his forward momentum.

He continued in this way, day after day, until he realized the peaks now all lay behind him. In front of him, the eastern flanks stretched out as far as he could see. Pine forests and thick mists blanketed the slopes. He would find plenty of food here, he thought as he began his descent into the valley.

He preferred to travel at night now, and he'd find a sunny spot to sleep during the day so that he could recharge his body with the sun's warmth. He could tell that spring had arrived in these parts, and that he was a lot further north than he had anticipated. He must have travelled in a northeasterly direction over the mountains, and now he continued to move northwards, through the forests.

As he progressed, his memory returned in bits and pieces. He remembered almost everything now. He realized he could not return to Rhiannon. At least not yet. He knew that he had lost control of everything, and that someone else would have taken the reins of power as soon as they thought him dead. To return without knowing the situation may mean a death sentence for him, so he must first take his revenge, and then he'd return and plot his rise to power again. He hissed to himself as he realized that he was now over the mountains—in Mannanon! Aelfar and Mernoc lay to the east, as did their capital, Three Rivers. He could take this territory. Who could withstand the powerful Amrafalus? He was not only a survivor, but a conqueror of worlds. When he was ready, he would unleash the Arrach! But, he told himself, find Blaidd first. He found comfort in his thoughts as he continued his lonely trek through the wilderness.

The sounds of the forest unsettled him as he softly slithered through the undergrowth and over rocks and fallen trees. He wondered what they were. A couple of times he'd see eyes that glowed through the trees, and they were often accompanied by howls that chilled even his blood. Dark and silent shapes scurried around him and he'd open his mouth to catch the scent of whatever it was. The odors were foul and caused him to gag, but now he would be able to detect the presence of anything before it came near him.

Sometimes he found a sheltering cave, but he always vacated it before venturing in too deeply. Every cave was occupied by something. His sense of smell told him long before he could be trapped by whatever was in residence inside.

He also found some unusual food along the way. Fish had been the bulk of his diet up until now, and occasionally small creatures that roamed at night fell into his trap as he lay in wait alongside a trail through the forest. These creatures were smaller than the average human was, but misshapen and ugly. Their skin was yellowish and their eyes bulbous. They also possessed strong jaws and teeth so he had to be careful. He snapped their necks before swallowing them. He didn't want them biting him on their way down his gullet.

Branwyn

After her conversation with the Arrach and Blaidd, Branwyn hastened back to Rhiannon, arriving at her home in the early hours of the morning. Anfawl, who was now sharing her home, was still asleep. Branwyn needed little sleep, so she waited for him to rise and greeted him outside on her shady terrace as he emerged for breakfast.

"You're back," he said. "I missed you. I hope your father is well?"

"He's doing much better, thank you, my love. He wants to know when I am getting married. He says he is tired of waiting for grandchildren as his life fades away."

Anfawl ordered his breakfast from a silent Marko, and then turned to Branwyn. "My coronation is to take place next week. I hoped you would be here for that. Perhaps we can combine the coronation with a marriage ceremony?"

"Well, don't be so romantic about it, my love. But yes, I think it's a good plan. That way all the citizens of Rhiannon will see me beside you on your throne. By the way, is it ready?" Anfawl had commissioned the kingdom's best artisans to craft a wooden throne for him inlaid with gold, silver, and precious gems.

"It's ready. But I don't have one for you, beloved! I never thought about having two made." Branwyn looked at him in disgust, but she quickly changed her expression to one of adoration. They would not need two thrones. Not for long anyway.

"Never mind, we can always commission another later. I assume I am to be crowned queen at the same time?"

Anfawl looked perplexed. He really had not given it any thought. Now he wished he had. "Er, yes ... yes, I will get on it right away." Now he had to find another crown.

He sighed. He didn't have time for this, but Branwyn was right.

As his queen, she needed all the trappings. Women liked that sort of thing, and he would do his best to accommodate her.

"I would like to set off for Galon, right after the coronation ... um, wedding ..." Now he didn't know what to call it. His confusion irritated Branwyn. How could he expect to lead a kingdom when details escaped him? The sooner she was rid of him, the better. Anfawl looked at the sun. "I really need to be getting back to ... I have a session today with the council. We need to go over the plans for the invasion of Galon."

"How is that going, love?"

"The council want to wait. I would like to get it into action right after my—our—coronations—wedding. I never liked wait-ing on anything. If we wait too long—"

"My love, I agree with the council."

Anfawl looked at her, astounded, but she continued.

"While I was traveling home, I heard rumors. Travelers on the eastern side of the Osgoi have spotted troop movements from the north. Apparently, Brenin is simultaneously planning his own in-vasion of Galon."

"What has that to do with us? Wouldn't that mean more haste for us? Why should they get there first and claim Galon?"

"Because, my love, they will draw Ortzi's troops to the north to fight them, while we sneak in with our navy and take Galon from the south. It will be important to find out exactly when Ortzi's troops begin their march northward—as I am sure his spies will inform him of the invasion from the north in plenty of time—and then we make our move via sea. Then we will deal with Brenin. His army will be exhausted by then and not expecting that anoth-er force will attack from the south."

Anfawl looked at her in admiration. Sometimes he really un-derestimated Branwyn. She was more than a beautiful face.

She was right; the navy was their only chance. Sending troops over the mountains—well, that was impossible. "And we can deal with whatever is left of Ortzi and Brenin's troops later," he added. "We'll send as many of our own troops by boat, as possible."

"We need to construct more troop ships," said Branwyn.

"I think you'll make a wonderful queen, my love," said Anfawl as he rose from the table. He was thoughtful as he mounted his horse and set off for the council chambers. He would make sure they understood this was all his planning, his brilliance. He might even gain their respect.

As Branwyn left the breakfast table, she too was deep in thought. There was work to be done. She had another plan, one that would take care of Anfawl. But it would have to wait until after the ceremony.

29.

A Convenient Man

The coronation, combined with a wedding ceremony, had as much pomp and grandeur as Branwyn and Anfawl could muster up in the short amount of time they had to plan. Branwyn did most of the planning. A holiday was declared for the kingdom, except for the slaves and servants, of course. For the Trueni it was business as usual. Feasting and parades, with Anfawl and Branwyn making the rounds of the city in their newly commissioned chariots of inlaid gold and silver. The best horses were decked out in feathers and finery, not to mention the ladies of the city, who competed with each other in attire and the best seating. It was a day that Rhiannon would never forget.

Branwyn understood the importance of ceremony. The image of their beautiful queen, decked out in silks and jewels that made them gasp in envy, would remain in the memory of the citizens for years to come. She was already a living legend, and her citizens would do anything for her. Anfawl would not be remembered or revered as she was. He sat like a statue through most of the ceremonies and looked uncomfortable when she told him to wave at the crowds. He scowled most of the time, and she knew he'd much rather be with his troops planning a war than taking part in this "ridiculousness," as he called it. It suited her well.

They ruled from their temporary palace for a while, but returned to her residence when they felt they needed a break from governing. It would be more difficult for her to get away, to check on Brenin's troop movements now that she was queen and always in the public eye, but she would find a way to manage.

Anfawl was not happy with her trips home anymore. He said it was unbecoming, not to mention dangerous, for a queen to travel. She could bring her family here, and they would take care of them.

"But Anfawl, they love their home and would not be happy here."

She would have to move her plans up a bit. Thank goodness her Merkaba was still working. One night, a month after their coronation, she slipped out of bed, taking care not to awaken her husband. In an instant, she was in her Merkaba, and, faster than light, she found herself in Abena, hovering over the Keep. There were lights burning in the Hall of Justice. Someone must be there.

She moved herself, still in Merkaba, into a large room. Ortzi sat at the head of a long table along with his council. They were in some kind of an emergency session. It looked as if he had just rousted them all from their beds.

"My lord, are you sure these spies are reliable?" asked one member.

"They are men I would stake my reputation on," said Ortzi, his face dark with anger. The doubtful member shrank back in his seat. "I put them in place many years ago to keep their eyes on troop movements from Aelfar, and now they have justified my trust in them. They have all independently and at great risk to themselves, confirmed that Brenin is moving a huge army south.

They made haste to return to Galon to make their reports through territory that is dangerous and hostile. Of *course* they are reliable!"

"What will we do, my lord?"

"Since you asked, I will tell you." Ortzi's voice dripped with sarcasm. "We will wait here for them, of course." He then took a deep breath. "What *do* you think we will do?!" he roared, pounding the table with his fist, and the members jumped. "We will meet them halfway! We will show them we are ready to fight and defend our land. I want you to get on this immediately. We'll send half of our troops northwards, and we'll keep the rest here to defend an attack from the sea. If I know Brenin at all, he'll be sending his navy into the bay to attack us from the south. He was counting on me not finding out about the northern attack." He stood up and pushed his chair back. "Get on it!" he said as he left the room.

All the members, except for one, scuttled out behind him as quickly as they could. The one member who remained behind— Branwyn slid over to look at the seal of authority he wore around his neck—was Peio, the Minister of War. Ortzi apparently did not easily intimidate him.

He took his time gathering his papyrus papers together and putting his seal away in a pouch that hung next to the dagger on his waistband. The room was empty. It was time for her to make a move.

As she deactivated her Merkaba in her usual flashy way, an alarmed Peio fell off his chair, raising his hands in front of his face as he lay on the floor. She knew he could not get a good look at her due to the brightness of the flash. She quickly stepped over to him and pulled his hands away from his blinking eyes.

"Look at me!" she hissed. Peio blinked again, in surprise, but his eyes were now trying to focus on hers. She gazed deeply into his cold eyes and began to talk, her voice hypnotic and compelling. It took a few seconds, but Peio finally relaxed and fell into a deep trance. She activated her Merkaba once again, and pulled his unconscious body in with her.

It took only moments for her to arrive at the temporary palace in Rhiannon. Finding an empty room that she knew would not be checked, she deposited Peio there, briefly woke him, issued more instructions, and then put him back to sleep again. Reactivating her Merkaba, she flew to her home. Anfawl had not awakened. She silently slipped back into their bed. All was going according to plan.

She arose early the next morning, and woke Anfawl up before his usual time. "We've been summoned to the palace, my love. There's news of the invasion."

Anfawl sleepily stirred, and sat up. "News?"

"Yes, we need to get up there immediately. I've ordered our carriage. We'll eat later." She wanted to get Anfawl up there before Peio was discovered. She helped him dress, and they hastily left.

The sun was coming up and the shadows were long and cool. The city was beginning to stir. She shivered, wrapping her cloak more tightly around her. She wondered if she had the stomach for this. Not for the killing—she could do that—but to be there ... to *witness* it. But she had no choice. Her performance was essential. It was all part of her plan, and she must go through with it.

As they walked into the council chambers, she noticed with relief that they were not the first ones there. A few members of the council were already seated. She had known that some of them liked to arrive early before the hustle and bustle of the day set in, and she'd been counting on that. The guards were posted at the doors, but they looked sleepy and disinterested. All the better.

She entered the room and turned to look at the first guard. She signaled, a quick movement with her hand, as she passed him. Immediately, his face went slack, and his eyes blank. She walked close to the next guard and did the same thing. His face too went slack and expressionless. No one noticed, and the guards would have looked normal to the casual observer. *Excellent*, she thought.

One of the council members looked up as they entered. "You are here early, Your Majesties! What brings you—?"

Branwyn quickly interrupted, talking over the member. "We received your message, Anafu, and came as quickly as we could. Let's go over those plans again."

"Message ...?" But Anafu's attention was taken up again as he noticed another person walking into the room. A man he'd never seen before, with strangely unfocused eyes, who was dressed in a way that was not common in Rhiannon, walked into the room. What was even odder was that the guards did not react. Anafu noticed that Anfawl had his back to the door, and did not see the stranger enter. He did not notice Branwyn's deliberate positioning of herself between Anfawl and the guards.

Before anyone could say something or make a move, the stranger hurled himself towards Anfawl as he drew his dagger from his belt. The guards were slow to react, but Branwyn screamed, and rushed toward the stranger. Instead, she seemed to get in the way of the guards who were also trying to reach the stranger. They both stumbled over her as the man plunged his dagger into Anfawl's back again and again.

Chaos ensued. Branwyn screamed, and lashed out at anyone who was in her reach. When the soldiers finally leaped to their feet, and pushed her out of their way, they ran towards the stranger who now stood dagger in hand, silent and unmoving over the body of Anfawl. Both soldiers, swords already drawn, slashed downwards, and the body of Peio fell on top of Anfawl's. Branwyn continued to scream as she threw herself on top of them both. Covered in blood, she was finally led away by a shocked Anafu who sat her down on a chair and handed her a container of water. She knocked it away, still crying, but Anafu did not see tears. Her face was dry, although red with effort.

"Check the body of the assassin," ordered Anafu. "Perhaps there are some clues as to who this man is and why he killed Anfawl."

Branwyn slyly looked sideways towards the soldiers as they pulled the body away, and searched the man's robes. Her look of triumph was unmistakable as they pulled out the Seal of Authority Peio carried in his waist pouch. Anafu snatched the Seal away and looked at it in amazement.

"It's the Seal of Galon's Minister of War! His name is Peio—"

Branwyn screamed again. "*Galon!* I should have known! They fear ... feared my husband. They sent this assassin to kill both of us. I have heard the Galonese know witchcraft. This man must have used it to gain access to this building. How did he get past the guards?" She looked at the guards, who now had frightened looks on their faces.

"Your Majesty, we don't remember this man entering at all! The first thing we knew ... he was past us and had already stabbed our king. It must be witchcraft!"

By now, the palace had been alerted and more people were running into the council chamber. Word was sent out, and all the council members who were not yet present, arrived in due time. The story was repeated over and over. An emergency session of the council was called, as soon as Anfawl's body, and that of the assassin, had been removed. Branwyn refused to go home.

"I must complete my husband's work," she insisted bravely, still wearing her bloodied robes. "It's what he would have expected me to do." She took her place at the head of the table and looked around at her councilors, seated and ready to do her bidding. Each one of them gazed at her reverently, as if she were the most courageous woman they had ever seen. "Now, let's discuss our invasion of Galon. We'll show them what happens when they send assassins to our land."

The men at the table all raised their hands in agreement. She wasn't sure about Anafu though. He was looking at her strangely. She resolved to keep an eye on him. Udfa stood at attention behind the table, and she nodded her head at him to take a seat. He too would bear watching.

His face was inscrutable, and she never trusted a man who

didn't show his emotions. She tried to probe his mind, but encountered a blank wall. No matter, she thought, he was not difficult to understand. He'd resented Anfawl and would express no remorse at his death. He'd wanted the leadership for himself. Maybe she'd offer him a bone if he performed well.

Sierra

Catrin and Deryn found shelter in many farmhouses, and the generosity of the farmers never ceased to amaze her. There were a few farms where they were driven away by suspicious occupants, and some who set dogs on them, but these were rare, and they always managed to outpace the dogs or leave before there was any trouble.

They now found themselves in a long trek through forestland where no farms existed, not even a village where they could find food or rest. The road almost disappeared in many places, and Catrin had to navigate by the sun. She discovered that Deryn was good at this; he had learned navigation from his tutor.

The weather was not friendly to them either. It rained almost constantly, and the road, where it existed, was a river of mud. She decided to travel alongside it as much as possible. Pine needles and thick undergrowth were better than the bog-like conditions on the road. She wondered how the conditions that slowed her and Deryn down significantly would affect Brenin and his army. She couldn't imagine leading an army through this muck.

The rain often turned to sleet, and she and Deryn found shelter in caves and rocky overhangs. The landscape here was not the flat plains of the east, but rather hillier and rockier as they drew closer and closer to the mountains. She could not see the mountains yet, but she knew that they couldn't be too far away.

After many days of endless riding, they were both exhausted and dirty, tired of the hard conditions they encountered. Catrin hoped that her son would survive the trek. He was not strong, and she had to stop more often than she had intended so he could rest and she would rub the warmth back into his legs and fingers. More than once, they hid in the thick forest as bands of men on horseback made their way past them. They looked rough, with hard faces. They were heavily armed, but they were not soldiers. She felt instinctively that they were cut-throats and bandits, and they would remain silent in the shadows of the trees, hands on horse's necks to quiet them as they passed. She always kept her dagger close now, hidden in her sleeve instead of her boot.

One morning she woke up and discovered her horse was lame. He must have stepped on a large thorn, she thought as she examined his hoof. She removed the offending barb, but his underfoot was swollen and red. She must find a farm or a village soon. Walking down the road with a limping horse would slow them down too much, but they must continue. To her relief, they found a small settlement a few leagues ahead. It was so small that it didn't even have a name, but it had a blacksmith and a few inhabitants who could supply them with food. The blacksmith looked at the horse.

"This 'ere fella ain't fit for riding," he said. "I 'ave another though if yer interested? Bought 'im from—" He stopped and she wondered if the horse was stolen property.

He brought the horse for her to look at. It was a young stallion, healthy and strong. He quoted her a price that she knew was exorbitant, even for a beautiful horse like this one, but she paid without complaint.

"'Is name's Sierra, 'cause 'e's black."

His dark coat glistened in the sunlight, and he nuzzled her hand as she greeted him by patting him on his noble forehead. They removed their belongings from the lame horse, which she left with him. He promised he'd be able to restore him to health, and she thought he had made a good bargain at his price for Sierra with another horse thrown in.

"How far is it to Meadowfield?" she asked.

"Meadowfield, eh?" He thought for a bit, rubbing his stubbly chin. "That's around three day's ride from 'ere, I would guess. Don't have much cause to go there myself, but plenty of merchants come through 'ere from Meadowfield, and parts yonder. We get our supplies from them. There's a fairly decent road too."

Catrin felt joy when she heard that the road was passable. She could use some good news for a change.

"Watch out fer bandits! Plenty in these parts!" he called out, as they cantered out of the settlement.

They did not encounter any bandits, only a few travelers who looked more like farmers on their carts, carrying goods to the settlement she had just left. They too warned them about bandits, so she and Deryn kept a sharp eye and ear out for approaching horses.

As soon as they heard hooves or voices, they would leave the road and find the deepest, shadowed tree they could. It served them well, and they were not accosted.

30.

Meadowfield

It had taken four more days of difficult riding before they had finally reached Meadowfield. Catrin wanted to get off Sierra and kiss the ground in the quaint village square, but she decided on discretion instead. She enquired of a passerby if there was an inn, and the man pointed to a building not far from the square.

"It's the third building on the left," he said. "*The Golden Sheaf.* Ask for Alberth."

They tied their horses at the posts outside the building. A sign with three sheaves of wheat creaked overhead as she opened the door. Alberth was a large man in a dirty apron, standing behind the bar, but at least the inn looked clean. The old wood beams were blackened from age and smoke, and she could smell the stale odor of ale and whisky spills that permeated the interior. A morose looking man sat at the bar and stared into his ale. He did not glance up at the young travelers as they entered.

"Can I help you, young sirs?" Alberth's voice was rich and deep. It felt somehow comforting to Catrin.

"We are travelers bound for Mannanon," she said. "We need to rest here for a while. Do you have a room for my brother and myself?"

"Mannanon, huh?" He looked at her more suspiciously now. "What would two young lads like you want in Mannanon? No one goes there ..."

No one except bandits and cut-throats, thought Catrin, who were on the lam from the law. But she'd already thought this through. "We're looking for some healers," she said. "My brother is not well, and I heard there might be healers from this village."

"Hmmm ... no healers in these parts, but others have asked. It seems every week we get someone here asking about healers. It's puzzling to us, since we have not had healers in this village for generations. We've plenty of scoundrels coming through though." He laughed, and pulled a key down from a peg behind him. "Not the least of which are the king's army! Only last year they came and took several of our best young men." He gave a sidelong glance towards the fat man at the end of the bar who continued to pay them no mind, and leaned over the bar, his voice a whisper. "Haven't seen them since."

Catrin looked at Deryn. His face was unreadable, but she wondered how he must feel to hear, once again, how unpopular his father and his army was. She didn't know how to explain things away. They both had been confronted with the truth, the reality of the kingdom, and now she stayed silent. Alberth nodded towards the man and whispered softly, again.

"His son was one of them." He handed her a key, and then spoke in a louder voice. "Your room is the second one on the left, upstairs. I don't have many guests this time of year. All I have besides you is a young couple, so if you don't like your room, let me know and I'll find you another. You can put your horses in our stables out back. I have a groom who will see to them. His name is Dan."

"I wonder," asked Catrin, "if the young couple you mention are named Corrick and Callum? They're friends of mine. I was to meet them here."

"Yes, they arrived a week ago. They're not here right now. They had to go to Potter's Hill. But they should be back soon."

Catrin and Deryn went up the creaky wooden stairs and unlocked the door to their room. It was a small room with two beds, but it looked comfortable, and it overlooked the village square. Leaving Deryn in the room, she went downstairs again so that she could put the horses in the inn's stables and see to their feeding. Later, Alberth directed them to a table where they could eat a hot meal. She and Deryn slept soundly that night, exhausted from their trip.

Alberth was a never-ending source of information. He seemed to know all the village gossip and nothing escaped his notice. "If you're still asking about healers," he said as they came down for breakfast the next morning, "I don't know of any, but the only missing people from this village are those three boys I already told you about who were taken by the king's men last year. We haven't seen them again. Your friends were also asking about these healers, and I told them the same thing. That's when they decided to go to Potter's Hill. I don't know what they think they'll find there. It's even smaller than Meadowfield." He noticed the look of disappointment on Catrin's face. "But if it will help, I thought you should talk to the parents of those boys." He told her that Arall, the Baker, was the father of one, and Trent, the Blacksmith, was the father of the other. "The other one—you saw him in here yesterday—he's a drunk. Don't bother with him. He don't remember his own name half the time."

He told her how to find the smithy and the bakery, and Catrin and Deryn set off to find the baker first.

THE SIX AND THE GARDENERS OF IALANA

Arall was busy. Ever since the army had taken Jarah, he'd had no one to help him in the mill or bakery. His other sons were still too young, and he'd have to wait a few summers yet for the second son. In the meanwhile, he'd employed Mehin to take up the slack, but Mehin only showed up when he was sober, and that wasn't often. At first he was reluctant to talk to Catrin, who introduced herself as Roland. This Roland seemed to be the same age as Jarah. He wondered if he needed a job.

"Yes, the army took my older boy," he said, a sad look on his face. "My wife is still inconsolable. If he'd been killed in battle we could understand it. Our grief would be terrible, but we would at least know. We hear rumors of wars, and we've seen the cruelty of the army towards its conscripts. Every day is torture for us, wondering if we'll ever see him again."

She heard the same speech from Trent. He hadn't seen his boy and didn't know where he was. But she had names now. Adain, Blaidd, and Jarah. If these were not the boys, she'd be back to where she started. Perhaps these boys were part of the missing healer party, or perhaps not. It was better than nothing. She'd wait for Corrick and Callum and see if they'd found anything in Potter's Hill.

She didn't have long to wait. They returned that same evening, shortly before sundown. Catrin waited in the inn for them to arrive, and as soon as she heard hooves clattering over the cobbles towards the inn, she ran out to meet them. They were tying up their horses at the posts in front of the inn when she walked up to them. She didn't want them giving away her identity to any observers inside the inn, and Callum looked at her indifferently as she walked up to them.

"May I help you with your horse, sire?" she asked.

"Yes, you may. Are you a groom here too?"

Catrin smiled. Her disguise was better than she thought! "No sire, I am your queen, Catrin. Do not react."

Corrick quickly looked up, recognition dawning in her face. "Milady!"

"*Shhh*…Corrick." Catrin put her finger to her lips. "It is I, but please be silent."

Callum looked annoyed. "I thought we'd agreed you would not come here milady."

"Call me *Roland*, please. Yes, we did, but there were more developments after you left. I had no choice but to come here with Deryn."

"You brought Deryn?" Corrick gasped. "How did he fare with the long trip?"

"He fared well! He's stronger than we thought. He doesn't know the details of why we are here, but he knows we search for healers that can help him and that we must not be discovered."

They took the horses to the stables and handed them over to Dan, then they returned to the inn. Deryn was asleep already, so Catrin went into Callum and Corrick's room where they could speak freely.

She told them everything that she'd learned since they left; that the healers were most likely still in Mannanon, and that Brenin had sent a troop after them to watch the last spot where they had been seen. "We need to go there," she said. "Or at least, I do. I think you and Callum must wait here with Deryn, and I'll bring them back—"

"You'll do no such thing, milady," said Callum. He knew he risked a charge of treason by not obeying his queen, but he was determined to protect her at all costs. "You and Corrick must remain while I search for the healers in Mannanon. *I* will bring them back."

"Callum, I'm going to pull rank here," said Catrin, equally determined. "If you are discovered by the king's men in Mannanon, you will lose your head without a trial. If I am discovered, it will be bad, but not as bad. It is something I can talk my way out of. I thought of taking Deryn with me, but you are right in that it is too dangerous. I will leave him here with you, and I don't want to hear any disagreement. I will leave tomorrow, and that is all I am saying on the subject."

Callum and Corrick knew when they were outranked, and although not pleased with the arrangement, they had to agree someone should remain here and protect the heir to the throne. Catrin made them promise they would not leave him alone for a moment. Callum told her what they'd found out in Potter's Hill.

"The name of the missing girl is Tegan. Her father is Rhaol the shoemaker. We now have four names, but it seems unlikely to us that these young people are the ones we seek. They lost their daughter when a Captain Eglog, an army recruiter, attacked their village."

"They didn't really want to talk to us about it," Corrick added. "But from what we could gather, she must have run off into the forest and gotten lost."

Callum gave her a crossbow and arrows. "Do you know how to use this, milady?"

She nodded. "Yes, we royal womenfolk are not entirely helpless, you know. I was trained to use the crossbow by my father."

Callum smiled. "I meant no disrespect, milady, but this will be more helpful to you than the small dagger you carry." He gave her a sword, as well. "This sword belonged to my father. I am sure he'd be happy to know it is in your possession."

Catrin accepted both weapons, gratefully. She felt she might need them.

The next morning, before anyone awoke, she gathered her belongings together and mounted Sierra, heading south, towards Potter's Hill.

Potters Hill

It was a day's ride to Potters Hill. There was no inn, but she enquired from a villager if any parents were missing children in case Corrick and Callum had missed any. "Yes," said a woman who was drawing water from the well. "Last year the soldiers came and burned down some houses, killed three people. One of our girls, daughter of Rhaol the shoemaker, ran into the woods and that was the last we saw of her. Name of Tegan."

"Can you direct me to her father's shop?" asked Catrin. The woman looked at her suspiciously.

"Why are so many people asking about missing children? Only yesterday we had two people who inquired about missing children, and the week before—"

"I am looking for specific missing children," said Catrin. "I don't know if this missing girl is the one I am looking for or not, but I have to start somewhere."

"Well, all right then. Her father's shop is over there." She pointed to a small store where a man was closing up for the night. Catrin walked her horse over, and the man looked up.

"I'm closing for the night, but if you need shoes—"

"No, it's not shoes I need. I want to ask you some questions—"

"Not another one!"

"Another what?"

"Another one asking about my daughter," he said. "As far as we know, she's dead. She probably died in the forest when the soldiers came ..." His eyes misted over, and a tear rolled down his cheek. "I told them yesterday ... everything I knew. They were a nice couple, and you seem like a nice lad, but last week there were soldiers here looking, and that frightened me. What could soldiers want with my daughter?"

"Sire, please. I ask your indulgence for one more enquiry. It's important to me. It is important too that these soldiers not reach your daughter first if she is indeed the one we seek."

Rhaol looked at her closely. "Come home with me, boy. You can talk to my wife, Mellyndra. She can tell you what happened."

Catrin walked with Rhaol to his and Mellyndra's home, a small cottage nearby. Mellyndra was a motherly woman who welcomed "Roland" into their home, and while Rhaol took Sierra to a nearby stable, she and Catrin talked.

"Please stay with us tonight," she said. "If you are going to Mannanon, you'll need a good night's sleep. There are no villages or inns south of here." She wiped her eyes with a rough hand. "Every night I think of my daughter, still out there with no shelter or bed. I wonder how she's doing. Is she cold? Is she hungry? Is she frightened? I can't stand it anymore. I wish I knew ... I can't allow another mother's child to ..."

Catrin almost cried herself. She couldn't imagine not knowing the whereabouts of her own son. Mellyndra told her what had happened the day Tegan disappeared.

"My husband was in his shop when a soldier arrived. This young soldier seemed polite and kindly, and asked my husband to make six pairs of boots for his troop who were encamped in the woods nearby. My husband already had six pairs made, ready for sale, so the soldier took them. He came back a little later to say that one of the pair did not fit their smallest recruit, so my husband made him a smaller pair.

"The same day, after this soldier had left, another troop arrived. This one was not as friendly. The captain—a man named Eglog—he was hideous, I tell you! All covered in tattoos! He wanted to know where we were hiding the escapees. We didn't know anything about the escapees he spoke of. Tegan was in the house with me and we watched as Eglog beat my poor husband almost unconscious. His soldiers then went to some of the houses and set them afire. I told Tegan to run ... *run into the woods, Tegan! Get away*! I ran towards my husband, and as I looked back, I didn't see Tegan anymore. She was gone. I have not seen her since. They did kill some people, but they did not kill my daughter. I would have seen that. After Eglog and his men left, we set up a search party for Tegan, but we could not find her. We searched for days, and she was gone. She simply disappeared." Mellyndra was crying openly now. She sobbed, "I feel so bad that I told my daughter to run into the woods. If she'd stayed here, she would have been alright ..."

Catrin was aghast. Now she wondered that, if not Tegan, the party who had come to Rhaol that day for boots were the six she was looking for. She hoped Mellyndra's daughter was alive. She wished she could do something—say something—that would help. But she didn't know what to say. She silently ate the food Mellyndra put in front of her. Rhaol had returned and he talked about the road south.

"Or what passes for a road," he said. "At its best, it's a track, and that disappears completely at times. It used to lead to Mannanon, but from what we've heard, all villages and settlements in Mannanon no longer exist. They were wiped out by terrible creatures—creatures that no one here has ever seen, but travelers speak of them, of hearing them in the forests at night."

"Oh, Rhaol," said Mellyndra. "That is nonsense. Those creatures are simply forest animals such as wolves, bear, and cougar. Sometimes, packs of wild dogs. They hear those and think they are big monsters."

"Well, you can scoff Mellyndra, but I've spoken to men who have come up that way and barely escaped with their lives. It's not only bandits—there are man-eating beasts in Mannanon!"

Catrin realized that Mellyndra didn't want to think of bandits and man-eaters while her daughter was still missing. She changed the subject.

31.

The Six

They looked around them. The forest, in daylight, was no less frightening than it had been the night they'd escaped the wolf-men. The sun barely penetrated the thick canopy above, now in full summer leaf. Tall ferns around them added to the gloom. They did not know in which direction to walk, so they headed uphill, following a small incline. They hoped it would lead them to a more open area where they could get their bearings.

This strategy brought them to the crest of a hill, where the trees thinned out enough for them to find the position of the sun. They determined which way north lay, and continued to walk. They noticed that the moss grew on the northern side of many trees, and when they'd lost the sun they used this as their rough compass.

As night fell, they once again looked for shelter. They were careful to avoid areas that were too open, and instead found an area where the trees were thickest, where they could hide in the undergrowth using the ferns and leafy branches to make shelters. They remained silent at night, avoiding fire, eating what did not need cooking. Tegan and Jarah were glad Anywn was not with them. It was difficult to keep small children silent, and even though she was advanced for her years, she was still a child. When they heard the roars and screams from the forest surrounding them, they were even more grateful that Finn had offered to keep her. It felt as if the forest came alive around them at night.

They huddled together and hoped nothing would discover their shelter. No one slept much, but morning arrived with its dim light and the cessation of the frightening forest noises.

They proceeded this way for several days, always heading north or east. They picked up the Garden River again, feeling a great joy when they found it. They could follow it all the way to Aelfar! There was no more need to look for sun or moss, and they'd always have a water supply. On the western side, they were in Mannanon, and the other side was Mernoc.

It didn't make any difference which side they remained on though. There were noises and signs of beasts on both sides; beasts who did not obey borders and territory decided by man.

The Bandits

The road south of Potter's Hill lived up to its reputation. It was worse, if that was possible, than the road to Meadowfield. Catrin began to rethink her decision to come alone, or even do it at all. There was something about these woods that made her skin crawl.

She kept her weapons close to her at all times, even when she slept, which wasn't often. It felt like she slept with one eye open. The slightest sound would jerk her awake, and she'd reach for her sword and pray that it was a deer or a small forest creature. The further south she travelled, the fewer forest creatures she saw. She wondered where they had all gone. There were no humans here to hunt them into extinction, but she couldn't find a rabbit, let alone a deer. Even the birds seemed scarce. There were fish in the streams, but they were difficult to catch without nets or a pole. One day, she caught a fat trout with her bare hands. It had swum a little too close to her as she bathed in a stream. It gave her some much-needed meat, and she hoped that her cooking fire would not attract predators. She also hunted for berries and dug for roots.

She came to another small settlement a few days south of Potters Hill. It looked strangely deserted, with no women or children visible. A rough man accosted her as she entered the settlement.

"Boy! Who are you? What you want, eh?"

"Excuse me, sire. I merely require passage through your settlement. Is there somewhere I can find food and shelter for the night?"

The man looked at her, suspicion etched on his dirty, stubbly face. "It's costly, boy. What can you give me?"

Catrin had a bad feeling about this. More rough-looking men emerged from the few shanties at the side of the road. They all held knives, swords, or other weapons. She did not reach for her own sword or crossbow. It would ratchet their suspicions up even more, and she would come off the worst in a confrontation. They were looking closely at Sierra now.

"Fine steed, boy. Fine animal. We'll take him."

Silently, she dismounted, and removing her weapons and food satchel, she handed the reins over to them. She had thought about leaving Sierra somewhere anyway. The further south she'd come, the less grass there was for him to eat. With his oats nearly gone, she knew that she'd have to abandon him at some point. Better here than in the lonely forest.

She'd become fond of the horse though, and felt sad that she must hand him over to this lot. Her pouch containing her money was tucked away in a personal place where she hoped it would not be found if she was searched. However, if someone did search her, the game would be up, anyway. She kept a few coins for situations such as these, and she handed the satchel, with the coins, over to the men. They searched it thoroughly, taking everything except her blanket and some old bread. The men were now eyeing her crossbow and sword.

"Sirs, if you would leave me my weapons, you can have everything else. I need to travel south and the road is dangerous."

"We already have what we want," grunted a man with a scarred face, and his azure blue eyes seemed to regard her a little kindlier than had the others. "I don't reckon you'll survive boy, weapons or no, but as for me, I wouldn't send my worst enemy out on that road without his sword and bow."

The men looked disappointed but nodded. The scarred man seemed to have some authority over the other cut-throats. He led her to an uninhabited shack near the settlement limits and told her he'd make sure his men left her alone.

"I think if some see you as you really are, milady, things will go much worse for you. I can't control all of them."

Catrin felt a chill go through her. *He knew!*

"Don't worry. I don't make trouble with womenfolk—queens or not. I will see to it that you are safe tonight, but be out by first light."

Catrin nodded, grateful that there was at least one honorable man in this place. As she looked at him more closely, she realized he was younger than he looked. The scar that covered one side of his face made him look older and more frightening, but his eyes were kind. If he had a shave and wash, she thought, he'd be attractive, even—maybe especially—with the scar, but she put those thoughts out of her head immediately. She had no time for evaluating men, especially those who chose to live outside the law. Besides, she was still married, and she didn't want to be like her husband when it came to vows.

Later, the scar-faced man brought her food and a supply of

bread for the road. "Not much food where you're going, but here's a net. It's good for trout in the streams." He gave her a small fishing net, and a bag to replace the one the men had taken from her. Inside, she found a flint. That would come in handy. The man then handed her a jar. "Open it."

She opened it, and immediately an odiferous stench hit her nostrils. She gagged.

"What is it?" she asked.

"You rub that on you, ma'am. Not now, wait until you get into the forest. It's excrement from some of the predators—man-eaters—we have around here. Nothing will bother you when they get a whiff of that. It will cover up the man—or woman—smell. It works for me. These beasts track by scent."

"Thank you," she said, but he'd already melted into the night.

By first light, she was as good as her word. She was now really on her own.

She rubbed some of the foul-smelling stuff in the jar on her before leaving, and the odor was strong at first, but either she quickly became used to it, or the smell dissipated. She wondered if she should rub more on her, but thought it wisest to use it sparingly. Animals had a much better sense of smell than humans, and she hoped that the predator, whatever it was, would not mistake her for a rival.

She walked as fast as she could maneuver through the forest, following what was left of the road, now an almost invisible track, and sometimes not even that. She could see that it wasn't frequently used, and that did give her some comfort. At least she'd not be running into more bandits. She had little to give, and she did not want to be parted from her sword and crossbow. She had already been discovered to be a woman; her hair was growing longer, and she chopped at it again with her stiletto. She should have done that earlier, she thought, but the gods had been kind to her in spite of her oversight. She wondered, again, how the scar-faced man had known she was the Queen. Not many people in these parts knew what she actually looked like.

The nights were terrifying. She wanted to climb a tree and sleep in the high branches, but she was even more afraid of tumbling out and breaking a limb than she was of her vulnerability on the ground. She used the salve mainly at night now, and tried to hide herself under low hanging branches of pines, or in the bracken and shrubs so that nothing could see her. Often, she heard nearby howls and cries, and once a wet snuffling around the tree she was under, but after a few moments, whatever it was went away. She slept little. She realized that days were safer for travel than nights, and whatever creatures were in these forests, they did not emerge in the daytime.

After a few more days of walking, she came to a river. It seemed to be flowing south, so she decided to follow it. It was a significant stream, and gathered speed as it tumbled down the hills and slopes. She used her fishing net to catch a few small fish and she built a fire, quickly stamping it out again after they had cooked. She hastily ate, burying the bones and scales in the ground or under leaves. She continued in this way for many more days.

She had lost count of how many day's walking she had done. One day blended into the next, and each night seemed the same, full of terror and sleeplessness. She didn't know how much longer she could last. What was her plan? She didn't have one. What was her destination? She had no idea. All she knew was that she must keep walking south. She felt the healers she sought were somewhere in this region. She realized her chances of running into them were zero, but she must keep going.

Early one morning, she awoke certain that she had heard something. The sun had not yet risen and it was that dark hour before dawn. She didn't know what had awakened her, but she felt the hair on her arms rising. She reached for her crossbow and slowly sat up, looking around.

She couldn't see anything.

Fully awake now, she stood up and looked around her again. Yes, there it was—the noise that awoke her. A crackling of small twigs sounded nearby as if someone was walking over the forest floor. One step, then two. Silence. She reached for her sword, but then thought better of it and picked up her crossbow.

She knelt and notched the bow, pointing in the direction she heard the noise. She waited. There it was again! It was definitely closer. Suddenly, out of the gloom, a huge shape sprang towards her. She could see it as a dark shadow, taller than a man, as it moved towards her. She could also see white teeth that gleamed as its jaws opened.

Without hesitation, she released her arrow.

A howl of agony split the morning air as the shape twisted and fell. She could see it thrashing in the underbrush near her. Now she could also hear more noises, more footsteps, not moving silently now, but as if a horde of these creatures approached at a run. She continued to kneel as she notched another arrow.

She would fight to the death.

32.

King Brenin

Brenin deeply regretted his decision to move his army through Mannanon. What had possessed him to act on this insane plan? He blamed Branwyn. He should never have listened to her advice. Somehow, she had bewitched him, and now he was ready to turn his army around and go home— except, he'd look like a fool. He would lose face with his army and his council. He would never be respected again. He knew he must continue, even if they all died, and he felt that they would.

The forests of Mannanon were more frightening than even the rumors, and his men were spooked. Brave soldiers, with years of battle and experience, begged him to turn his army around. He had them all flogged. If they continued to insist, there would be beheadings. His word must be kept. He couldn't be seen as weak. He wouldn't last a month if he returned to Three Rivers without taking Galon, without ever even *engaging* the enemy.

THE SIX AND THE GARDENERS OF IALANA

They had left the villages of Meadowfield and Potter's Hill behind them a long time ago. His soldiers whom he had sent looking for the six healers had not been seen again. The villagers had told them that they'd been there, along with others, asking about the healers, and then they'd headed south. What others could be looking for the healers, he wondered? He would ask Branwyn when he saw her again, although he probably wouldn't see her until he arrived back in Three Rivers, after the war had been won.

They'd gone through another small settlement, but no one here knew anything either. They'd picked up a few cut-throats to add to their ranks. It couldn't hurt to have more men. Only one of them, he was told—a man with a scar on his face—came willingly, although he had not seen either him, or those who'd needed more persuasion.

Their horses were weary and there was no food for them in the forest. They were quickly running out of supplies for both horses and men. The forest sounds at night gave him and his men the shivers. He could well believe the stories and old legends of man-eating beasts in these forests, no matter what Branwyn had said. How had she come, alone, through these forests? Something was not adding up, and he felt increasingly uncomfortable with what she'd told him.

The feelings of dread grew the further south they progressed. It intensified when they discovered the remains of the troop that had gone missing, the troop he'd sent to look for the healers.

There were not any bodies left to bury, but they did find what was left of the men and horses. The leather armor clearly belonged to his army. The teeth marks on the remains frightened his men, and everyone was jumpy. He doubled the perimeter guard at night and put the horses in the center of their encampment so they would not be eaten.

The Six

Three days passed, uneventfully, as their northward trek continued. They felt the crystals in their possession protected them, but perhaps that was their wishful thinking. Or, they thought, they had just been lucky so far. They understood more now about keeping their heads down and sleeping in areas that were not on wolf-paths. They realized that the wolf-men left tracks, and Tristan and Kex could easily determine where they were. They avoided the commonly used pathways. They found tracks of other beasts that were unknown to them, and they avoided those areas too. They still heard the night sounds, and a good night's sleep became a thing of the past. Even the slightest noise woke them with a start, and it took them a long time to get back to sleep.

Early, on the third morning after leaving the tree portal, they were awakened by an ear-splitting howl. This howl was different to the other howls they often heard during the night. It was a howl of agony, and it was close. They packed their things quickly and began to run through the forest, thinking they'd been discovered. They thought the howl came from their left, so they ran to their right, approaching the riverbank. It was when they heard more howls that they realized the sounds were echoing around them, and they had no idea where the howls were actually coming from. They stopped running so that they could listen and determine which direction they should take. The sun was not up yet, but there was now a pre-dawn glow filtering through the trees.

They slowly and quietly walked towards the riverbank, thinking that perhaps they could cross the stream so that their scent would not be picked up. It was then that they almost stumbled over a dark figure kneeling on the ground. It looked to be a boy, about their age, aiming a crossbow at the trees. He had his back to them, but spun around when he heard their approach, tightening his fingers on the bow as if to release the arrow.

"Don't shoot!" Tristan yelled, holding up his hands, and they all stopped. The boy froze, but still pointed the crossbow at them.

"Take cover!" the boy shouted. "There are beasts coming. I just killed one!"

Tristan pulled out his knife. The boy stood up and they all stood closely together as dark shapes broke out of the trees ahead of them. The shapes crouched low to the ground, approaching cautiously now.

It was a pack of wolf-men.

"Put down your weapons," Jarah commanded. The boy looked at him, disbelief written on his face, but he did not lower his crossbow. "Use your fire-palms when I give the word!" Jarah said to the Six. They all remembered how the Gardeners had frightened the beasts off with their fireballs. They could now do it too, or at least, they *hoped* they could. They had not yet tried it in their own world. Jarah thought if that did not work they still had the Crystal, but he was reluctant to use it as a weapon. He would rather frighten the beasts off.

They sheathed their small knives and held their hands up, palms facing the wolf-men. The boy still knelt, keeping his crossbow nocked and pointed towards the shapes.

It was then that a creature appeared, a misshapen and hulking form that loomed out of the dark, just behind the pack. The Six immediately recognized it as the creature they'd seen battling the wolf-men, the one that Irusan had revealed as Blaidd. He had seemingly come out of nowhere, and he now towered menacingly over them. He turned to his pack and gave an unspoken command. The wolf-men stopped advancing.

The boy's dirty face froze in fear, his crossbow going slack in his hands.

"*Jarah! Tristan!* It I, Blaidd!" the beast's voice growled and rumbled from its barrel-like chest. It reached a hairy paw out and pulled the crossbow out of the boy's limp hands. With one squeeze, the crossbow fell in pieces at its feet. The Six looked at the beast—Blaidd—dumbfounded. Would he continue to pose a danger to them, Jarah wondered? Up close, he was even bigger than they thought. He gestured again, and the wolf-men fell back. He sat down with his palms up in a sign of surrender. "Yes, I Blaidd," he said. "Amrafalus use crystals on me. I change into monster. I no hurt you!"

"Blaidd, we know it's you," said Jarah. An expression of surprise crossed the beast's face. "Irusan told us."

"I no time to talk. Brenin come with army—close by. You must go. I tell my creature-men no hurt you. Safe passage to home." He looked at the boy. "I not know this boy, but he kill one of us. He must die."

"What do you mean, he must die?" asked Jarah, his relief replaced by fear. He didn't want to leave this boy to die at the hands of these creatures.

"It is law of pack. Life for life, death for death. Must obey."

"He killed one of you?" asked Jarah. "Show us the body, and then we'll decide."

"Iratz dead. Boy kill with arrow. But I take you to him and show."

They all followed Blaidd—it was difficult to think of him as Blaidd anymore—as he strode towards the spot where the wolf-man had been hit by the boy's arrow. They could see the body now, lying hidden in the bracken. Jarah bent over the body, and they all, except for the boy, looked down at it. Jarah felt along the beast's neck.

"There's a pulse," he said. Tegan knelt and placed her hands, palm down, near the wound. The arrow still protruded from the body. "It has not hit its heart," she said. "It's a bad wound, but I think we can do something." The wolf-man emitted a low, throaty growl, and they jumped back in fear, but then collected themselves and knelt around the prone beast.

Its breath smelled rotten, like spoiled meat, and Djana held her hand over her nose. "We can use the other crystal, and the fire element to cleanse. It should work," she said.

They had spent many hours, days, and weeks in Ardvale learning how to clean and heal open wounds using their palms. It was what Irusan had taught them, and it was how he had once healed Adain from his almost-fatal arrow wound. They also had the crystal from the cavern in Galon. They had never practiced using it on a living creature before, and this would be a true test of their abilities.

The sun slowly rose over the horizon, and the wolf-men gathered around, shading their eyes from the light. Blaidd seemed less bothered by the sun, as he said his eyes could operate in any light conditions.

It took them until the sun was high in the sky. They weren't as proficient as Irusan, but the wound finally healed with only a small scar in the hide to show that Iratz had ever been wounded with a crossbow arrow. The wolf-men whimpered and growled among themselves as Iratz stood up, looking in amazement at his chest.

"Life for life," growled Blaidd. "We keep word. Boy go with you."

"Why did you not kill us, Blaidd?" asked Adain. "You could have. You were extremely angry with us last we saw you."

To their surprise, they saw a tear form in the eye of the beast, and it slowly spilled down a vast cheek.

"I sorry," he said. "I do wrong. I look for you to heal me. I find your parent's, Djana, and they help."

Djana gasped.

"I not hurt your parents, Djana. I not hurt good people anymore. But the Raven ..." he stopped, and tears continued to spill down his cheeks. They could hear *m-m-mooing*, as his chest heaved, and then he continued. "The Raven ask that I help her. That I ... *we* ... help King Brenin army. I agree. It what is best for my people. I not ask for healing. Blaidd happy now. Blaidd like to be with wolf-men. Blaidd respected. My name now Yagmak. But I no kill you, and I no give you to Branwyn!"

They looked at him, still astonished. It would take a lot to digest everything Blaidd, or Yagmak, had said. The boy looked confused as Blaidd spoke. He had not said a word since they had first found him, but he was also looking at the Six with a new light in his eyes. *A look of recognition*, Jarah thought.

"You say the army is nearby. How nearby, and why are they here?" Jarah asked.

"There is war come to all Ialana. Raven must rule over all, she say. She use King Brenin to conquer, but will kill king soon. She now rule Rhiannon." This came as news to the Six.

"How long were we gone, I wonder?" asked Tristan. "Blaidd, how long has it been since you left Rhiannon?"

"I leave eight moons ago," said Blaidd. The Six looked at each other again, consternation in their faces.

"That means ... we've only been gone ...," said Jarah.

"Three moons!" finished Tristan. "It felt like years!"

"Well, Finn did say there is no time in—"

"You must go!" Blaidd interrupted their musings. "No talk!"

His ears twitched. He could hear sounds from the forest. The army was close—too close. His erstwhile friends had to leave before they were captured. He knew Branwyn would reduce him to a pile of dust if she ever found out he had them in his grasp and he'd let them go. They must go before any of her spies saw them ... before *she* saw them.

He looked up. He didn't see any ravens above, but with her one never knew. He signaled to his pack and they disappeared into the forest. They must sleep. Tonight, it would be busy.

As they followed the Garden River upstream, the Six looked again at the boy they had acquired. Who was he? Jarah had a strange feeling. This boy was not ... there was something wrong. He just knew it.

"Who are you, really?" he asked, looking at the boy closely.

"I can tell you, now," the boy answered, "that I have found you. You are the six healers, are you not?"

"First tell us who you are," Tristan insisted.

"I am Queen Catrin. I—"

"Oh! So pleased to meet you, Your Majesty. And I am Djana, Queen of Rhiannon!" said Djana, a dangerous glint in her eye. "Stop playing with us, and tell us your name, and what you're doing here."

"I just did," said Catrin. "I am not a boy." She looked at the girls. "Come over with me behind that tree and I'll show you!"

"She's telling the truth," said Jarah. "But that doesn't mean she's the Queen!"

"She smells bad," said Kex. "Worse than we do. Worse than the wolf-man. I didn't think *queens* smelled so bad."

"She's really dirty, too," said Adain, his voice dripping with skepticism. "What would a *queen* be doing in the middle of the forest?"

"I am telling the truth in both things," said Catrin. "I am Queen Catrin. I am here to find you—the Six. My son needs healing, and I heard of you from a woman who calls herself Branwyn."

This got their attention.

"We're listening," said Tristan.

As they walked, she told them her story, how she had discovered what the woman Branwyn was planning with her husband, and about her son and her husband's intentions for both her and Deryn.

"So I have finally found you," she concluded. "Please come back to Meadowfield with me. Deryn is there."

"We were going to Meadowfield anyway," said Jarah. "Yes, you may travel back with us, and we'll see what we can do about your son."

Catrin smiled her gratitude. It had all been worthwhile! She had found the healers.

They talked so much, ignoring Blaidd's warnings, that they did not notice the soldiers until it was too late. A troop on horseback, looking almost as surprised as they were, appeared unexpectedly through the trees in front of them. It was the advance guard sent out by Brenin, looking for the best path south.

"Halt!" cried the soldier in the lead. He nodded to the troop, who quickly surrounded the seven. "I think we have found what the king has been searching for! Who else would be crazy enough to be wandering these forests?"

"But there are seven, Captain, not six," said one of the soldiers.

"I can count! We'll take them back with us, and the king can sort it out."

Catrin looked stunned. "I can't be captured," she whispered. "My husband will kill me!"

"Unfortunately, there isn't anything we can do about that now," said Tristan. "We'll have to hope for the best."

The others looked at each other in silent agreement. They would do their best for Catrin, but unless another miracle happened, they were just as doomed as she was. The soldiers took their small knives away, and Catrin's sword.

There was nothing they could do.

33.

Capture

The soldiers escorted them through the trees, back the way they had come. It seemed that the Six would have run into the moving column soon enough, even if they had not been captured, but at least they might have had some warning. They rode through the column that had spread out through the forest, until they found King Brenin riding on his white horse, with his generals by his side. The Captain saluted. "We discovered these people in the forest just ahead, Your Majesty," he said. "Perhaps they are the six you seek?" The king squinted at them, and then looked again, this time closer. To Catrin's dismay, his eyes focused on her. She saw the recognition in them and her heart sank.

"Catrin! Is that you? *For the love of Idris...!*" The Captain looked startled, as did the generals. The queen? How could it be? Brenin's face darkened. "You'd better have a good explanation for this," he said.

"Yes, I do, Brenin. But I beg you, take me and do what you will, but let these people go." She gestured towards the Six. "They have done nothing, and in fact, saved my life from the beasts of the forest." She looked at them imploringly, and Jarah heard the unspoken words: *Please, find my boy and heal him!*

His nod was barely perceptible, but he didn't think Brenin would let them go. He was right.

"Sorry, Catrin. I have promised someone the capture of six healers, and I have to make sure these are the six we seek. I will keep them *and* you. We will talk later." He wrinkled his nose, looking at his wife with disgust on his face. "You stink!"

He instructed the Captain to tie them up by their hands, and the ends of their ropes were tied to the saddles on the horses of the troop that found them. In this way, they were forced to walk and run behind the horses as they moved through the forest. They walked all day, stopping once or twice to rest and eat. There wasn't much food. Brenin's army was down to survival rations, and what little food there was inedible, but they forced it down, not knowing when they'd get more. Their own supplies had been taken away too.

As they walked, Catrin noticed a soldier on horseback approaching them. The man had a scar that ran down his face, but she recognized the horse first. It was Sierra! The man approached, and then went by, an azure-blue eye winking at Catrin as he passed.

"Who is that?" whispered Tegan, who was situated the closest to Catrin. "Do you know him?"

"Shh!" said Catrin. "Yes. I'll tell you later."

That night, they made camp next to the river. The prisoners were escorted to a tent. It was to be their prison for the night. At least they would not be left out in the open, thought Jarah, but guards were posted both inside and out. After their evening meal, which wasn't really a meal, the king strode into their tent.

"All right, Catrin, speak," he demanded. "What are you doing here?"

"I heard of the healers, Brenin. I came to find them so that they would heal our son. But these people with me are not the healers. I thought they were, but they're travelers that I—"

"Quiet, woman! You think you can continue to deceive me? There are no travelers in these parts. Only sorcerers and beasts. I would wager my kingdom these are the healers that we look for. I will hand them over as soon as I am reunited with my next queen. Yes, I am replacing you, Catrin. You've been a disappointment to me, and I've found a woman more worthy of your position. You will be beheaded in the morning, for treason against your King. I'll make an example of you. When the troops see I can behead anyone, they'll not question my orders again. And you," he turned to the Six, "you will do as Branwyn desires, or you will suffer the same fate as this woman." He turned on his heel and left the tent.

They were silent for a while, and then Catrin spoke.

"I am so sorry ... I tried my best. I did not want my husband to find you first."

They tried to comfort her as best as they could, but she would not be comforted.

All they could do was wait for the morning.

Branwyn and Brenin

Affairs of State in Rhiannon had been going well since the assassination of Anfawl. Branwyn was now sole ruler of the land west of the mountains. It wouldn't be long, she thought, before the east would be hers too. Her subjects worshipped her, and the council was not a problem. They understood where their loyalties lay.

Admiral Udfa had been helpful, stepping into the breach with the military. He had demanded full authority over both branches of the military, and she had agreed. Udfa was more intelligent than Anfawl had been, she thought. He seemed to understand exactly what she needed, and she had no doubts about his competence. Yes, he had allowed the Six to escape, but that could have happened to anyone.

She would never underestimate them again either. They would either turn into either formidable enemies or extremely useful allies. She hoped for the latter, but her priority now was to find them. She would pay a visit to Brenin. She needed to keep an eye on him, anyway.

The fleet, under the command of Udfa, had left port for Galon. Now she must ensure that all went well with the troop movements in Mannanon. She had flown over the region not too long ago and seen the Galonese army heading north. Her planted spies had informed Ortzi of the approach of Brenin's army, and he had reacted predictably, exactly as she'd planned.

She activated her Merkaba and located Brenin's encampment. The night was dark with no moon, but the encampment was lit up like a Rhiannon festival and she could see it from leagues away. She knew which tent belonged to Brenin. She knew that he'd be frightened to see her materialize in his tent, but at this stage of the game, she didn't care. Either he would accept her for who she was, or he would be replaced. She hoped he would accept her though. He still had his uses.

Brenin was asleep, but she woke him up.

"What ... Branwyn? Who ... how did you get here?" He looked at the guard inside the tent, slumped over and fast asleep. He would have his head in the morning too. His, Catrin's, and anyone else's who had not alerted him to Branwyn's presence inside their camp.

"Wake up, my love," she said. "It is time you learn of who I really am; how I get back and forth over long distances, how I can get past all your guards."

He blinked at her, puzzled. His puzzlement changed to understanding, and then fear, as Branwyn talked. She told him of her origins, leaving out the parts she thought he would find too unpalatable and glossing over others that might put her in a bad light. She knew he was a weak and cruel man with ambitions, but she felt even he had some limits.

She ended with, "and I want you by my side, on the throne of Ialana."

Brenin thought for a while. He was shocked, but not surprised. He'd suspected something like this for some time now, and truthfully, he realized he didn't care. If she could help him attain his own ambitions to rule Ialana, he didn't have a problem with how that was accomplished. He realized now that he did not love her, he *feared* her, but that didn't matter, either. Together, they could develop a relationship of mutual respect, something he did not feel for his current queen. Well, she would soon be only a memory, and so would their son. Branwyn would produce an heir worthy of the name.

He rose. Now he must present Branwyn with his own gift. He felt she would be pleased.

"Come with me, my new queen, I have something to show you."

They stepped out of the tent, surprising the guards at the entrance. Where had the woman come from? She had not been in the tent earlier ... Brenin could see the confusion on their faces and laughed. He could think of so many uses for these skills of the new queen. They walked to the tent where the prisoners were kept, and, taking an oil lamp from the guard outside, they walked in. The Six and Catrin were not asleep. It had been difficult for them, and they looked tired and drawn.

Brenin looked at Branwyn as the light of the lamp fell on the faces of the prisoners. Her joy was everything he expected and more. He felt a swell of pride in his chest. He had done what no one else had been able to do: capture the Six! He didn't care what she did with them. Finding them was its own reward.

"Well, well, my love! This is a wonderful surprise. I won't forget it. Yes, I have been searching for these six healers. Well done!"

The faces of the Six and Catrin's fell. They knew immediately who this woman was. Could things get any worse? "I will leave you here with the king, for now," she said, triumph in her face. "I will be overseeing the battles and the defeat of Galon, so I'll be too busy to deal with you, but you will return to Rhiannon with me when the war is over, and if I don't get your cooperation, I *will* use my mind crystals on you. You will suffer a similar fate to your old friend, Blaidd." The Six could hear the menace in her voice and didn't doubt that she'd use her mind probes and crystals on them for one second. Branwyn looked at them again, confused. "But, my love, who is the seventh?"

"Catrin is the other—the former Queen of Aelfar and Mernoc. She is to be executed in the morning."

Branwyn laughed. "Oh dear, the lifespan of royalty these days ... we will have to ensure our own longevity, my beloved!" They both laughed, again, and Catrin and the Six felt chills go up their spines.

These two were truly unspeakable. What chance did they have of escape? They had thought long and hard since being captured, and they realized that they had no choice but to use their Crystal to help. They knew that it was not what the Crystal was designed for, but unless they did *something*, Catrin would die in the morning, and they would end up in the hands of this distorted woman. Jarah had made a suggestion to use their fire-palms, but they felt this would not work so well on humans who were not afraid of fire. They had tried to bring up their Merkabas, but with an amused guard looking on they had no success, and how would they take Catrin with them? They'd still have to leave her, and with the guard in their tent, any attempt to plan an escape could easily be thwarted.

As Branwyn and Brenin left the tent, laughing hysterically, the Six looked at each other.

"What now?" asked Tristan. "I'm all out of ideas."

"Me too," said Jarah. They sighed. They would not get any sleep this night. They wished Irusan would appear and save them, but they knew he was far away and probably had no idea of their predicament. They had been unable to contact him, telepathically. He must have returned to his world. They didn't feel as concerned about their own fate as they felt about Catrin's. She would die in the morning. At least they had time still to … .

At that moment, they realized something odd. Tegan mentioned it first. "Did you notice the forest is rather… quiet tonight?"

Everyone stopped talking and listened. Yes, it was quiet! The normal sounds of the wolf-men and other creatures were not out there. It had never happened before. Every night they'd been in this forest there had been a cacophony of sound. Tonight though, there was nothing. Not even the croak of a frog. It was too quiet.

They looked at each other, puzzled. What did it mean?

Tristan shrugged. "Perhaps the wolf-men have all moved south. Didn't they all make a pact with Branwyn to—?"

He didn't finish his sentence. There was a sudden uproar in the camp. Screams of men mingled with howls that shook their tent. Horses screamed in panic, and they could hear soldiers' footsteps pounding outside as they ran in all directions. Their own guard looked uncertain, as if he wanted to run outside to see what was happening, but afraid he would lose the prisoners if he did, so he stayed put.

They waited, trembling with fear. Even the guard's face turned white as the screams outside rose. Every now and again, something would hit the sides of their tent, and fall with a thud to the ground. They would then hear dragging noises, and high-pitched yells of terror. Over all this, there was a roar that drowned out all else, and it sounded close.

It was then that a huge claw swiped at their tent from the outside, and a large rent appear in the side. Looking at them from the hole was a creature the Six were all too familiar with.

The scorpion-like claws and spider-eyes of an Arrach.

34.

The Battle

They had just returned to Brenin's tent when they heard the commotion on the edges of the encampment. Brenin sent his guards to see what was occurring.

"Probably an encounter with a beast," he said. "Nothing to worry about, beloved."

"I'm not so sure." Branwyn looked concerned. "I told them to lay off our soldiers. This should not be happening."

"I am amazed at your talents, Branwyn. Speaking to beasts! That is incredible. I hope you're right, and they *are* on our side."

"Maybe it's a stray beast who didn't get the word," said Branwyn. But the commotion did not stop. They could now hear screams, howls, pounding footsteps, and cracking branches outside as men ran hither and thither. The guards had not returned to report back, either.

"Do you think we should leave the tent?" asked Brenin. He

hoped that she'd say no, that they should stay. He was frightened, but didn't want to admit it, even to himself.

"Let's wait and see ..."

Their tent lurched and Brenin turned pale.

"*I have to get out!*" he screamed, raw panic in his voice, but whatever was on the other side of the canvas did not wait for him to emerge. A large claw, that Branwyn could see now belonged to an Arrach, shredded the canvas from top to bottom.

What is going on? Branwyn thought. *Didn't I have their cooperation? Their promise?* Brenin was still screaming—sword in hand— as he slashed desperately at the claw coming at them through the gap. Branwyn took a deep breath and, raising her arms, used the incantation to call on the fire elementals.

She thrust her breath out as hard as she could to direct the flame towards the Arrach. Instead, a feeble jet of flame, one that would perhaps light a candle, sputtered from her palms. She tried again, this time calling louder and exhaling even harder. Nothing. What was happening to her? Was there another powerful wizard ... the Healers, perhaps? Yes, they must be blocking her. She would try other elements—anything—something must work.

She called on all the elements she knew, but there was nothing more than a small splash of water, a tiny rock, and a gust of air. It would not have been enough to deter a small child. Brenin was backing up now, running out of what was left of the shredded tent. That was not a good idea, she thought, but what else could they do? She ran outside too, and a sight she would never forget met their eyes.

Bodies lay eviscerated on the ground, soldiers ran screaming past, and monsters were everywhere. Arrach, wolf-men, and large creatures that she did not know existed fought side by side against Brenin's army. Some looked like apes, while others were smaller and goblin-like. All had large teeth and claws, and the soldiers with their weapons stood little chance against this army from hell.

In the center was a large shape, but she could see the sharp horns that towered above the horde. It was Blaidd.

She wanted to kill him. She would reduce him to a pile of dust! She aimed her palms out towards him and called on her inner Chi to ..., but it still wasn't working. Her fire-palms fizzled with a few colorful, but harmless sparks.

She hissed, eyes ablaze with fury. Blaidd's massive head turned in her direction and he began to move towards her. At the same time, she could see Brenin had lost his battle with the Arrach, the one that had been trying to get inside the tent. It was time for her to go.

"Help me, Branwyn!" cried Brenin, his face a mask of desperation and horror. The Arrach had him, helpless, in its large claw now. He had been stung, and his face was a purplish-black. She couldn't stay to see this.

With a cold look towards her erstwhile lover, Branwyn did the only thing she could still do. She pulled up her Merkaba, and in a flash of light, disappeared.

Amrafalus

The reptile had been watching the encampment for several hours now, trying to determine whether it was worth attacking or if he'd be outnumbered. He decided there were too many soldiers. He would have to move on. Maybe he could take out a few on the outskirts. Soldiers became sleepy at night and their attention wandered.

He was about to wander off himself to search for vulnerable perimeters, when he felt eyes watching from the forest. He realized the forest was quieter than it should be. He stayed where he was, deep in the shadows and under the overhang of a large pine. He could see them now, large, dark shapes that flitted silently from tree to tree. He could also smell them; the rank odor of wolf predominant, and other creatures he could not yet fathom. Was it Arrach? He didn't think they came this far south! But yes, here they were ... he could see them now as they scuttled side by side with the wolf-men towards the camp.

His mouth split open in a grin. He would eat well tonight! He cautiously emerged from his lair and glided silently towards the camp.

Blaidd's Last Betrayal

Blaidd had seen Branwyn. He threw aside the soldiers in his path as if they were mere twigs. He needed to get to her before she had time to recover. He saw her trying to use her magic on him and knew that if she succeeded, he'd be a cinder. To his relief, she stopped, hate and fear in her eyes. For some reason, something was not working right for her. He picked up speed, but she vanished in an instant. He was too late; she was gone.

He was glad that she was his final betrayal. He had led her along, thinking that he, his wolf-men, and the other creatures of the forest would help her, but he did not intend to help her. He'd called a meeting of all the forest beasts and they'd discussed, again, the merits and drawbacks of being the Raven's ally.

The Arrach thought it would mean more food, but he'd told them that the army that was approaching had more promise than the forces of Galon. He said that they'd start with Brenin's army and reclaim their land from the trespassers. "We will never be sovereign unless we stop all incursions now," he said. "Mannanon and the Osgoi are ours. Once the Raven takes Ialana, we'll be hunted down and exterminated. We must stop her."

They all saw the sense in his words, and, being what they were, their word meant nothing. They would go back on their promise.

Brenin was dead. He knew it was Brenin by what was left of

his clothing, clothing that only a king could wear. Gold chains, silk garments, all in pieces now and stained with blood. The Arrach that had consumed him like a sweetmeat in a wrapper now searched for other food. He hoped the Six had left this area quickly, and had not run into the Arrach—who he could not completely control—or the king's soldiers. It was then he noticed the Arrach that had eaten the king was now looking at another tent. It had already slashed its way through the canvas and a terrified soldier ran out as the Arrach pounced.

He moved over to the tent. Who could still be in there? Perhaps it was empty, but the soldier had been guarding something.

His question was answered as he saw Tristan looking out. He had taken up the soldier's sword, and was ready to do battle with the Arrach, who had now dropped the screaming soldier and was making its way towards Tristan.

Blaidd roared. The Arrach stopped and looked at him.

Leave this tent! commanded Blaidd. The Arrach looked disappointed, but it meekly obeyed. No one argued with the Beast.

"Blaidd!" said Tristan, "I am so glad it's you!" The others cautiously peeked out from the tent. "Be careful, the Raven is here!"

"I know," said Blaidd. "She go. King dead." Catrin couldn't stop her quick intake of breath. She hated her husband, but she also felt shock and sorrow at his passing. What would she tell Deryn? "You go now," said Blaidd, pointing north. "We take care of armies."

They didn't hesitate. Quickly gathering up swords and a small supply of food that had been kept in the tent, they ran through the chaotic encampment, escorted by Blaidd. He saw them safely into the trees, beyond the fighting, and as they disappeared into the dark forest, he turned back. He must get to—

It was then that something massive leapt at him from the trees, knocking him off his feet. He rose, but it ran at him again, hissing and spitting, claws gouging his face. This thing, whatever it was, was as big as he! In addition, it was strong.

With a roar, he rose to his feet again and the thing landed on his back. He could feel its teeth shredding his neck and shoulders. He fell back, pinning it under him. It stopped biting and tried to wiggle out from beneath him, but Blaidd kept pushing down. It finally wiggled out—its slick, scaly skin making it difficult to crush. Blaidd leapt up again, and this time faced it so it could not take him from the rear. He lowered his head and prepared to charge. The creature rose up, and now Blaidd could see it clearly.

It was Amrafalus.

Shocked, he came to a dead stop. It couldn't be! But it was. The hesitation almost cost him his life. The creature charged again, and Blaidd crouched, holding his head close to the ground. As Amrafalus rushed towards him, he waited. It wasn't until he was almost on top of him that, with an upward toss of his head, Blaidd rose, impaling the Reptile with his horns.

Amrafalus let out a screeching hiss that hurt Blaidd's sensitive ears, but he didn't stop. He shook his head again, and flung Amrafalus from his horns. The reptile bounced off a large tree, and then slumped to the ground. Before Amrafalus could rise, Blaidd hurtled towards him. He lowered his head again, and impaled him with his horns, one more time.

With another hiss of escaping air, Amrafalus' face relaxed— into a death mask. Blaidd shook the huge body off his horns and looked down as it lay in a pool of ichor, motionless, on the ground.

Yes, this time, he was *sure* he was dead.

35.

The Merkaba

Branwyn, from the safety of her Merkaba, observed as Blaidd stopped running towards the spot where she had stood with Brenin only moments ago. He stopped as she disappeared, then he turned his head to look at the Arrach who was now after the prisoners in the tent. She watched as he commanded the Arrach to leave them alone, hissing in rage as he escorted the Six and Catrin safely out of the camp. She followed in her invisible orb as they made their way through the forest to safety. *If only her fire-palms were working!* She tried again, but now she couldn't even produce a simple spark.

Blaidd turned to leave, as if to return to the battle, but she needed to stay with the Six. She must *not* lose them! Her revenge could wait.

Just after she'd turned to follow the Six and Catrin, the sound of thrashing, roaring, and hissing arose from the dark forest behind her. Confused, she turned around again.

All she could see was a tangle of thrashing limbs. Puzzled, she watched. What had attacked Blaidd, she wondered? But it was only when Blaidd lowered his head, impaling his attacker, that she took a sharp intake of breath. That beast looked familiar. She drew in closer. It was—it *was* Amrafalus! *So, he is not dead after all. But look how he's changed*! She watched, admiringly, as Blaidd finished him off, and it was in that moment that she realized she had almost forgotten something.

She had forgotten that Udfa, with his navy, was approaching Galon. Not all was lost! They could quickly take Galon from the sea, but she must get to the fleet and ensure their victory. Perhaps, by then, her powers would have returned. They could take care of Ortzi later—or maybe the forest beasts, with Blaidd, would take care of Ortzi's army. He had betrayed her, yes, but she could give him Ortzi's army as more food. These beasts were insatiable, and she must regain her powers and take care of them too. They were too dangerous to live, and they couldn't be trusted. She would have to find the Six again, later. She knew where they were headed, but she felt angry that they'd once again slipped through her grasp. That could be rectified though, and they were not her immediate concern.

She guided her Merkaba over the early dawn landscape. The sun was not yet up. But something still felt wrong. She needed to get to Abena before daylight, but her Merkaba would not move with the speed of thought. It was supposed to be instantaneous when she wished it to be. Now it jerked and wobbled, and sometimes she felt as if it was falling out of the sky towards the ground. Each time this happened, she quickly recovered, and it would fly straight again, but it could not seem to go any faster. At last, as the sun's first rays rose over the eastern horizon, Abena and the Bay appeared below her.

She wobbled as low as she dared over the Bay in her traitorous Merkaba, feeling nauseous and dizzy. *Were Udfa and the Navy there yet?* There *was* a fleet in the bay, but with a sinking feeling in the pit of her stomach, she could see now that it was not her fleet—not Udfa's navy. It was Brenin's navy. If Udfa wasn't there yet they had no chance against Ortzi's cannons. She'd—they'd all known he had cannons—but not having access to his guano supply, Rhiannon could not make the explosive powder needed to be on an equal footing in a sea battle. She had decided that it didn't matter, sheer numbers would overpower any cannon-fire, and the two fleets would easily overwhelm Abena. With Ortzi's army out of reach, they could easily win.

But where was Udfa?

The cannons roared from the battlements on the Keep and from the many stone castles situated around the bay. It took nearly all day, but Brenin's fleet stood little chance. They could not approach the land without a pummeling from the cannons. Ortzi's ships, also cannon-loaded, came around from their rear and hammered them from the back.

They were trapped. They could neither retreat nor advance. Finally, the last ship sunk under the waves, and Branwyn, still in shock inside her stuttering, malfunctioning spirit vehicle, limped slowly over the waves towards Rhiannon.

The Best Laid Plans ...

Her Merkaba was now useless. It threatened to plunge her beneath the choppy waves and she was no longer able to keep it airborne. With a frustrated sigh, she quickly changed into her Raven form. At least she could still depend on that. It took her longer than she'd have liked, but she finally made it back to Rhiannon, tired, furious, and hungry. She'd make someone pay for this. *Udfa!* What had happened to the navy? He would pay for this, by Idris, he would!

THE SIX AND THE GARDENERS OF IALANA

She shape-shifted back into her human female form as she entered the council building, the current seat of government, through a window. While flying towards the city, she'd noticed her navy still moored in the bay. Had Udfa misunderstood her orders? Not possible, she thought. She had overseen the navy's departure herself. They must have turned back, as soon as she was gone. She would have Udfa's head! She had to get to the council chambers quickly and see what had gone wrong. They would have to find another way. She would not drop her plans. It was a setback, but she'd recover.

A servant, startled, dropped his tray as she appeared out of no-where. He screamed and ran down the corridor. That was careless of her, she thought, but it didn't matter. She could always claim he was delusional. As she continued to walk down the corridor towards the chambers, more people moved out of her way, gasping in horror. Some like the first servant, screamed and ran, while others cringed against the wall as she passed. What was the matter with these people? They saw her all the time! However, she had no time to deal with crazy people. She must gather her council members together and find Udfa.

She knocked a few of them over as she passed since they were rooted to the floor, terror in their eyes. It was then, as she pushed a female servant out of the way, that she noticed something odd. Her hands weren't human. Nor were her arms. She looked more closely at them now.

Her arms looked like the wings of a hatchling, and her hands were scale-covered claws that ended in talons. She looked down at her feet, peeking out from under her long robe. They too were tal-ons. She hadn't changed back properly! No wonder everyone was terrified. She stopped and took a deep breath, willing her Bran-wyn form to reappear.

A flash of light and she looked at her hands again. Now they were worse. Large, pus-filled sores appeared where stubby blue quills pierced her skin. Her hands were still clawed and scaly. Wait, she must find a mirror! Running down the hallway, she located a mirror on the wall, and looked at herself.

She wailed in horror as she sank to the floor. She covered her large, horny beak with her talons—a beak where her face should have been. Pin feathers poked out all over her head where her hair ... *her beautiful hair* ... it was gone! She tried to change again, but now nothing happened. Nothing at all. She was no longer recognizable as a human.

As she looked up guards ran towards her, their swords drawn.

"I am your queen, help me!" she tried to say, but all she could hear was a hoarse squawking issuing from her throat.

The last thing she saw was the bright flash of a sword as it descended towards her neck.

36.

King Udfa

"**M**y brothers of Rhiannon," Udfa spoke. It had been a week after the death of the sorcerer. He now sat in his new place at the head of the council table with Anafu, his second-in-command, next to him. "We are fortunate in our decision to not go to war with Galon. We were wise to keep our fleet out at sea, just outside our own harbor. Our spies have returned with terrible news of the massacre of Brenin's army in Mannanon. Ortzi's weapons destroyed his fleet. Our own sorcerer queen is now dead, and her ashes scattered in the ocean. We enter a new era of prosperity and peace in Rhiannon!"

Anafu smiled. "Yes, brother, we have the ability to recover from the unfortunate times this city has experienced. I foresee a time when Rhiannon will return to her original splendor. We, as your council, and with you my lord as our new ruler, will work tirelessly to ensure we meet our goals."

"How did our queen turn into that monster?" asked another council member. "I've never seen anything so terrifying in my life. She frightened even our Trueni!"

Udfa smiled and shrugged. He wasn't going to tell anyone what he'd done. One day, before Branwyn had left for Mannanon, he had found her seamstress and offered her a generous bribe. He'd then given her a handful of small crystals, with explicit instructions: to sew them in the hem of the queen's robe, one that she would wear soon. He didn't know when she would wear it, but the seamstress said it was her favorite robe and that she wore it often. He'd told her the crystals were for 'good luck'.

The crystals were part of a collection that had once belonged to Amrafalus. Udfa had stolen them when Amrafalus ruled, and they'd not been missed. He didn't know what they were programmed to do, but he remembered Amrafalus saying that too much exposure to them was dangerous, so he'd kept them in a small, lead-lined box. The body of the sorceress had died with this robe on, and he'd recovered the crystals from the robe before anyone noticed, placing them back into their box. They might come in handy for another time.

"Who knows?" he said. "But I always knew there was something wrong with her. She was a sorcerer. Spells go wrong all the time."

The council members looked at each other, agreement on their faces. They would not enquire further.

"Our goals now are to return Rhiannon to its ancient days of glory," he said. "We have all heard how crystals were used by the Wise Ones to protect the city."

"Didn't do much against the Dherog," said one council member.

"We aren't going to be like old women," said Udfa. "That was a mistake. We will do all we can to obtain real crystal technology; technology that will never allow our country or city to be invaded again. Blaidd, or Seryn, was not the only person who could have helped us in that. There are others. We will find them—the

Six. They will help us. I hear from my spies that Ortzi has the crystals we need, and the Six know where they are. They are experts in crystal technology. We have not yet located the island of Mu'A—the Chimera of Amrafalus, who discovered the location—died in the destruction of the Citadel, but the Six know where this island is. I am a patient man. We'll find them, eventually, and bring them here."

The council agreed again. It was what they must do. Their survival depended on it.

Homeward Bound

After leaving Blaidd behind them, the Six, along with Catrin, hurried through the dark forest, each with their own thoughts.

As the sun came up, Catrin was grateful that it would not be her last sunrise. She would live for many more, and she no longer had to fear her husband. She hoped that Branwyn would not return to Aelfar. If she did, she'd kill her herself.

Jarah thought that Blaidd had more than made up for his previous betrayals. Without him and his assistance, all would have been lost. He'd told them before leaving them on the outskirts of the camp that no beast would attack them. They were under his protection for as long as he lived.

Adain, Jarah and Tegan were thinking that now, finally, they could return to their homes and families while Djana thought that she would visit with the Six in Aelfar for a while, then return to Abena. Kex thought she would stay with Adain, and no matter where he was, she'd be there too.

As the sky grew brighter, they heard a sound behind them: the sound of horse's hoofs. They stopped and crouched down behind some bushes. Even though the beasts would not be their problem, there were still bandits and cut-throats to contend with.

The horse drew nearer, and they could see a man on its back. To their dismay, Catrin stood up and revealed herself. "Don't be alarmed, I know this man," she assured them. "He's not a bad person." The man saw them, and he stopped and dismounted. He was the one who had passed them the day before, the man with the scar on his face, and the blue eyes. He looked at them and smiled.

"I am Ambros," he said as he stopped the horse and dismounted. "I will not harm you. I only needed to return some items to milady here." With that, he handed over Sierra's reins to her and a sword. "I retrieved your property from the soldier who took it from you. He won't be needing it anymore."

Catrin thanked him. She was relieved she had not lost Callum's father's sword, and she was delighted to have her horse back. She'd grown fond of him for the short time she had him, and was thankful he'd escaped the massacre. "How did you escape the attack last night?" she asked.

"They didn't like my smell and stayed away from me while I made my escape," he said. "I did not give you my whole supply of salve! I have been following you. I saw that big beast escorting you out and stayed well behind him where he would not sense me. What you don't know, is that he was attacked by a ... thing ... almost as big as he."

There was an intake of breath from each, and Ambros smiled.

"I can see he's a friend of yours. The good news is, he killed the other beast. Your friend lives." They all looked relieved.

"Why are you so ... kind ... to us, if you're a cut-throat?" asked Kex.

"I would like to travel with you," he replied. "I need to go back to Aelfar. I heard the beast tell you that the King is dead. Now that he is dead I have nothing to fear, and you have protection from the beasts. I will be safe traveling with you, and I can help you defend yourselves against bandits. I know their methods."

"Did you know my husband?" asked Catrin.

He had a strange look on his face as he answered. "Yes, many years ago. We were deadly enemies, and I had to flee Three Rivers. He did not see me yesterday, fortunately, but he probably would not have recognized me anyway. I will tell you about it, one day."

"You knew who I was, too," she said. "You will tell me how you knew that as well."

Ambros nodded. "I will, but not right now."

"You and Catrin smell the same ... bad!" said Kex, wrinkling her nose.

They found Ambros intriguing. They would all like to know more about him, thought Jarah, and they agreed that he could travel with them. It would help to have a horse, too. They turned north and began to walk.

END OF BOOK TWO

The Ialana Series

The Six and the Crystals of Ialana Book One
The Six and the Gardeners of Ialana Book Two
Anwyn of Ialana Book Three
www.katlynnbrooke.com

Visit my web page to download a free copy of my novella, "*The People of the Damned*".

As an author, I rely on my readers to help me get the word out about the Ialana Series, and you'll be helping me out in a big way if you take a few minutes to write a review.

Every review helps me understand what's important to my readers, which in turn helps me.

By telling others how you enjoyed the Ialana Series, you'll be helping them make a decision about buying the book.

Just go to the Amazon page where you purchased the book and click on "Review this Book". If you are a member of Goodreads, a review here is also appreciated.

If you enjoyed *The Six and the Gardeners of Ialana*, you will also love the third book in the Ialana Series: *The Six and Anwyn of Ialana*.

Anwyn of Ialana is possibly the most exciting and action-packed of the series so far. An old enemy of the Six returns, and a deadly weapon must be stopped before it destroys the world. This book picks up where the second one leaves off, and the adventures of the Six continue. It too is a book that can stand alone, but you will not be disappointed with the quality, pace, or the many plot twists and turns.

The Ialana Series is in the process of being made available in Audio (Audible.com). So far, the first in the series is available in audio, and I hope to have the other two available soon. Stay posted by going to my website, or my facebook page below:

https://www.facebook.com/katlynnbrookeauthor/

About the Author

Katlynn Brooke was born and raised in Zimbabwe. She has lived in the USA since 1979, and has travelled extensively, living in India and Indonesia.

She has always enjoyed reading fantasy fiction, such as the novels of Tolkien, Robin Hobb's Fitz and the Fool trilogy, R.A. Salvatore, Madeleine L'Engle, and many other fantasy authors who have inspired her Ialana Series.

Katlynn Brooke is also deeply inspired by the mystical and paranormal. She has studied many spiritual paths to find her own truth and answers to age-old questions. She tries to incorporate as much of her discoveries about the more mysterious aspects of the universe and nature of reality into her books as possible.

While she spends much of her time writing, she is also an accomplished watercolor artist.

She lives in Virginia with her husband, and a cat named Aurora.

www.ingramcontent.com/pod-product-compliance
Lightning Source LLC
Chambersburg PA
CBHW050026180626
46810CB00002B/586